Totally Bound Publishing books by Ellen Mint

Happily Ever Austen
Pride and Pancakes
Rash and Rationality

I0663127

Happily Ever Austen

RASH AND RATIONALITY

ELLEN MINT

Rash and Rationality
ISBN # 978-1-83943-904-9
©Copyright Ellen Mint 2020
Cover Art by Erin Dameron-Hill ©Copyright July 2020
Interior text design by Claire Siemaszkiewicz
Totally Bound Publishing

RASH AND RATIONALITY

Dedication

This book is for all the hopeless romantics
keeping the world spinning.
Special thanks to Kristi for being the best alpha
reader I could ask for, my editor Rebecca Baker
Fairfax for helping to whip this book into shape and
Jane Austen for inspiring generations of women to
not take societal confinement lying down.
Also to my dog, whose constant need for walks
lets me create characters and stories from the ether.

Chapter One

It is a truth universally acknowledged that a store nearing closing without any customers will be the epicenter of employee mischief.

In the midst of re-stocking the latest airport thriller, *Blood on the Tarmac*, Brandy heard the pre-programed soundtrack skip. The classical piano and violin CD—which made her both ache to nap and also homicidal after a twelve-hour shift—changed, and a rhythmic beat rumbled from the three speakers crammed above the giant bookshelves.

Shaking her head, she resumed unboxing the books despite a smile climbing up her cheeks. Just when her arms were full, a head popped around the long corner. With windswept hair never tamed even by a comb, Marty was a wiry man in both stature and height, but his exuberant smile and deadly cheekbones more than distracted from it.

As the song rolled out of the musical intro, he mouthed along, "Snow falls from the skies, forgetful and pure…"

"It's June," Brandy said, but Marty ignored her.

He slapped a hand to his forehead and collapsed against the bookshelf. "I reach out to feel, glass cold as a grave..."

"Shouldn't we be working?" she said and bit her lip to keep from laughing. Marty, not about to give her an inch of relief, started to shake his hips.

Hands extended far, as if he was stretching, he cried out along with the singer, "Reach for me, reach for me. Give me a chance. Sing me a hope, gift me a dance."

Brandy doomed herself by turning to the man pleading for her attention. A glint struck his boyish brown eyes and he fluttered his fingers while straining for her. With a laugh, she dropped the paperbacks and accepted his hands. Together, the pair swung in a tight circle, the shelves pressing them so close he was nearly on top of her.

Marty dipping her caused Brandy's no-nonsense ponytail to smack into the display of big-headed collectibles. One carrying a surfboard rebounded from its stand, falling into the arms — and giant head — of a woman in a parka. *Ah, plastic love.*

"Reach for me, reach for me," Marty sang, his sweet voice barely competing with the artist's baritone. Not that it mattered to Brandy, who laughed along while joining him.

His hands locked tight around her waist, the pair galloped up and down the walkways of the store. Brandy could barely keep up with Marty, who managed to raise his knees nearly to his chest with each step.

"You're such a dork," she called to the man twirling her with abandon. Marty waggled his eyebrows at her in response, too busy mouthing along with the song to respond.

They dashed through the shelves of thrillers and horror, hovered around sci-fi, and he gave her a deep dip at romance.

Brandy skimmed her palm along the floor, which needed a mopping by one of them later. But she didn't care about work, not with her unending laughter trapped in a cascade of giggles and Marty sweeping her around in a circle. Marty kept her from smashing into him, but the two lingered barely a breath away from each other as the love song drifting through the air reached its climax. His gaze beamed into hers and he sang the final words in a gentle whisper.

"I reach out to hold a hand fit for mine. Hearts become bold, and our stars align."

Brandy rose, staring in wonder at the lips singing to her. She reached out, about to touch his cheek, when a jangle burst from the front door. Marty opened his hands and she danced back, a silly blush burning up her neck. What was she doing? It was just Marty, who always acted like a fool nearing closing time. *Good friend. Nothing more.*

"I guess one of us has to do that work thing they pay us for," he said with his smile in place. It'd never dimmed in the two years she'd known him at Turn The Page.

A loud horn erupted through the speakers, causing Marty to flinch. As the DJ for the local station launched into his spiel, Marty made the 'I'll just go and fix that, you deal with the customer' gesture before skittering off to the back room.

Absently, Brandy tugged on her requisite green work polo. She glanced down the rumpled mess to find the ring she wore around her neck had displaced itself with Marty's dancing. Tucking it back safely between her shirt and skin, she walked to the front.

Admiring the multitude of fliers for bands, lost pets and author signings stood a lithe man in a three-piece suit. His hair was gelled into an impenetrable helmet that neither rain, sleet nor hail could shift. A pair of glasses with thin gold frames perched upon his rounded nose and he kept pulling on the pomaded mustache below.

"...and word is Harty wrote that new hit about a mystery woman, who gossip believes to be – " The DJ's 'very interesting story' snapped back to *Für Elise* on the cello. The disconnect caused the man to turn around in surprise and Brandy sighed.

"Where is he?" the customer asked.

Before she could respond, the answer rounded the shelves. "At least I beat it before they got to the daily fart..." Marty began, running a friendly hand across her shoulder before he caught who'd walked into the store. "Eldon."

"Martin," he responded, adjusting the cuff on his fancy linen shirt like he'd fallen out of a spy novel.

Staring from the tall, academic and slightly anemic Eldon to the short, bombastic and dusky Marty, it was impossible to believe the two were brothers. The fact that Eldon Dashwood moved as if he feared a single spot striking his suit while Marty all but bathed in mud drove the confusion home.

"Shouldn't you be knee-deep in nougat right now?" Marty asked.

Eldon seemed engrossed in the tin of magnetic poetry on the counter. But he glanced over at Marty once to say, "There was a clog in the peanut mixer."

"So? Say you invented a new peanut butter parfait flavor. It brings all the kids without deadly allergies to the yard."

A soft laugh rose from Eldon, who wrapped a hand around his brother's shoulders in a half hug and half strangle. "I will take it under advisement. But I don't think management enjoys their QA department telling them what to do."

"And you used your free day to come spend time with me? I'm touched, truly. It brings a tear." Marty pointed at the edge of his eye and squinted as if to bring one out.

For his part, Eldon sighed and shook his head. His gaze drifted from his silly brother to the only other worker in the store. "Evening, Brandy."

"Hi," she called, feeling out of place amongst the family bonding. Eldon often stopped by, sometimes with 'discount candy' from the factory he worked for. And Marty would talk and complain about him. But that familiarity didn't become family.

"Glad to see Martin hasn't been left alone to man the store. God only knows how many days it would be until the entire place burned down."

"Hey, that was one time and it wasn't my fault. Fire Marshal said as such."

Eldon shot Brandy a sympathetic look. "How you suffer him I will never understand."

"He's...he's not so bad," she said, catching the mock pain from Marty as he slapped a hand to his heart. It brought forth a laugh from her, which he always managed to do.

"Did you just come here to prod at my weeping self-esteem?" Marty poked at the packs of gum. "Because you're slacking off on the job."

"Ha." Eldon always said it rather than laugh. A single, sharp 'Ha.' He shook his head, then slicked back the hair that didn't move. "Martin, what day is today?"

"Is it someone's birthday?"

Eldon clacked his tongue against the roof of his mouth. "Nearly, with it almost being July. And what did you say you would do?"

The laughter evaporated to understanding and squeamishness as Marty tried to bury his face in the cash register. Brandy's curiosity was stoked now. She drifted closer, pulling the old broom from the crook to swipe at the floor.

"I...I was going to, but I've been busy. Working. As one does when not suffering from clogged peanuts." He said it fast enough that the *t* in peanuts vanished, causing Eldon to scowl deeper.

"You've had over two days to get it, Martin. You expect me to believe your boss had you working for forty-eight hours straight?"

"Oh yeah. Mr. Fensin chains us to the break room after dark. Feeds us fish heads from a slop bucket," Marty tried. "Okay, I'll get Mamá's present after my shift."

"I need to have it engraved, which means you need to get it now," Eldon said, digging into the pile of self-help books.

"Why are we even...? *Fine.*" Marty threw his hands up. "I know better than to argue with you. About anything. Ever." He pretended to yank off an apron and wadded the imaginary cloth onto the counter.

Increasing his exasperation pantomime, Marty slid in front of his brother with his hands on his hips. "One teeny, tiny, so insignificant you won't notice it problem."

"What?" Eldon sighed.

"I don't have my car."

"How do you not have your...? What's wrong with it?"

Marty held both hands up as if about to plead for his life. "Nothing. It's good. Fine. I just, I want to do my part to save this big blue marble, so I've been taking the bus. Which won't go anywhere close to Ol' Micks. So, um...?"

"There isn't a force on this planet that will ever cause me to loan you my keys," Eldon declared, his arms crossed.

"Well, I don't know what you want me to do. Last I checked, I can't teleport. Beam me up? Hello?" Marty tapped at his chest. "Is this thing on? Guess I'll have to stay here where there's A/C. Such a shame."

"You could borrow my bike," Brandy said, causing Marty to wilt and Eldon to bloom. The latter gave his signature laugh and slapped Marty once on the back.

"There, problem solved. You can pedal to pick up Mom's gift."

A series of curses slipped under Marty's breath. He cast a dark glare at his brother. "You are the worst. And since when you are in league with him?" he whined, jabbing a finger at Brandy.

With a smirk, she took the padlock key off her ring and passed it to him. "Here. Careful, the brake's a little squeaky. And make sure to chain it back up when you're done."

"You're a brave woman to trust him with so much responsibility," Eldon said, easing to the door. He paused on the threshold, looking like he had a hat to doff to the pair. Instead, he gave one last glance at Marty. "Mamá would wash your mouth out if she heard your language."

"Oh yeah, well...I don't see why you don't just get the gift yourself!" Marty shouted.

"Because it's not my responsibility," were Eldon's parting words as he slipped back out into the blazing-hot day. A trio of tourists wrapped up in full Liberty

Bell regalia stumbled past the odd man dressed for banking.

Marty stared in his wake, digging his fingers into the key trapped in his palm. "Well, I guess I'm off. I shouldn't be too long, but if the boss arrives..."

"I'll dress a mop up and say it's you," Brandy answered.

Marty winked. "I'd almost say I like you for that." He dangled her traitorous key off his finger and added, "Almost." With that, he vanished out of the door.

Chapter Two

Because trying to balance a six-foot-long pole in one's arms while pedaling down Frankford Avenue is a breeze, why not have it start raining? Might as well give me a real challenge. Marty had tried holding his mamá's specially ordered fly-fishing pole across the bike's handlebars, but after nearly taking out three trashcans, a rotted newspaper box and a cop, he'd switched to holding it under his arm.

That left the front half of the bicycle wobbling and rain that should have been cooling his sweating brow drenching the back of his shirt. He glanced over his shoulder. In his mind's eye, the green dye leeched into his skin and stained it until he looked like the Incredible Hulk's svelte cousin.

Cars crammed full of dry and properly cooled people blared their horns at the wet sop pumping his weary legs. *Yes, how dare I slow them down. They might suffer the unending agony of sitting in place for an extra ten seconds. The horror!*

Another honk sent him ramping upright, the fishing rod nearly falling from his hands. While it was in the usual protective plastic case, he doubted it'd survive long against Philly drivers with vengeance in mind. Their mother had been hinting at wanting a new pole for months, less than subtly 'accidentally' texting them links to this fiber-weight something or other, then apologizing for it.

Marty had joked they should get her a cookie bouquet, but Eldon had given him a sour look and insisted they do as their mother sort-of asked. Locking the wobbly pole under his arm, he risked wiping his eyes and caught a beautiful sight.

Giving a jolly ring of the bell he'd bought Brandy for her birthday, Marty raised his hand to signal, then pedaled as fast as possible to make the turn. A car nearly clipped his ass for his troubles, but he ramped up onto the sidewalk and down a back alley. As long as no angry cops, or the ghost of one, were walking the area, he should be fine.

The buildings untouched by the sweeping hand of gentrification leered closer to him, their faces cracked. Marty hunkered deeper into the low collar of his polo, which he kept flat on principle. He stared directly ahead, the bike bobbing below him as each grind of his leg grew longer and slower.

How the hell does she do this every day? Brandy must have thighs that could crush a bowling ball. Hm… He might have to check when he got back.

"Stop blubbering!" a voice shot out from the dark. It came from a twisted, narrow alley that led to a cul-de-sac of dumpsters. Shadows flickered amongst the garbage, easy to dismiss as nothing more than flotsam in the storm — until lightning cracked overhead.

A man with a black hood cinched tight around his meaty face had a hand gripped around the thin wrist of a thin woman. Even at this distance, it looked as if he could snap her bird-like bones with a single squeeze. She cried out, which caused the man to fold his hand into a fist.

Anger surged through Marty, which overrode common sense in an instant. He rammed the bike to top speed, his feet flying. The pole shifted to the left, his sights burning through the man prepared to hurt a defenseless woman.

"Unhand her," Marty shouted above the rush of rain and traffic. He raised his helmetless head high, his armor drenched instead of shining. But the trusty ten-speed steed didn't let him down. The man turned away from her, his bug eyes widening as he took the full momentum of a grown man at top speed wielding a fishing pole turned into a lance straight to the gut.

The attacker flew back, falling ass over end. Marty and the bike kept rolling. A wall was coming up fast, and he slammed a foot down. Shaking under him, the bike came to a palm-grinding stop. Steam hissed off the tires, which squealed their last as Marty watched the man rise to his ham hocks.

He stared at the woman left quivering by the brick wall, then glared at Marty. Raising his finger, Marty jangled the bell thrice, then aimed the bicycle as if he was a bull about to gore the man again. That must have been enough, as the attacker turned on his heel and ran like the coward he was.

"Run all you like, I'll still... Oh, he's gone." Marty tried to shout after the man and dug for his phone to call the police when a gasp reminded him of why he'd turned into a jousting knight.

Leaping off the bike, making the handlebars crash to the ground, he ran for the poor woman. "Here, miss," he said, holding out a hand to her. She was slow to take it, barely laying her long baby-pink-painted fingernails against his palm. Marty didn't tug her up, but waited. Her white-blonde hair was drenched to her forehead, obscuring most of her features. But as she turned, raising her chin, she beamed a pair of ice-blue eyes on him, and all the breath was knocked from Marty.

"Janeth. Janeth Willows," she whispered on the wind as Marty raised her to her feet. For a moment she buckled, her fragile body falling into his arms.

She blinked her big eyes at him, her pale lips quivering from the chill.

"Dashwood. Uh, Marty. Martin Dashwood is my name," Marty stumbled.

"Pleased to meet you." Janeth smiled so sweetly Marty's heart went into cardiac arrest. When she wrapped her hand around his, the jolt restarted his heart. As she raised and lowered their conjoined hands, she said, "My hero."

* * * *

A mountain of steam erupted from the bronze contraption, and Marty stared in wonder, clogging up the counter space quickly cramming with rabid business people. He waited until the last two poofs of tiny clouds popped free from the ancient espresso maker before he let the zombie denizens re-caffeinate themselves.

"Eldon, it happened!" he said, settling down at the table.

"You got that bunion removed?" Eldon asked with a soft sigh.

"Ha, as if you're one to talk, Witchy Feet."

That got him a glare, Eldon's sharp eyes shooting lasers through his glasses. Marty waved it off. "So many warts, wooo! Does Elena know about them?"

"She is..." Eldon paused and shook his head. "You said something happened."

Marty sighed. "I met her. The one."

"Oh, wonderful," Eldon said in his crystal-clear 'I don't care and am ignoring you' voice. Marty frowned deeply.

He'd been preparing for this moment since last night, when the pair of them had run through the rain to a shop where she could call a friend. With his polo shirt extended above her head, he'd kept her safe from the rain and stared in rapture at her. The woman he was destined to be with.

"I did," Marty thundered, trying to slide around to catch his brother's eye. "Last night, I rode in like a shining knight in a Renaissance painting and rescued her."

"From an insane man on a bicycle?"

"No! From a mugger."

That caught Eldon, who finally laid his phone down, though the dubious eyebrow was still in play. "You stopped a mugger for a random woman on the street. Did he have a gun?" The nonchalance snapped to 'concerned brother' in an instant.

Marty shook his head. "I mean, I didn't see one on him. There may have been a knife? That isn't the point! It finally happened, I found her. My...my one-to-be."

The great eye roll made it clear where Eldon sat on matters of kismet and love. For him, kismet was a simple matter of the brain piecing together two coincidences, and love was a score in tennis. He wasn't incapable of emotion—Marty knew how to push just the right buttons to get that Dashwood blood to boil. But Eldon was the biggest wet blanket when it came to romance.

Which was why it didn't surprise Marty in the slightest when his elder brother plucked off his glasses and pinched the marks on his nose. "What about this woman you've known for...what? Twelve hours?"

"Probably more like ten," he admitted, checking his old watch from their *abuelo*.

"And from that long courtship, what in her manner has made you declare her the one?"

"Did you not hear me? I saved her from a mugger. I rescued her from who knows what, took her hand, and she...she called me her hero." He'd been walking on air since that moment, his lips mouthing her name when she wasn't staring at him. *A hero.* "Come on, there's no better love story."

"What are you on about?"

"The story you tell your grandkids. How pop-pop and meemaw met. You know it's an eternal match when your story is full of drama and romance."

Sure enough, Eldon scowled at the mention of romance. "You can't be serious? Eternal match? For fu...fudge's sake, Martin."

"I'm sorry if we can't all 'Bump into our long-term steady girlfriend while trying to turn in a paper about goat milk' as our meet-cute," he said. "Us mere mortals simply have to make do."

"It wasn't goat milk — it was the acidity of bacteria strains in cheeses."

"My mistake. You're a regular ol' Casanova."

Eldon practically puffed up like a cat in the rain at that comparison. It was a mystery how he'd wound up in a relationship at all, never mind with someone as patient as Elena. Four years and they'd gotten as far as moving in together. Even pointing at the word *wedding* caused him to break out into hives and run for the bathroom.

Diving back into his daily news from around the world, Eldon turned away from his brother. Marty thought that was the end of it, when a soft voice said, "Tell me about her."

"What?"

"If she is your supposed soulmate picked by God Himself, then I should know something of her."

His grin rising, Marty was unable to stop shimmying in his chair. He popped up onto a knee to lean higher over the table. "Her name is Janeth. Rather exotic, right? Tight body that says 'I work out but only use those little pink weights.'"

"And...?" The eyebrow quirk was back.

"And she's got hair that metal-blonde color."

"Platinum?"

Marty nodded hard, remembering the smooth locks wafting back and forth against her jacket. Well, he assumed they were smooth. They'd looked it. "And her eyes are this unforgettable aquamarine. Catching her gaze is like looking into a snow globe."

"Snow globes contain numerous...never mind. What else?"

"What do you mean?" *She was gorgeous, vulnerable, tender, hot. What else does he need?*

"What does she do for a living? Where is she from? What is her family like? You've declared her your soulmate and all you know about her is what you'd find on a driver's license. Even less than that, unless the status of her organ donor registration came up while you rescued her."

Marty frowned. He could always count on his brother to turn a molehill into a massive mountain.

"We didn't talk much. She was in shock, from the attack. But she was so kind..."

"To the man that saved her from a would-be mugging."

"And sweet, and did I mention blonde? Like, long-long blonde." Marty passed his hand over his head and down to the small of his back.

Eldon slammed an elbow on the table, then cupped his chin in his hand. Telltale condescension rose in Eldon's face as he glared at Marty. "So your soulmate could be a dressmaker's mannequin with a blonde wig for all you care."

"Don't be a dumbass. I know there's more there, okay? We just didn't have the chance to connect because she had to get home to calm down and file a police report."

"Martin, do you have plans to see each other again?"

"Uh..." Things got rather hectic when this guy she said was her friend arrived. "She's got my number," he said, hope gleaming in his heart.

His brother gave one last withering look before resuming his reading. "Watch out, Romeo and Juliet, step away, Heloise and Abelard, beware, Cleopatra and Marc Antony. We have a true romance of the ages here."

The sarcasm wasn't lost on Marty, but he dragged his chair closer to say, "You know those were all doomed relationships, right?"

Eldon caught his look and, in his bitchiest voice, answered, "You don't say."

"Morning," a far too cheery and friendly voice announced, keeping the brothers from tearing each other apart. "I've got a black tea here." The barista eyed the cups in her hands.

"That would be mine." Eldon pointed at the table before him.

"And a" — she turned the cup around to read the receipt below — "fluffy unicorn latte."

Marty raised his hand and took the mug overflowing with pink foam. "Thanks," he said.

After Eldon returned the gratitude, the barista left the two alone to glare across their morning beverages. It was the eldest who waved the first white flag. Raising his mug of plain black tea in the air, he said, "Here's to love."

Marty bounced his latte against it, declaring, "To love." In doing so, a dollop of pink cotton candy foam fell directly into the tea, and Eldon sighed while drinking both down.

Chapter Three

"Brenda!" The shrill, nasal call of her boss came from the front of the store. Sighing, Brandy put down her home-brewed coffee and slipped out of the break room. The summer sun lanced directly through the windows, burning in her eyes and casting long shadows against the back wall.

"Yes, Mr. Fensin?" she asked sweetly, stopping before both the withered gaze of the store owner and the display they'd put up last night.

"What is this?" Their boss stabbed a finger at the setup that'd been Marty's idea.

Her coworker had lit up with mischief the second they'd unboxed the latest summer thriller with a cover of a bikinied woman swimming in the ocean. Now, that book swung from fishing line he'd tied around the ceiling pipes, and below, nestled on a pedestal covered in a blue tablecloth, sat all the books on sharks they had in the store.

It was obvious to anyone with a passing knowledge of pop culture what Marty was referencing. But seeing as Mr. Fensin had climbed out of a Colonial crypt, wandered down the road until he found a store front and opened a bookstore, it went above his head. *Literally.*

"It's a summer display. For sharks. Lots of people are interested in sharks," Brandy said as diplomatically as possible. She could almost hear the indignant huff rattling in Fensin's ribcage.

"This is bullcock," Fensin said. A year and a half on and she didn't flinch at his conflation of two different nonsense words into one. Good thing Martin wasn't here yet, or he'd be saying 'bullcock' all day.

"Do you want me to get rid of it?" she asked, standing in place and not moving.

"Yes!" Fensin ranted, his arms flailing above his head in the most dramatic fashion possible.

Brandy reached a hand out, as if about to dismantle the whole thing, when she paused. "What should I replace it with?"

"Eh...?"

"We'll need a new summer display. What do you think would go best?"

In an instant, the big bad wolf deflated to a yapping lapdog. Fensin clawed at his ear, his crusted eyes glaring out of the window at the sticky morning. "Do whatever you want." For someone who owned a bookstore, Fensin had little use for the written word and even less for creativity.

But he couldn't deny the impact Marty's unfocused brilliance and Brandy's more subdued innovation could have on the bottom line. With a smile, she eased around the old man to stand guard over the cash register as if the store was crammed with customers instead of no one.

Usually, that was the end of it, but Fensin's beady eyes dashed around the stacks before he homed in on the only one there to browbeat. "Whose idea was that?"

Marty's.

"A collaboration between us," Brandy said to a deeper scowl. He couldn't single them out if they took the blame together.

"Dunno why I have two of you anyway. Times being what they are, everyone's buying their books with these." He pulled from his suit coat a flip phone which could only be on the internet if it was set on top of a modem.

Brandy ignored the familiar threat unleashed whenever it was approaching payday. But Fensin wasn't done yet. "Where's the other one? In the back making box snowmen again?"

"No," she said as if the very idea was silly. It was June, after all. Marty only did that in winter.

Fensin rounded on her, no doubt about to press the question, when the man of the hour arrived. He swept in through the front, his polo fully unbuttoned and a bakery bag in his hand. *Ah.*

"Morning, dear." Marty called his familiar greeting. He walked closer, his gaze fully on Brandy, when Fensin stepped in the way. Eyes wide, Marty slipped back but an inch before he smiled bigger. "And it's nice to see you too, Brandy."

Oh, that wasn't good. Brandy hustled around the desk, prepared to stand between the two, when the door opened.

"See we got a customer. Do your damn job," Fensin ordered Marty before turning and snorting once at Brandy. With that, the old owner stomped out of the door and back to whatever mausoleum he called home.

Brandy cast a look to make certain it was Eldon on Marty's heel before returning to her vigil behind the counter. "You're late," she said, punching in her employee code. The number was zero-zero-two.

Flipping around his wrist, Marty stared at the watch. "Says I've got another two minutes till my shift starts. Oh, got you a cronut." He deposited the bag on the counter.

Brandy couldn't even pretend to be angry as she peered inside at the poor-man's cronut, a croissant dipped in frosting. Still, she hadn't had breakfast yet. "It's nearly the end of the month, remember."

"Damn it, how could I forget? Culling time. I keep thinking one of these days I should wear a pig costume so Mr. Fensin can just chop my head off right then and there."

Brandy cast a single look up from the brown bag. "I'd like to see that."

"Me as a cute little piggy, or with my head on a stump?" Marty asked while sidling around the counter. The space was crammed tight thanks to stacks of milk crates full of books. To fit, he had to slide his hand around her back, the palm splayed to the wall as he leaned closer.

"If you don't mind, I have a book I put on hold," Eldon said to his brother, who glanced over.

"Let me guess— *How To Be Even More Boring in a Boring Recession*?" Marty turned to dig through the stacks as if he knew right where it was.

That left Eldon standing in front of the counter watching Brandy trying to eat a sloppy breakfast pastry. The man who dressed like he was due at Wall Street at any second hovered around a woman praying she didn't cover her green polo in frosting.

"How are...how's Elena?" she asked, clinging to one of three safe facts she knew about Eldon — there was a stack of dirty laundry Marty revealed whenever he had a chance, all of which she tried to banish from her mind while watching the gray-eyed man scrub at his glasses.

"She's well," he said and blinked at her through the smudge-less lenses. "Brandy, you will be attending our mother's birthday party, yes?"

"I...I dunno. That's more of a family thing. Not really for friends of family."

"Nonsense. Besides, you already met her at the block party last May."

That had been awkward to say the least. When her new coworker had asked if she had anything planned that night, the next thing she knew, she'd been standing in a park while a massive family had shared barbecue and shot off fireworks.

"Here's your stupid book." Marty handed it to his brother. "What's he bugging you about?" he asked Brandy directly, but Eldon answered.

"About attending mother's birthday. And you should not hand over the merchandise until a customer has paid. What if I ran off with it?"

"I'd kick you in your knees." Marty grinned wide as if would do it. "And come on, Brandy, you've gotta. It's her fiftieth, so she's gone all out. Please. Please, please! She likes you."

"She likes me?" They'd only traded a few words a year back and maybe one or two sentences when she'd stop by the store to round up her son. Did Marty talk to his mother about her?

A confounding churning that had to be the sudden sugar rush dropped in her stomach. She hadn't done the mother-meet since what felt like another lifetime.

But that wasn't what this was. *Marty's a friend. Nothing more.*

"Okay," Brandy gasped, causing both brothers to smile wider. "I'll come. Should I bring anything?"

"Your bright smile," Marty answered, causing her to grin and blush in response. "Now, if you'll excuse me, I have to ring up my brother before he pulls a runner."

Eldon crossed his arms as Marty yanked the book back and prodded at the old cash register. "I had no intentions to steal it. I was only pointing out a potential flaw in your business dealing."

"Uh-huh, right. I've got my eye on you. Try anything and you're going on the board." Marty slapped at a blank wall, which his brother stared at. "I'll make a board, then put you on it. Banned from the store, danger to society. Think of the scandal for our poor mamá."

Grabbing the bag with his book, Eldon sighed at his brother. "I don't know why I bother. Good luck with him," he said to Brandy. "I'm afraid he's going to be in an even more obnoxious mood than usual."

"Oh?" she asked, but Eldon was already out of the door, walking crisply away. Marty whistled to himself as he dug through the other holds. He looked the same to her.

It wasn't until she'd vanished into the back that it hit her what he was whistling — a love song.

* * * *

She had nothing to fear. Marty was his usual happy-go-lucky self, even if Brandy took the front while he put his back to work unloading the latest shipments. A handful of customers wandered in, mostly to escape the omnipresent heat baking the sidewalk to sweatbox standards. They all got a chuckle out of the *Jaws* reenactment above their heads, then slipped back out into the heat.

The tourists always grew thick as deer flies the closer it got to the fourth. When the streets were flooded with marching bands, firework casings and drunks in flag regalia, she was lucky to get a second to see Marty. Most days she tolerated the job, but that week ranked worse than Christmas and Black Friday combined.

Sticky, exhausted and no doubt sweating because the A/C had broken down for the tenth time, Brandy wished she had somewhere to escape to in July. But taking a vacation was out of the question. For starters, she had rent to pay, and there was no money to go anywhere else.

A handful of kids paused outside the store, one hanging off the massive gorilla statue they'd 'inherited' when a tattoo parlor went out of business. The phones were all out, snaps taken as they dangled back and forth around the unimpressed ape. Brandy felt ancient watching the people who were maybe a couple of years younger. At their age, she'd already been...

It didn't matter.

As a distraction, she yanked up the box Marty had dropped off. She wouldn't risk the counter, as thirty pounds of hardbacks could shatter the cheap glass. Instead, she placed it on her chair, slit the tape and ripped open the box.

Headlights, blood smeared on the grill and hood, a body crumpled below tires. The images strobed against her vision, Brandy's hand lashing out to grip the wall. She struggled to swallow back the rising bile, her head spinning when the word *Car* leaped from the title.

"Damn it," she cried, knowing she was running away from nothing more than a box of books, but having to. "Damn it, no. Not again." Brandy knocked against her head as if a small gremlin would answer and get out of her skull. The acrid stench of spilled oil and gas burst from her memory into her nose.

In a panic, she reached the back room and yanked open the door. A cleansing breath filled her lungs, then another. Instead of ripped-apart mud and flashing lights, she soaked in the piquant smell of afternoon sun striking a back-alley dumpster.

"Hey."

Crap. "Hi," she said, a crooked smile knotting about her lips as her gaze focused on the man curled up amongst the maze of boxes.

Marty wiped off his pants and stood. He was maybe a half an inch taller than her if he wore new shoes. But in that moment, she felt like he towered above her, both as a protector and source of shame in one. A powerful urge to fall into his arms rose from her traitorous brain, but she turned away to stare at the mountain of packing peanuts in the trashcan.

"Don't tell me, the register's on fire," he said as if completely unaware of her near panic attack.

Brandy slotted on a wider smile and turned to him. "No. No, I just..." *Wanted to see you.* "I was wondering if you were doing anything tonight."

What?

He shrugged, then slung a box up onto his shoulders. Marty had what she'd call a dancer's body, sturdy yet also willowy. But when he'd hoist fifty to sixty pounds of merchandise like it was nothing, she couldn't deny watching his surprising muscles at work. *In a totally platonic way. As friends do.*

"I shall check with my trusty butler," he said with a laugh and twisted around his phone. "Jeeves says that I am available for a fortnight. Whatever that is. So...?"

"Oh, I... Mel, she gave me this pack of super-cheap DVDs, and I was wondering if you wanted to come play movie roulette tonight."

They'd been doing it on and off for a few months. Get together, pick a random movie from a DVD collection that cost a buck, then watch it. The last time, she'd even broken out some of her old gear and made parmesan cheese popcorn, which he'd inhaled — literally. Marty didn't do anything by half measures.

Soft brown eyes caught hers, and he asked, "What shall be our poison of choice?"

"Um, there's a comedy pack with tons of Laurel and Hardy. An old spooky horror one."

"So lots of cheesy skeletons and bats on strings," Marty said with a laugh.

They'd spent all Halloween lost in the Vincent Price oeuvre, hiding under a small blanket fort. It'd been fun. It was always fun with Marty. That was just him. "And, uh, one romance collection. Which, you know, we don't have to..."

"What? You think I'm too young to handle the kissing scenes?" Marty laughed when his phone jangled to the same song he'd been whistling before.

He dove for his pocket, his movements frenzied as he prodded at the screen. Furious typing commenced, then deleting, then even more typing. All the while, Brandy stood there, uncertain if she should leave him to whatever it was. Mr. Fensin didn't like it when no one was at the front.

"Yes!" Marty cried. He clutched his phone tight to his chest and bounced in a full circle. "Yes, yes, yes!"

"What?" Brandy asked, enthralled with his exuberant but uncoordinated dance of joy. "Did you win the lottery?"

"She agreed to a date!"

Her smile dropped. "Oh. Who?"

"Janeth Willows." He damn near purred her name, holding his phone close to his face. Was he taking a freaking screenshot of her texts?

He hadn't talked about anyone lately. Anyone like that. Brandy furrowed her brow, trying to remember, when it struck. "That woman you..."

"Rescued from certain doom." Marty sighed in rapture.

"I was going to say bent my bike for."

"Oh, shit!" He stared at the same green polo he always wore. "I have to get ready. I have to... Can I ask you a tiny favor?" Marty's mania switched to sweet begging so fast it whipped Brandy's head around.

"It better not be to use my bike again." The dent she hadn't cared about before instantly became a major issue.

"Would you mind closing tonight?"

Oh. So his date was... "Um." Her tongue burned and her face flushed, but Brandy nodded her head.

"Thank you." Marty grabbed her hands and pulled her close in a half-hug. She went limp, trying to not be aware of the body she'd almost run to for salvation. After glancing around once, he dashed for the front of the store.

Brandy trailed after him, watching as he punched his code into the cash register to sign out. "Why are you clocking out?"

"There's so much I have to do." He glared out of the window. "I don't know if there's enough time."

"Wait, what? Are you leaving work *now* for a date?"

Marty dashed for the door, not even pausing as he left her fully in the lurch. "It's got to be perfect!" he shouted one last time before escaping out into the street crammed with pedestrians.

"So I guess movie night is off," she muttered to herself. Pausing beside the display window, Brandy watched him until he turned around the block. It wasn't like she had planned it, really. Or was invested. It just seemed like a nice thing to do, with him. *Not with him, with him. Just as friends.*

Always friends.

"I'm sending that Willows woman a bill for my bike."

Chapter Four

"Damn it!" Brandy raced to yank the pot off the stove, but she wasn't fast enough as the milk spilled over the sides. It hissed in boiling rage, causing her to curse stronger under her breath while flipping all the dials off. The evil pot rested right smack dab in the middle of her electric burners, daring her to try to warm it up again.

That was what she got for wanting some homemade mac and cheese for once.

"Problems?" Mel called from the dining room. It also happened to be the living room and laundry in her tiny place. She'd thought about getting one of those fancy dividers to pretend she had a real dining room, but had never gotten around to it.

"I miss gas." Brandy switched on a new burner and began the long wait for it to heat up. "My old kitchen was..." Her voice cracked and she glared into the small pot on a tiny stove in a minuscule apartment.

"Hey." Mel's voice cut close, nearly causing Brandy to whip the spatula against the wall. Her friend paused beside the fridge, taking in the mass of take-out magnets, before she continued, "You thinking about him?"

"Right now, the old stove," she said, really not wanting to pick at that wound. It should be five layers thick in healed skin, but somehow it kept getting ripped open.

That was the problem. There was no way of escaping what she'd lost because he'd...it was all around her.

"You ever think maybe it's time to let go?" Mel asked in such a soft voice that Brandy took a moment to make certain she heard it right.

"I'm hardly hanging on."

"You still wear the ring."

Even knowing it wasn't there, Brandy glanced at her left hand. The tan line had faded from a long winter without a gold band on it, but the lump above her heart lingered. Thanks to the ring's exposed prongs, scratches that never seemed to heal were etched into her skin. Her hand hovered right above the small bulge in her bra that hid a shattered dream.

She didn't want to cry. Two years on and Brandy was sick of it. Sick of having people learn about her tragic story, coo in false sympathy and tell her that things would get better. If she had to hear about God and doors one more fucking time...

"B." A warm hand caught her arm and Mel's no-nonsense face softened. "If you ain't ready..."

"I am. I think, I mean, I want to be. But then I feel like I'm, I'm letting him down. How dare I move on when he's..."

"What would Kevin have wanted?"

Her slow stirring through the bubbling milk paused. Brandy stared into the creamy depths as if it was the veil between the living and dead. "He'd want me to add mustard to this," she said to her friend.

It brought a single laugh from Mel, who shook her head so her tight spirals of hair all boinged perfectly. "Have you thought about getting back on that horse?"

A flash of Marty smiling as he ran out of the door burst through her skull. He was so damn happy rushing off on a date with this strange woman. *Practically danced down the streets.* And what did she care? He could date whoever he wanted. She'd never given him a second glance before.

They were friends.

"I don't even know how to do it."

"Come on, it's like riding a bicycle," Mel said, causing Brandy's entire face to turn as red as her liquor's namesake. "All you need are the proper tools in your hands and it'll come right back."

Now burning clear up to her hairline, Brandy wished the damn milk would boil over so she could cool off. "I don't use, there aren't a lot of...what do you mean?"

"Don't be coy. I know you've got a piping bag around."

"Oh! You meant about the..." Brandy gasped as she realized her friend was talking about her previous life in baking. But at the glint of mischief across Mel's face, Brandy collapsed right back into her black hole of misery. "That's been a long time too."

"You made those cakes for my Christmas party."

"Right, and the fondant cracked, my marzipan wouldn't set and I covered the whole thing in a cinnamon buttercream to hide the mess. Hardly good work."

At seventeen, Brandy had met the love of her life. Not only had he been sweet, handsome, funny and caring, he'd believed in her. It had felt strange at times to be married while almost every other girl she knew was in college, but they'd lived in a cozy place together, and thanks to Kevin's parents, she'd had her first ever bakery to run straight out of pastry school. It would have been a perfect life.

"Can you hand me the cheese?" Brandy asked, pointing to the mass Mel had helped her grate.

As the cheddar and swiss melted into the milk, Mel said, "I don't want to push you or nothing, but I've got a gig."

"Really?" That drew her full attention from the cheese that still needed its mac. "I thought Seasons Caterings was shut down for good?"

"I got a boost from a certain crowd funding source and it's back. Even booked a few parties for the summer. BBQs mostly, so ribs and sides. But I could really use help from the most talented baker in the city."

"Mama Moe's won't give you the time of day," Brandy said, folding in the noodles. She had to add a few spirals to the elbow as her pantry was getting bare.

Mel slammed a hand to her hip. "Don't go playing that humility song, girl. You're good. And if I had your desserts, it might give Seasons Caterings a fighting chance against the big boys."

"I'll…" She wanted to say no. That she barely turned on her oven unless it was to throw a frozen dinner into it. "I'll think about it."

"Great," Mel responded as she gathered up both bowls and forks to trek out to the dining area.

They were always walking on eggshells around her, Brandy knew. Well, the few who'd remained in her life after the accident. Even the ones she'd thought were good friends had started to fade. Maybe they'd missed Kevin too much to be near his widow, or maybe they'd been annoyed at how she'd shut herself up in the apartment she couldn't afford anymore.

Widowed at only twenty-four, she'd wanted to be veiled to the world. Like those old Victorian ladies in mourning for decades, shuffling around the house in a black robe while cobwebs built up across the windows. But those windows and robes cost money, which a meager life insurance wasn't going to pay for.

And, she hated to admit to herself, sometimes she enjoyed being out in the sun meeting new people. Living her life without him.

"While I love the chance to hang," Mel said with her fork half stabbed through a macaroni, "the invite for tonight came about rather suddenly."

Brandy didn't wince or give any hint that the probing question had hit pay dirt. In a nonchalant voice, she said, "I asked Marty to come over too, but he's busy."

"Oh? Seemed like he'd run ten miles to your place if you were cooking."

"He's got a date. With some woman, Janeth Willows." Brandy scoffed, making air quotes.

"That name rings a bell," her friend said.

"Janeth. Ba! How up your own ass do you have to be to add an h to Janet?

"Uh-huh." Mel smiled wide.

"What?"

"You know what. Them brown eyes are looking rather green."

Brandy laughed so hard she parted her congealing cheese. "Please. Jealous of what? Marty? He's just a..." She frowned at Mel's knowing smirk. "He's a friend, okay. Nothing more. Never been, never gonna be."

"Then what do you care if he's seeing someone?"

"They aren't seeing each other, it's a date. First one. And I'm not jealous. I'm annoyed at him for running out on me."

There was that damn look again.

"At work! It was his day to close up, but I had to stay late. Not that I had anything to do. Still. Oh, and he smashed up my bike. So...yeah!"

Her gaze drifted away from her phone long enough for Mel to stare in confusion at Brandy. "He broke your bicycle?"

"Not on purpose. It was when he was saving that Janeth lady." Because he got to ride in and whisk her off her feet, hair blowing in the breeze. Probably lifted her in his arms across the handlebars, the pair riding off into the sunset while he leaned closer to... "The brakes are completely shot because of it." Brandy scowled, hating that she put even a second's thought into his romantic rescue. That was also Marty's fault, since he couldn't stop going on and on about it.

"Right. Sure." Mel kept on with the 'I'm not listening and don't care enough to fake it' answers, before her head shot up. "I knew that name sounded familiar."

She spun her phone around to reveal an Instagram page in predominantly soft pastel colors. Brandy barely gave it a glance before Mel said, "Janeth Willows, she's one of those influencers."

"A what?" Brandy took the phone. The first handful of images were of various cotton candies artfully placed beside flowers.

"Someone who gets paid to take pictures of themselves eating vitamins and sitting on beaches."

"Sounds grueling."

"I followed her when she did more traveling and food recommendations. Now it's all about vitamins to make your hair grow and teas that make you shit your pants."

It didn't take long until Brandy came face to face with a woman created in a lab to walk down a runway. Her face was perfectly symmetrical, with features so fine they almost vanished in her over-exposed pictures. Only her eyes stood out against the thin nose and lips. Ice blue, they were the kind that followed a person around a room before asking to see the manager.

Absently, Brandy batted at her freckle-dusted cheek. While the Instagram model had the kind of cheekbones a person would expect to find on a model, Brandy's were flat as a pancake. It didn't help that her mother had given her a long, almost rectangular-shaped head with a forehead that could sustain a forest.

"Of course she's blonde," Brandy said, trying to not notice how willowy Ms. Willows was. It could be photo manipulation. Maybe, in reality, she had a peg leg and one eye and... *You're thinking of a pirate. Marty's not dating a pirate.*

What do I care?

I don't.

"Here." She tried to toss the phone back to Mel, but her friend had her arms crossed. "It's not like I'm Marty's keeper. If he wants to go after a woman who spends her days taking a dozen pictures of a donut, who am I to stop him?"

"Are you sure you aren't just the tiniest bit jealous?"

Brandy glared. "No. I'm not."

She could see Mel winding up to ask her if she wasn't jealous or wasn't sure when the feed refreshed itself. The rosy golden colors switched to a deep indigo, drawing her eye to an image that sank her stomach. It was Marty dressed in a full suit, clinging to Janeth's arm. She'd turned her face away from the camera in order to plant her lips on his cheek.

The caption under it read, *Giving my hero a big smooch*, followed by three lip emojis.

It was Marty that Brandy stared at. She'd seen him smile and laugh nearly every day since they'd met, but in all that time it'd never been so big. He was ecstatic.

Why shouldn't he be? What was stopping him from finding that great love he kept talking about?

"Here." Brandy solemnly passed the phone back. From the corner of her eye, she caught another refresh and a second picture of the date.

Mel inspected the feed herself, her eyebrows rising as she asked, "Don't you want to watch their date play out?"

"No," she said truthfully, dropping her fork in her dinner. Her appetite was completely drained. "It feels like spying."

"Hardly counts when the person is posting it all publicly. But fine, putting it away." Mel slipped the cursed phone into her pocket. It should have yanked away the lingering sickness seeping into Brandy's veins too. "So, what movie are we taking on tonight? The romance pack? Comedies?"

Somewhere out there, Marty was having the time of his life, entertaining and enchanting a woman who could be a literal angel. *And here I sit, deep in mac and cheese, dressed in sweats, prepared to waste my night watching discount bin trash.* It didn't sound so fulfilling anymore.

Pinching her nose, Brandy said, "The thriller collection." She'd had enough romance for a lifetime.

* * * *

Don't screw this up.

As his name rebounded around the exotic bus station, Marty turned…and picked his jaw up off the concrete. A straw sunhat—white as snow—nestled on her head. She struggled to keep it in place as vehicles whizzed past to his right. It also caused her skimpy dress with those straps so thin they were barely there to billow about.

He watched with rapt attention at how the light cotton molded around her legs, which had to be ten miles long.

"You're…dressed well," Janeth said as she came to a pause before him. People unaware of the epic romantic saga about to be made continued walking past. Some of them slumped onto the bench to wait for another passing bus.

Tugging on the lapels of his only suit, Marty smiled wide. "I wanted to make a good impression." Lucky thing he hadn't grown much since high school, either up or across.

After dancing her perfectly painted gaze across his body, Janeth pursed her lips. "Well, it suits you quite well, my dashing hero."

All the anxiety that'd been knotted down his spine melted away. He hadn't had much time to throw this together, but Marty had run himself ragged to get everything just right. And it was all worth it just to hear her call him a hero.

Janeth dashed to him, wrapping her hand around Marty's head. He stood taller, his brain buzzing in shock. But she didn't kiss him. It was to her phone she turned, curling her fingers around a case decorated in watercolors.

"I think the man who saved me last night deserves a kiss," she said in a near giggle. Before Marty could answer, she turned, placed her ruby lips to his cheek and pressed down.

His heart leaped higher at her touch and he raised a hand to hold the small of her back when Janeth turned away to inspect her phone. She typed nimbly while talking to him. "What's your Instagram name, so I can tag you?"

"Oh, I..." Marty shifted on his toes, growing aware that despite his body remaining at the same teenage length, his feet hadn't. It was all good — *girls like men with giant...shoes.* "MCDashwood," he said.

Janeth giggled at that, her entire face brighter than the summer sun. He wanted to burn in it, but she returned to her phone. "What's the C stand for?"

"Cruz."

"Your middle name is Cruise? Like the ships?"

That caused Marty to snicker. "More like in Penelope. It's my mother's family name and also my middle one. An old tradition of... Not that any of it matters. What about you?"

"Hm?" Janeth kept typing even as she watched him.

"Do you have a middle name?"

"Yeah, of course. It's... Oh no! Something must be wrong. Says here you've only got fifteen followers."

She twisted the phone around and held it to Marty's face.

"Really? Fifteen? Last I checked it was thirteen. Probably that deli I'm helping to pay the mortgage for thanks to their Monte Cristos."

Janeth didn't answer, all her focus on the phone. *Crap. Did I already blow this?* He hadn't even got her out of the starting gate.

"Well." She sashayed to his side and wrapped her arm around his far shoulder. Before he knew it, their faces were pressed together and she held her phone out. "That won't do. People need to follow my hero."

Marty gazed in wonder at the woman beside him. She'd scrunched down on her heels to compensate for his lack of height, which pulled him directly into her enchanting face.

"Say cheese!" she demanded in pure exuberance and snapped a picture. But Marty didn't say it, and he didn't turn away to look at the camera.

"Ooh, that's a good one," Janeth declared, showing him the image of an angel and a love-struck man gazing in awe at her. "Please help him out. He needs all the followers he can get," she narrated, then hit Send. With that, she turned away from Marty to the Schuylkill River rolling under an overpass bridge.

"I haven't been here in ages. Though" — she flapped her hands in front of herself — "in this heat, I fear my face is melting off."

"You're beautiful beyond measure," Marty said, his heart blundering in awe. "And, if I may, I thought we could walk along the river for a stretch." He extended his elbow to her and bowed.

Janeth shrugged then looped her arm around his. "Why not?" she said as he guided them around the traffic and down the river trail which snaked out onto the water. Railings kept them from falling into the river and needing to be rescued, but as the crystal blue water rolled around them, he felt as if they were walking on the surface.

A soft breeze blew not a refreshing crisp air, but more baked-in heat from the city. It stifled Marty's heavy suit more, sticking his shirt and pants to parts of his body he'd forgotten existed. Those vengeful shoes continued to pinch tighter and tighter to his toes, the heel rubbing haphazardly into the skin. Oh yeah, there were going to be blisters.

But none of it mattered. He was walking arm-in-arm with Janeth, who fell quiet to take in the open water and clear skies before them. Even beyond her beauty, it was clear from how she held her head that she was confident, graceful. He knew from how soft her hands were that she'd be an excellent mother, wiping away a baby's tears and tickling tummies. Her gentle nature was evident in the soft sway of her dress, tenderly floating around her hips like an ethereal spirit. And her eyes were piercing with intelligence. No doubt she had a dozen favorite books.

Still, it was a bit strange that she wasn't talking. Maybe she needed a nudge. She could be shy, a delicate flower hiding from the burning sun in a meadow.

"How are you feeling?" Marty asked, certain the gurgling in his gut was love and not any unease from the awkward silence.

"Hm? I'm good. Why?"

"Your ordeal, with the mugger. I mean, if I'd been in your shoes..." He paused and glanced down at her heels. "I'd fall over a lot." That brought a laugh to him and a vague look of indifference from her. A serious, delicate meadow flower. "But I'd be terrified to go anywhere outside. You're so brave."

"I didn't think of it like that, but I suppose I am. It was a shock, one that didn't hit me until I was home. He could have been planning to do any horrible thing to me." Her voice sharpened at that, a sneer lifting her lips. But those soft eyes danced back to Marty and her body caressed his. "Thank goodness you were there to save me."

"Uh-huh." All brain functions shut down as he felt the graze of her hip, the clasp of her palms against his biceps and the small breast glancing against his ribs. *Warning! Warning! We have boob touch!*

Focus. Romance. This has to be perfect.

"If you wouldn't mind, I have a little something set up ahead," Marty said, turning them away from the winding on-the-river trail. They drifted away from the setting sun to face a park of greenest grass. A handful of kids were slumped on a bench, phones in hand and one nudging a skateboard with his foot. But they didn't matter.

He'd planned for all contingencies.

"Are you certain this is safe?" Janeth asked, eyeing up the kids like they were carrying switchblades.

"I'll protect you, I swear," Marty declared and she once again melted in his grip. The teens didn't even glance up once at the pair of love birds walking up a rising hill. Marty struggled with the incline, but supported Janeth, helping to guide her up to his next surprise.

"Wow," slipped from her as she stared in wonder at the checkered tablecloth laid out on the grass. A woven basket sat in the middle, its top opened to reveal an array of cheeses and a moderately priced wine inside.

But the real centerpiece was the battery-operated phonograph placed on a small table. It needed a fully flat surface, otherwise the damn thing didn't work.

Marty left her side and pulled out an old record of crooner songs. It took him no time to line it up, ushering in a soundtrack of smooth music to accompany his lifting the wine and two glasses.

"This is..." Janeth blinked her baby blues in shock, staring from the setup to the glass Marty handed her. Suddenly, she reached into her bag. "I have to take a pic of this."

"Of course," Marty said uncertainly. He tugged the offered glass back, watching his date fiddle with her camera settings.

Uncertain what to do, he was about to take a drink, when she said, "Wait. Hold it out to me again, like I'm...I'm the luckiest woman in the world."

His smile resumed tenfold, Marty extending the wine as asked. "You are," he whispered, his full charm cranked to eleven. Janeth snapped a picture of a man in a suit handing the viewer a glass of wine while a record played in the background. Beads of sweat dribbled down the glass, slicking Marty's hand, which he struggled to keep horizontal.

"A real picnic. I never even..." She finally turned from her phone to find him in the same position. "Oh, thank you." And with that, she accepted his gift, taking a quick sip of the rosé.

Thank God. Marty's shoulder ached from holding that awkward pose, but he wasn't about to show it. "Please, sit. Would you care for anything to eat? I brought brie and toasties to spread it on. There's also a salami in here."

Everything was going perfect. The walk along a dazzling river arm-in-arm. The beautiful picnic spread across verdant grass. The melody swaying through the sunset streaking across the sky. So...

"Do you know what I want?"

Me? "No," Marty said through gritted teeth.

Janeth swept her skirt under her and she fell to her knees on the blanket. "For you to sit here with me, and listen to this lovely record you brought," she said, taking his hand with hers.

A million butterflies burst inside Marty's heart and he dove behind her. His hip bashed into ground much harder than it looked, but he kept the pain off his face. Curling his fingers under her hand, he brought it to his lips. "There is nothing I'd like more," he whispered before placing a soft kiss to her knuckles.

She smiled serenely, her hair aglow from the light streaming behind her. He'd finally found his angel.

As the sun's vibrant reds glistened one last time across the river's ripples, Janeth turned to him. "This was a lovely surprise. Thank you."

The words were right, but the tone was too formal and final. Ah crap, there came the panic again. Marty kept his smile in place as he shrugged. "It's just the kind of guy I am."

All she did was smile politely and return to her phone. *Damn it.* How was he losing her already? Was the music wrong? Too hokey? She'd barely touched the cheese. *Dumbass, what if she's lactose intolerant? Think!*

"Martin?"

He hated his full name, but the voice that'd been distant melted to warm caramel. In that moment he'd have let her call him Martin until his dying day.

"Yes?" he asked, his limbs frozen as Janeth inched closer along the blanket.

She extended a single long finger, the nail painted like a plaid kilt. When she landed it on Marty's chest, he stopped breathing. As it began to rise higher up his lapel, his heart clocked out. Hanging on the edge of death, he floated in a dream as Janeth rustled through his gelled hair and pulled him closer.

Right before they touched, he took control, kissing her. This was everything he'd scraped and worked for, the moment he'd been wanting to have for ages. Her lips fell flat below his, but he didn't mind. Cupping her jaw in his hand, he gave it his all. Tender but not weak, wet without being slobbery, hot without dragging it into triple-X territory in public.

The limp woman seemed to respond, pursing and molding her flat lips around his. Just before parting, Marty caressed her bottom lip between his, leaving a touching reminder behind. Slowly, her heavy eyelids raised, radiant blues beaming at him as she licked along the mouth he'd ravished.

Movement from the periphery caused Martin to turn his head. Her phone hovered to the side of them, her finger right on the button to take a picture. Well, why not? Some day in the future, their grandkids would want to see pictures of the first time they'd kissed.

"How's the date going so far?" he asked.

Janeth quirked her lips to the side, the smile of heaven blanketing everything from him.

* * * *

"Bye." Brandy waved to Mel, who walked away with a container full of mac and cheese. Why had she made so much in the first place? Even as leftovers there was no way she'd eat it all before it went bad.

Wiping at her eye, Brandy limped back into her empty apartment. The loading screen from her game console and shitty movie player bounced its homicidal music through the air. They'd wound up going with three slasher flicks back to back, Brandy trying to focus on the fake blood splattering on the camera. The last movie had been *real* special, a murderous advent calendar that somehow predicted a person's death.

"I should save that one for Christmas and give it to Marty," she said to herself before wincing. They'd gone the whole night without her mentioning him once. Mel had sure tried, bringing up this Willows woman every few minutes in the first hour. But even she'd gotten tired of Brandy's lack of reaction, and they'd settled into hacking and slashing.

Having watched so much death should've probably sent Brandy dashing through her puny loft to find a killer hiding in her shower or the cupboards. A very tiny killer, like if Thumbelina were a mass murderer.

But those stories didn't get to her. They felt fantastical and impossible. Serial killers didn't chop up sexy teenagers one by one in a cabin in the woods. No, what chewed on her brain and left it in mulch were the love stories. The promises that if she found him, if she put in all the work and made that one true soulmate hers, happiness was guaranteed.

She only watched them for Marty, anyway.

What's he doing now?

Despite her best efforts, that damn thought wouldn't leave her. It'd take nothing for her to search for Willows' Instagram feed and see.

But no. *No!* That was what crazy stalker ladies did. She'd hear about it tomorrow at work. If there was even anything to talk about. Probably not. It was hard to see someone like this Janeth lady falling for Marty.

Sure, he was cute in that 'boy next door who also a bit hyper like a cocker spaniel puppy' way. And hilarious. No one could deny how funny Marty was. Smart without being fussy about it. Creative to a sometimes-dangerous fault with their boss.

Brandy caught her reflection in the hall mirror, her eyes glazed over and a smile straining her cheeks to the breaking point. It fell in an instant and she stomped into her bathroom. Squeezing a massive dollop of toothpaste onto the brush, she attacked her bicuspids.

So he took her to the river. Lots of people go to the river. He didn't have to ditch me to do it. Ditch his job, not me. Not like we're anything but friends. And there's always other movies to catch together.

Her angry brushing transformed to vigilant pacing, Brandy circling around the table where her phone was charging. She kept glancing down at the black screen, then away. More tartar met its end, the harsh bristles clawing into her gums.

He saved her from a mugger. What woman wouldn't fall for that? Man sweeps in from nowhere, out of the shadows, and chases away a villain about to hurt you.

It'd work on her.

Foaming at the mouth, Brandy yanked her phone up and searched through the feed. It didn't take long for Ms. Willows' carefully cultivated photos to arrive. There was Marty and the awkward cheek kiss. And more in a park with a picnic. Was that a record player?

Little over the top, Dashwood. Brandy was snickering to herself when a new photo refreshed and her heart sank to the floor.

Marty had cupped her jaw in his hand, a thumb caressing her chin, while the two kissed in front of the setting sun. His eyes were closed so tight, as if he was pouring his soul into that one touch. And below the image was the caption, *We're dating!* It'd already racked up a hundred and fifty comments and was growing.

What did she care? He was just a friend. A coworker. A guy that sometimes came over for movies and brought her donuts. She didn't have any claim to him…not that she'd want to.

After spitting in the sink and rinsing, Brandy wiped off her toothpaste-stained face. She vowed she wouldn't look at Janeth's Instagram feed ever again, and wandered off to bed to sleep away her old heartache.

Chapter Five

Her promise lasted all of three days, Brandy eventually subscribing to not only Janeth's Instagram feed but her videos as well. It was all Marty's fault. He couldn't stop walking into work with the fattest grin on his face, and judging by the whistling that wouldn't cease, his dates were going great.

And with each snoop, Brandy had to agree.

One night he took her to the museum and they painted portraits of each other in a room he'd rented. Surrounded by art from some of the greatest painters the world had ever seen, *she* did a little line doodle of Marty. Meanwhile, he made a finger-painting of *her* portrait complete with an angel halo.

But that was nothing compared to the date from the night before. Some little Italian restaurant for dinner, pretty typical until one saw the massive J and W hanging on the wall, made from roses. There were a good five pictures of Janeth posing in front of it, and one with Marty shrugging in pride with his hand wrapped around her waist.

Oh, Brandy noticed all right. She knew every picture where there was a sliver of Marty's olive-tan hand, or a cheek, or even just his leg right out of frame. It became a demented game for her, scrutinizing each new image from Janeth to see if she could find any sign of cracks. But it was all angels and heaven, no demons allowed.

A loud jangle nearly sent her phone flying against the wall. She caught it in her palm, her heart racing as she banished the thing to her pocket. It wasn't until she tried to convince herself she had no reason to feel guilty that she realized it was the bell.

In waltzed Marty, a bag slung over his hip with the strap across his chest. He dashed inside, grabbed one of the shelves and panted. Hard. "Made it!" he declared to Brandy and the one student winding around their philosophy section.

"Almost didn't—alarm here seemed to think that when I told it to shut off, I wanted it to. Silly thing," he said, waving his phone at her. "But I made it."

"Um." Brandy turned to look over her shoulder at the clock which showed it was fifteen minutes after nine.

"What? That thing's wrong. See?" He wafted his wrist around as proof. "My watch says..." Marty paused and tapped the face. "Damn it, I forgot to wind it again. Old piece of..."

He cranked on the dial, revealing neon-colored bandages taped to nearly all his fingers. Pointing at them in concern, Brandy asked, "What happened to you?"

"Oh, that? Turns out when you buy roses wholesale, they come with the thorns still attached." He laughed as if his appendage mutilation was hilarious, even waving his right hand's fingers, which bore the brunt of the attack.

So he took all of that just for… Oh.

Marty remained face down in his old watch. "Had a bathtub full of 'em. Just me, a hot glue gun, a very unhelpful video tutorial which I swear skipped steps and so many angry roses."

His bag struck the counter, the thud drawing Brandy's eye. Were there more presents inside for her? Had he bought up every chocolate truffle in the city and planned to spell her name out with them? Or maybe he'd gotten a pile of oysters and was going to try to find a pearl just for her.

Keeping every thought off her face, Brandy poked at the register as a distraction. Her coworker finally got to the 'work' part.

"How am I already clocked in?" Marty asked.

Brandy shrugged. "I knew you'd get here eventually. No reason for the boss to know about your thorn battle."

"Ha." Marty laughed once, his shoulder barely grazing her in a bit of fun, before he stuffed a fist around his mouth. It couldn't disguise the massive yawn rumbling past. "I just hope I got all the little buggers out of my tub before I take a shower. Gonna be a fun call to the plumber if I didn't."

For a brief moment, Brandy stared at Marty. Not a cursory glance to make certain he was standing there, or a polite watching his face while talking together. No, her eyes traversed up his forearms which were on display as he'd rolled the polo to his elbows. She stared across his chest and swerved down his stomach as the idea of him in the shower played about in her brain.

When her gaze was nearly at the swimsuit bit, she spun back to the register. Her cheeks burned hot, her fingers flexing against the cheap plastic as if they wanted to hammer out an epic novel across it.

"Welp, back to the back with me, the book mule. Which I hope doesn't mean I ever have to carry any contraband books across the border."

Brandy snickered at the thought. "That would be really uncomfortable."

"And a tight squeeze," he said with a laugh. She didn't take the bait that time, keeping her gaze focused away from his sitting area. Marty lingered as if he expected a response, but when nothing came, he slipped out to find the newest stock to slot on shelves.

"I hope it was worth it," Brandy said fast, catching him off guard. "The roses and thorns. I hope she liked them."

She knew all about his dates thanks to her snooping, Marty never talked about them at work. He didn't have to—his massive grins told novels. This was the first time she'd ever acknowledged the fact that he had someone in his life who wasn't a nosy brother or a friendly coworker.

Marty squinted as if he couldn't see her. Then the big smile loped across his face. "I'd say it was a rousing success." He laughed and vanished to the back room.

* * * *

It wasn't until after lunch that Brandy saw Marty again, thanks to the store getting swamped with an 'impromptu' book signing. They could have them, as long as there was no calendar and their boss didn't know. She was busy folding up the card table that'd held the local writer's books when Marty dashed through the stacks.

With a stage-magician flourish, he dropped a book into her just emptied hands. Brandy stared at it in confusion. Did he need her to shelve it or was it a request? "What—?"

"It's Excerpt-O'clock," he declared, causing her to groan.

"We haven't done that in... I can't even remember."

He held his own book tight to his chest, his eyes blazing with a familiar mischief. "Exactly the reason to bring it back. Audience favorite, really play on the nostalgia vote."

Brandy finally took in the cover. It was one of those airport novels written by a late-middle aged man who wanted to pretend he was a twenty-year-old who drove every woman wild. *And* he probably stopped the president from being exploded by bombs attached to pirates, or something like that. They had more important work to do.

Still... Marty danced back and forth in place, his shoulders doing most of the moving. She sighed. "Okay."

"Yes!" Marty pumped his book in the air, which looked like it bore a fancy dress with the woman's head cut off at her chin. *Oh, boy.* "Twenty-three," he said, setting off the game.

Brandy grimaced at having to go first, but she flipped to the twenty-third page in the book and read the first full sentence. "'Armed only with the M1 Garand I pulled from the mannequin's cold, plastic fingers, I knew it was up to me to stop the terrorists from taking over the Smithsonian.'"

A snort erupted from Brandy at that perfect summation, and she stared at Marty. "Sixty-nine."

"Nice," he said, cracking open the book. "'For today is not a day to be a…' Wait. Sorry." He coughed, raised his voice an octave and slipped on a 'Southern belle' accent. "'For today is not a day to be a wilting flower. I shall become a vengeful desert rose.'"

So they were working with an armed vigilante about to protect the Smithsonian from Scarlett O'Hara. *This should be fun.* "Forty-seven," Marty said, guiding her to the next page.

"Ooh, this one's dialogue. 'Tell the devil Clint Hardback sends his regards!' Clint Hardback? Holy…okay, um, one hundred and five."

"'He lingered near my bridal trousseau, his hand caressing the sanded wood as if it'd touched every woman in this town.' This is getting juicy," Marty said, and he kept reading further down the page.

"Hey, stick to the rules you made up," Brandy said, slapping a hand over the book.

"Fine, next number."

As they kept trading sentences, Clint Hardback sent numerous nameless goons to their gory deaths, and the Duchess of Cottonwood Cove lingered behind the scenes. In their jumbled retelling, it seemed as if the duchess wanted to take control of the Smithsonian in order to screw over her second cousin who had tried to marry her under false pretenses. Clint's motivations were that he had a gun and that seemed to be it.

"…'And now the entire county knows your dark secret,'" Marty said, his voice cracking from the overuse of falsetto. "Well? Don't leave the duchess hanging—she might chop off your finger to convince the priest you were consorting with witches."

"I need a number, remember?" Brandy said.

"Oh, right, uh. Let's skip to the end."

With a smirk, Brandy flipped to the back. "'Thank you, Mr. President, but I can't accept your offer to become Secretary of Protecting the Homeland. I'm so dangerous it would only encourage more terrorists to try and take me down.' Well, Clint is certainly confident. Okay, your turn."

Smiling wide, Marty crushed open his book to the end. His bandages flew like a neon blur until he landed on the page. "'However did...'" He coughed and rubbed his throat. "Sorry, gotta go back to regular me. I hope the duchess will forgive me."

"After you take your lashings, of course."

Marty laughed and dove in. "'However did I miss you? Your genteel company, your hand forever by mine? Your golden eyes peering from across the parlor? It is as if a veil has been lifted and, by God's graces, I can see what He laid before me.' Well, that wasn't what I was expecting..."

Silence, save for the tick of the clock, permeated the room. Brandy gouged at the back of her neck and glared at her book. She could feel Marty staring at her, only amplifying the confusing pit in her stomach. *Say something. Tell him that...*

"Marty, you should know," she said, her voice soft. She kept flipping through the vast pages of machismo in her hand. When bright green and yellow bandages cupped over her fingers, she turned to focus on his eyes. Whatever hid in those deep brown depths, she had no idea.

With a snicker, she said, "I like my book better."

"Yeah." He reached over and took it back. Absently, he pressed both together as if the cover models were kissing, despite one not having a head. "The explosions get all the applause. I should go and...you know. Go. Do the going things."

"Right." Brandy nodded, turning away to focus on the door. For the first time, she prayed for a stream of customers to stampede through it. For the first time, she had no idea how to talk to the man hiding away in the back room.

At that moment, the front door opened, depositing another Dashwood before her. Eldon's glasses fogged up in an instant, telling her how muggy it was away from their air conditioning. As he tried to buff off the condensation, he said, "Afternoon, Brandy."

"Hi. Chocolate still clogged?"

"No, personal business. Where is my brother?"

Absently, she pointed at the back room. "Probably making a fort out of the boxes," she said, as if she hadn't helped him some late nights. As if it hadn't been her idea to make a working drawbridge with leftover twine they found. Why did she act more like a kid at twenty-six than she had at nineteen?

Because you were married and working through school.

She clutched her ring and Eldon vanished behind the scenes to speak with his brother. Thinking about Kevin, or Marty, or how much the existence of Janeth kept bugging her, was out of the question. Needing anything to do but plunge into her weeping psyche, Brandy picked up a random puzzle book.

At first she thought it was one of those fancy newspaper crossword ones, but the page asked her to find things hidden in the image. The ice cream was easy, but the damn beachball was giving her a headache. She nearly had it all, including finding every Christmas tree, when Eldon emerged.

He wore Marty's bag around his back. Was that not another date idea for Janeth? Before Brandy could ask, Eldon paused and turned around. "Now you're certain you have it booked?"

"Yes," Marty's voice whined. She didn't realize he'd followed, his shorter stature eclipsed by his lanky brother. He glanced once at Brandy before focusing on his brother. "It's all ready to go. What about you?"

"What of me?"

"Maybe you're failing to uphold your end of the bargain. The eldest son forgetting his poor mamá's birthday. Truly, it is a heart-wrenching crime."

Eldon rolled his eyes at Marty's prodding and they landed on the poor woman dragged into his family bickering. "Will you be bringing anything, Brandy?"

"Hm? Am I supposed to?"

He shrugged. "No, but I've found that even when asked not to, food still appears."

Crap, that was in two days. What could she make in time for Mrs. Dashwood?

"You are still coming, right?" Eldon pressed, throwing her baking calculations off.

Glancing first at Marty, then back to Eldon, she said, "I...I thought so. Had planned to, anyway. Did you not want me to?"

"What?" Marty spun on his heels. "Of course you're wanted. Wouldn't be a proper party without Brandy Benson there. Hollar!" He threw his hands up and wafted them around, causing both of them to smile. Only Eldon remained unmoved, his eyebrow in a permanent snit.

"Well, glad that's all settled. Martin, do get dressed up, at least." With that he walked out of the store, mystery bag in hand.

"Dressed up," Marty mumbled to himself. "Show him. I'm wearing my gorilla costume with the tiny swim trunks. Ha!"

"How...?" *Tiny are they?* She meant it as a joke, a little light prodding back and forth. But as Marty turned to her, the awkwardness burned through her and she switched tactics. "How big will this party be?"

"Oh, don't worry, homebody. It'll be a small one. Mom insisted."

Chapter Six

That's a lot of people.

"Excuse me." Brandy whipped around at the voice, and a mariachi band wheeled a massive amp up the plastic path placed on the grass.

She knew the Dashwoods weren't hurting, but this backyard birthday party stretched up a hill and back down so far she couldn't see the end. Proper banquet tables lined the stone walkway up near the porch. There was no food yet, but the chafing dishes prepared to keep it warm said enough. Climbing the hill behind the band, she caught where they'd be set up.

Not only was there a dance floor placed next to a koi pond, but a stage on wheels kept beaming lights across the party. As it was still seven, the spotlights didn't get far against the sun. Chairs littered the grounds, placed in a haphazard fashion as if they intended to be there for a person to sit for a moment instead of the night.

No chance anyone paid that much money to not expect their guests to dance for hours on end.

And she'd come willingly to this. Clutching the plastic carrier tight to her chest, Brandy felt the urge to turn and run as fast as possible. It'd be another half hour until the next bus arrived, but she had a book on her phone. *And it's rare for anyone at a bus stop to expect you to dance.*

"*Hola,*" a voice whispered behind her. She spun, nearly whacking into the man with her heavily shielded baked goods, when soft, warm eyes smiled at her.

"Glad to see you made it," Marty said.

"Yes," Brandy said, trying to act like she hadn't planned to turn tail and run. Absently raking her fingers through her for-once-down hair, she took in Marty. The requisite green polo and dark khakis had been traded for a sea-blue shirt he'd abandoned buttoning to expose a dangerous level of chest. He must have something against cuffs, as they were rolled up to his elbows, exposing the forearms that in the golden light looked even more cut than usual.

His gaze drifted from the sudden burst of excitement on the hill back to her, specifically what was in her hands. "Did you bring something?" He reached for it, and on instinct Brandy swatted at his grubby fingers.

"You can't have any until the birthday girl does."

A pout emerged, his lower lip glistening in the disco lights. "Ow," he whined and placed the finger she'd barely touched in his mouth. "You're a cupcake dominatrix, lady."

She laughed at the thought, but happily fell back into their light games. In a soft but stern tone, she said, "I only punish those who deserve it."

"Oh, if I was with you, I'd never be able to sit down," Marty answered with a shrug. Her smile strained for a second at the ludicrous thought.

"I doubt you could afford my services, cupcakes or otherwise." She clung to the absurd idea of her being some baker clad in a leather apron about to whip a pair of buttocks with a whisk. It was so stupid to even think of… She drifted her gaze from the ramping festivities straight to the ass in question and how well his black pants framed it.

Marty turned, causing her to panic. But there was no look of disgust in his gaze. He must not have caught her staring. "For you, I'd take out a loan," he said.

"Baby!" A soft squeal of excitement broke over the tuning of three Spanish guitars.

"Hi, Mom," Marty said, as if a woman in a cream business suit hadn't run across the lawn in heels and scooped him up in her arms. Mrs. Dashwood was the type to be called imposing without having any of the physical characteristics required. Despite being slight in build with average height, her fine features matched Eldon's more than Marty's. Though, as the pair stood side by side, some of her younger son hid below her aristocratic demeanor.

The deep-set eyes, shrouded by her forehead and mystery, glimmered in excitement at the prospect of her party. Her lips, which were a perfect shade of mixed berry, crinkled at the edges in the same smile as her younger son. And both had their hair pulled back for the celebration, Marty's in a small ponytail while Mrs. Dashwood's rested in a loose knot at the back of her neck.

A bunch of Spanish flitted off his mother's tongue, which Marty sighed and laughed at before pointing to

Brandy. In an instant, the motherly-love assault was turned on her. "You made it," she cried.

"And she brought a treat." Marty couldn't stop eyeing the carrier.

"*Feliz Cumpleaños*," Brandy said to the woman's rising smile. "And I'm afraid that's all the Spanish I know. Oh, except for *Donde esta la biblioteca?*"

His mother laughed liked a tinkling of bells and wrapped a comforting hand around Brandy. "The library is in the west study, and if you're concerned about the location of *el baño*, it's down the hall and on the left."

"Your house is…beautiful. I mean, all I've seen so far is the backyard, but I'm certain the rest is lovely."

"Uh oh, Mamá, she's on to us and our cardboard facade," Marty said.

"Pay no heed to him." She shooed at Marty, who acted as if he took serious offense. "I'm happy to say the real estate business has been kind. Not as kind as previous years, but kind enough."

Brandy couldn't even imagine what this place was worth, probably in the 'we could own a fancy boat if we wanted' range. And yet Marty lived in an apartment barely nicer than hers, while working the same job.

"Oh." She shook her head, remembering what she'd brought. "These are for you…I hope that's okay. I didn't realize this was fully catered."

"Don't be silly. Just my friends bringing what they can to share, as you have."

Biting her lip, Brandy tugged open the carrying case to reveal a dozen cupcakes. She hadn't had much time, so she'd iced them in a star swirl of blue and white buttercream, then added pressed sugar molded into small fish.

A new squeal broke from Mrs. Dashwood and Brandy risked glancing up. His mom practically glowed in delight, her hands clapping together so her mass of gold bracelets clanged. "They're fish! Oh, look, fish on the water. I adore them," she said, waving around a cupcake first to her son, then the woman who had made them.

Carefully, she peeled down the wrapper. "I almost don't want to eat it, it's so pretty."

Brandy smiled as she always did when someone said that. The compliment was nice, but if she didn't want her art to be eaten, she'd have taken up painting. Clenching her toes in her sandals, Brandy watched the woman bite through the layers of buttercream and down into the cake itself.

Blue smeared across her cheek, smudging her perfectly applied makeup. With a bright smile, she pointed to the treat in her hand. "Is this blueberry?"

Mrs. Dashwood inspected the small cake. Two layers of blue, stained with both the natural dyes of the berries and food coloring, hugged a white cake layer. "It's the flag!" she said, twisting the cupcake around to show to Marty.

"I thought, with you being from El Salvador, that it would be an acceptable—"

"Acceptable?" She took another big bite, her question hanging in the air as she chewed. "Dear, it's wonderful. Thank you so much for this. For coming. I told you she's good people."

That part she aimed at Marty, whose cheeks shifted a strange pink. "I was the one to tell you, Mamá."

She began to pat Marty's cheek in a patronizing way, when a crash broke from the direction of what was probably the kitchen. "*Puchica!*" Mrs. Dashwood cursed. "Forgive me, I think your father is in over his head. Again."

Bustling away and muttering more curses under her breath, Mrs. Dashwood left the two of them. "I need to try one of these Salvadoran cupcakes," Marty said.

Accepting defeat, Brandy held the tray up for him. Judging by the mass of people already clustering around the tables, there was no chance she'd have enough. Maybe she should drop her carrier off in the kitchen and hope for the best.

"Good. Not like anything my *abuela* would make," Marty said with crumbs scattering down his shirt, "but that's a good thing. She can burn water, I swear to God."

Just like his mother, he too had blue frosting smeared across his cheek and didn't seem to be aware of it. She tried to swipe at her own face in the same spot, but Marty wasn't getting it. With a smile, she leaned over and placed her thumb right beside his lips.

He glanced over in surprise, his chewing stopped dead. With her heart in her throat, she wiped away the staining buttercream, leaving only a slight blue tint in its wake. "You had a little something…" She stared at the frosting now on her thumb.

"Oh." He touched where she had, both of them breathing slowly while the frosting melted from her body heat.

"So," Brandy began, growing more aware of the lack of someone on his arm, "could Janeth not make it?" *Because you didn't want to invite her?*

Marty blinked and turned away from her. He swallowed the last of the cupcake and took to licking the paper before answering. "No, she had some important shoot to get to, but she'll stop by later. Can't wait for her to meet my parents."

"That's...great." Brandy closed the lid on her cupcakes. "I'm sure they'll love her."

"Yeah."

Marty swiveled his head to follow, but she shifted so even her peripheral vision couldn't find him.

"Everyone does."

The party was off to its usual smashing success. He wished he could take the credit, but most of that was his father's doing. Though their mother's eyes did light up when she unwrapped her gift, even as she pretended she had no idea what the six-foot-long cylinder could be.

"Okay, okay." He dipped his arms, extinguishing the sparklers he held in both hands. The kids groaned, but he held firm. "Uncle Marty is very tired. Why don't you go annoy Eldon?"

Their little mischievous grins rose and, like a flash, they all took off after the man in a full suit who didn't want anything to do with the sticky-hand sort. All their second cousins danced around his brother, pleading that he set off more fireworks. It wasn't even eight and they'd already torn through half.

Eldon took in their pleas with his usual flabbergasted look, then glared at Marty, who tried to sneak off and wolf down a couple of hot dogs before they were all gone. He'd nearly made it to the meat table when a hand grabbed his arm and steered him away.

"Marty, could I have a moment with you?" his mother said, pulling him closer to the dance floor.

"Do I have a choice?" he asked. The hot dogs were even farther away than before. And the street corn. How did he miss that in all its buttery, cheesy goodness?

But his mom had her 'we need to discuss something important' look on, so he turned to her. "All right, Mamá. What is it?"

"The woman you brought to the party…?"

"Isn't she wonderful?" Marty sighed, his gaze skipping past the clusters of cousins, aunties and uncles, to his angel leaning against the dessert table.

"I suppose. It's only that, well, is she okay?"

That ripped him away, his head shaking. "What? Why?"

"She's been trying to eat that churro for the past two minutes."

A groan rattled from Marty as he watched Janeth pose with the cinnamon sugar treat perched on her lips. Her phone switched positions thrice. "Mom, it's normal."

"In my day, anyone who couldn't figure out how to eat a churro *estaba bayunca*."

"Mamá!" He turned on the woman he'd thought would be giddy to meet his girlfriend. Instead, Janeth had gotten a polite but cold handshake and little more. "She's not crazy—she's taking pictures of the party. It's…it's what she does."

"Takes fifty pictures of a churro?" his mother asked slowly as if he too was *bayunco*.

"What's with the negativity? Do you not like her?"

"No, she's…fine. Rather aloof."

Marty scoffed. "So's Eldon, but you don't hold that against him."

"What am I?" said aloof man asked, striding closer. "Aside from covered in sugar. Thank you for that, Martin."

"Doing my part to liven this party up," he answered with a snicker at his brother.

Their mother eyed up the white handprints now decorating Eldon's suit. "I was only inquiring about this new woman in Marty's life," she said to her firstborn.

"She's quite…something, isn't she?" Eldon said.

"Yes, very, what's that word they use now? Bougie."

Both men stared at their newly minted fifty-year-old mother. She glared back. "I use the internet, the same as you."

"Look, okay. I get that she's outside of our strange Salvadoran and Italian family loop, but I thought you of all people would welcome her."

Their mother sighed, her arms crossed as if she had to enter her mental palace to confront him. "Of course, dear. I only was thrown off guard. You arrived with that delightful Brandy and I thought…"

"What?" Marty asked, but he turned away from her to find the new woman in question having to field a barrage of questions from Uncle Edward. She seemed to be holding her own and wasn't going for any mace or flails in her purse.

Odd—he'd never noticed how va-va-voom she was. That thin sundress she had on struggled against her curves, especially around the back. With her hair down, one side kept falling in front of her eye. She'd push it back behind her ear, only for it to come tumbling back out. Marty had almost done it for her when they'd stood in line for carnitas, but she'd turned to him and his hand had frozen before making contact.

"She's a friend," he said. "I mean, sure, she's nice."

"Delightful young lady," his mother said, as if Brandy hadn't won her heart for life with those cupcakes.

"But we're…we're friends, okay? Don't." Marty shook his head. "I'm with Janeth and you're going to have to accept that."

"Of course," his mom said. She patted Marty's cheek, making him feel two feet tall, but then she shot a look at Eldon, a look that Marty couldn't read, but he knew they were up to something.

"I only wish for your happiness, because someone doesn't seem to want to settle down yet." The sweet lady transformed to a viper as she turned on Eldon. His eyes bugged out and he stumbled back a step.

"Mamá, we've been over this. Elena and I can't find a reason to waste such expense on a wedding."

"Wedding, schmedding," their mother thundered, "I want grandbabies! You don't need to have a wedding to give me a grandchild. All my sisters and brothers have some. Why is it taking you so long?"

Marty chuckled as his brother squirmed harder in his shoes. "Yeah, Eldon. Why can't you give Mom a grandbaby?" he said, earning a withering glare for his troubles. But Marty shrugged it off, leaving Eldon to suffer. It was his own damn fault. He'd been with Elena for four years. Elena who came from a Mexican-American background, who spoke three languages, who was a neurological something or other. Who probably needed a warning before their mother swooped down and sabotaged her birth control.

A soft gasp had him turning. The kids found a new sacrifice to their fire god, poor Brandy trying to blow out the sparklers they held near her face.

She gave it her all, her cheeks puffing out like a chipmunk's for air. But it was all for nothing. The kids giggled like mad, demanding she try harder, and damned if she didn't answer that call.

Oh shit! Marty dashed forward and drew back her hair. Her profile pivoted to him for a second, before the kids shook their sparklers closer. "You looked about to turn into a sparkler yourself, there," he said, to explain why he was holding her hair.

God, it was so soft. He rested his hand right above the nape of her neck, her mahogany hair lying in his palm. The longer he stared, the more distracted he became by the glisten of her dark locks as she moved. An urge to bunch up the ends and tickle them over his face walloped him in the back of his head. *What?*

"Thanks. I'd look terrible bald," Brandy said, between huffs and puffs.

He twisted to the side and stared her up and down. At first, it was just to try and visualize her without her mass of hair, but his gaze found its way down through her cleavage, which even one of those lacy undershirts couldn't hide. Coughing, Marty said, "I think you could pull it off."

Gah! Realizing what he was doing, he turned to the kids and shouted, "Okay, you little terrors. That's enough. Go find someone else to torture."

They pouted but scampered at his command. "I swear, I don't have nephews and nieces, but demons with access to incendiaries." Marty released his hold, watching the waves fall back to rest across her naked shoulders. There was probably a strap there, but he couldn't see it through her forest of hair. Or maybe he didn't want to.

She smiled at him and rolled her hands through the thick locks. "They're just having fun."

"Do you like kids?" he asked, completely out of the blue. Obviously it was to her, as she stumbled back a step, but to him as well. He'd never brought up kids with her before because...it didn't matter. To their job—not many little kids hung out in a dusty old bookstore without any fun coloring books or dinosaurs.

"I do," Brandy admitted, her hair combing slowing down. "I mean, I always wanted to have a couple. Maybe three. But..."

Her pause turned into a cliff with Marty dangling off the edge. Shit, why did he ask about that? The urge to apologize, to try to joke about how Eldon was under the microscope with their mother, danced through his head. But he knew that'd only make her feel worse. Brandy drifted her head down and tapped a toe into the ground.

She needed someone to talk to. To listen to her. To hold her and tell her everything would be okay.

"I should go check on Janeth." He chickened out.

Not even a sign of pain lingered on her face as she gazed at him. "Yes, of course. Keep her away from the fire hazards too." She smiled as if gritting through a chipped tooth and Marty turned away.

He caught sight of Janeth moving on past the churro photoshoot to the cake. Before he left Brandy, he said, "I've always wanted kids, too."

After fending off a mass of personal questions from damn near every Dashwood family member, somehow Brandy wound up right beside the last person at the party she wanted to talk to. Dressed in an opalescent skirt and bright red bodysuit, Janeth stood out amongst the crowd, which took some doing as the outfits ranged from Eldon's stuffy three-piece suit all the way down to kids in hoodies with their thumbs hooked through the cuffs and jeans falling off.

Seeming to have moved past the picture portion of the night, Janeth was plaiting her hair into three small braids and watching the band perform. When the impenetrable glare shifted, Brandy realized she'd been caught staring.

"H-hi," she stuttered, feeling like the knock-kneed weirdo who stumbled into the captain of the dance team in between classes.

Janeth smiled. "Hello. Which one of Martin's many relatives are you?"

"Oh, I'm not. He's my...coworker. Yeah, we work together at the shop. Bookshop, I mean. Turn the Page." *Holy shit, shut up!*

The smile didn't dim, but the edges of Janeth's lips pinched tighter as if she was fighting the urge to grimace. "Interesting," was her single response as she turned to focus on the guitar players in the midst of a battling duet.

Even with her skin itching and scalp tightening, Brandy remained rooted to the spot. "I like your hair," she said, spitting out the first compliment she could come up with. It was best to be nice to the girlfriend, after all.

Running her hand down said silvery-white hair, Janeth said, "Thank you. It's a pain to keep it from not breaking off in chunks."

"You're not a natural...?"

"No." She laughed at that. "All bottle. I think my natural is close to your blah brown. Been so long I can't remember."

Brandy was about to reach up and tug her hair forward to inspect the boring color, when she shook off the urge. "If it's so much work, why do you keep bleaching it?"

"For the clicks," she said so breezily that it felt like a simple fact of the world. "I didn't get much traction until I switched to white-hot blonde, and boom, a million followers and counting."

"That sounds..." *Sad. Exhausting. Marty likes her. Be nice.* "Thrilling," Brandy said, forcing her lips to turn up.

Janeth gave a little bow of her head, no doubt trying to dismiss the tiny peon with only twenty-three people who followed her nearly dead account. Wanting to vanish into the dark, Brandy was about to do that when the pulsing lights of the stage formed a spotlight on the dance floor.

Marty's father, Angelo, stood in the middle with a guitar strung across his chest. He strummed it then stared out across the massive gathering. "Where is my beautiful wife?"

It took the crowd parting to reveal Mrs. Dashwood. Even through the harsh gold and green light, it was evident she was blushing as her husband pulled a chair out to the middle of the floor. Angelo gestured once to it. With a shake of her head, she sat down.

"Fifty years," he said, catching her hand. The pair stared deep into each other's eyes. As he raised her knuckles to his lips, he said, "And she doesn't look a day older than the summer we met at the Tuscany villa."

"You old softie." She laughed as he kissed her hand.

Angelo shifted the guitar around and began to play. While Mrs. Dashwood kept her face turned to him, her gaze drifted around the crowd all watching. Then her husband began to sing. Not well, not even close to what one would call in tune. But it was so heartfelt and genuine, the abject apology she seemed to beam to the crowd didn't feel necessary.

He didn't care if he made a fool out of himself. It was all for the woman he loved. And now Brandy knew which parent the brothers took after.

She heard the snap of a shutter and turned to find Janeth's phone propped up. The woman kept silent, but the rictus on Janeth's jaw and laugh in her eyes told her enough. An urge to shout at her to put it away rose, but Brandy cause sight of Marty shifting through the crowd and her indignation died.

Who was she to tell his girlfriend what to do? Maybe he found his father's singing as hilarious as Janeth. What was she doing getting in the middle, anyway? His life had nothing to do with her.

A sting burned through her ears, and not due to the strained singing. Brandy slipped away. Past the banquet tables ransacked to little more than chicken bones, she found herself dashing through the french doors on the patio.

She stared in a confounding terror at the caterers dressed in chef's whites. They must have been shooting the shit before a random party guest wandered in. A dozen memories struck Brandy at once. Of the long hours she'd spend tramping dishes and produce up winding paths and stairs. How they'd all cluster outside to smoke, even if she never picked up the habit, to get away from the homeowner. The little doggie bags of treats she'd crack into with Kevin at two a.m. as he listened to her day.

"I need to use the bathroom," Brandy called out at the top of her lungs.

The chefs all stared askance at each other before one was kind enough to say, "Through there."

Gasping, she nodded in thanks and made a beeline through the swinging doors out into an American West-styled living room. For some reason she'd expected the house to be a cold, pristine white. Yet rich earth tones filled the couch, the walls, the sandstone sculpture and the paintings.

What if the caterers were there to stop any guests for gawking at the artwork? Not wanting to drown in embarrassment, Brandy turned away from the picture of a ghost coyote. A helpful sign marked 'Guest Bathroom' hung above a door. Fairly certain she had it right, she turned the knob and walked inside.

Arms were wrapped around nearly naked skin, a head was suffocating in exposed cleavage and pants lay on the floor. Panic seized Brandy's body, her hands flying up to block her eyes and her damn legs locked in place. "Sorry," she cried. "I didn't know anyone was in here."

In trying to scramble away, Brandy slapped at the lights. Naked skin in full spotlight blinded her, sending her dashing for the door.

At least she didn't smack her head on it in the escape. Slamming the door behind her, she tried to pull in a breath to cleanse the shame prickling up her legs. Another evil thought bounced through her head — at least it hadn't been Marty and Janeth.

"Are you okay?" a voice called from the kitchen.

The idea of a caterer grabbing her by the ear for peeping on a couple in flagrante sent Brandy flailing away. It wasn't until she was halfway up the staircase that she realized they probably didn't want a couple fucking on the sink either. But she kept going up, each step chasing away another decibel of the party. As the sound fled, so too went the churning in her stomach that she didn't realize was there.

Here, the air smelled crisp and cool. The A/C blasted on high to make up for all the bodies shifting in and out below. On a small credenza, she spotted a potpourri bowl filled with seashells and wicker balls scented like the ocean. Pictures lined the walls of the long hall. There was one of what had to be Eldon at his college graduation, with Marty pretending to steal the diploma. Another with Marty wearing some kind of uniform and showing off a scar on his arm.

Curious, Brandy kept walking deeper into their lives. Some of the frames held their parents, usually standing hand-in-hand beside a famous landmark. But one picture caused her to stop and stare. Two kids, maybe six and four, were photographed on a playground. The eldest stood rod straight, his hands behind his back, and the youngest flopped down in the mud.

Even when he was a preschooler, Marty's come-what-may smile was recognizable anywhere. It stretched wide enough to show a missing tooth, baby Marty sticking his tongue through the gap. No cares, not for him. Only happiness in a loving family.

A sound burst from outside, causing Brandy to whip her head to the East. Were they starting the fireworks already? She circled her fingers around a doorknob, knowing it would be impolite to enter, but curious. Maybe it was the upstairs bathroom. That had to be around here somewhere.

Another loud hiss followed by a pop set her on her path. Turning the knob, she stepped into a bedroom just as a spray of purple and red stars faded from the window. She walked over close enough to see without looming over the party. Sure enough, there was Eldon with a fire extinguisher in hand, directing people on where best to wait. And Marty, holding three lit punks between his fingers, ran about adding the fire.

The show played out for their mother, who stood front and center. As the impressive display approached the end, Marty pulled out a massive artillery shell the size of a cooler. After securing it on the ground, he lit the fuse and ran.

For a moment, nothing happened. Both brothers looked about to inspect it when the full payload shot into the air. The explosion snapped back so hard that the entire house rattled under Brandy and the light in the room clicked on.

Like an anthropologist who had stumbled upon a mythical tomb, Brandy stared at her surroundings in wonder.

The colors ranged from blue walls to purple rugs and a green bedspread. One desk was covered in knickknacks and trophies. What didn't make it there spilled over to the dresser. And leaning against that was an old acoustic guitar.

Did Marty play too? He was always pretending to sing along to songs, but she'd never heard him try. Maybe he was as tone deaf as his father, but had enough sense to know it.

Shaking her head even while smiling at the thought, Brandy inspected the cork board. Here were pinned pictures that came from the family printer. The ink had faded until the flimsy paper was mostly yellowed and stained, but she could make out the idea of what had been. There was another image of a slightly older Marty in the same camper uniform. This time, instead of showing off a scar, he was posing to bring out barely-there teenage biceps.

Beside that was a picture of him standing on a theater stage dressed like he'd run out of a renaissance fair. Brandy peered closer, noticing that the white tights suckered to his legs had a hole in the knee, when a voice shouted from the hall.

"I know it turned all the lights on, that's why it was worth so much…"

She didn't have time to run, to flip off the switch or leap out of the window. All she could do was stare as Marty pushed open his bedroom door and caught her standing in the middle of his memories.

His mouth opened in surprise, but a snicker escaped first and he shouted to his brother, "I've got it! You can get back to the party!" With that finished, he turned to her. "I wondered where you got to."

"I wanted to use the bathroom, but it was occupied…" She gulped, her face shifting to full-on chartreuse.

Marty raised both eyebrows as if he expected more, but Brandy clammed up, afraid she might spill everything in one go. "So you wandered in here instead to check out my dashing turn as Romeo."

Of course they'd pick him to be Romeo. *Lucky Juliet.* "That would explain the tights," Brandy said with a smile.

To her relief, Marty returned it. "There was this half-cape that dangled off my shoulder as part of the costume. Loved that — made me feel like a stuffy Batman. Memorizing all those lines, however… Pretty sure I'm the reason the drama teacher took an early retirement the next year."

Marty slipped inside and closed the door. "Haven't been back up here since...that Thanksgiving flu. Oh, that was fun. Whatever you do, never eat Eldon's potato au gratin. He'll swear up and down he didn't poison us, but I know better. It's the quiet ones you've got to look out for."

Poor Marty had been so green for that Black Friday that he'd matched their store uniforms. She'd even brought him some of her leftover turkey stock to try to ease his stomach back from the brink. And now he had Janeth to help heal him. "I'm sorry for wandering in here."

"My fault for not giving you the proper tour. Let's see, this is my desk where I'd pretend to do homework when leveling up my Orc mage. Ah, that dresser was perfect for hiding all the bad report cards before my mom saw. And the closet..." He moved to yank open the shut accordion doors, only for a great shift to rumble inside.

Slamming them shut, Marty said, "Is best left the way I found it. What else do I have? Oh, the bed." He waved his hand out, inviting her, and sat by the flat pillows.

Brandy sat beside him, shuffling her purse into her lap. Marty tugged back the cover to reveal perfectly placed sheets. "I knew it. Eldon's been making this again."

"Your brother would make your bed?"

"Every damn morning while I was eating Pop-Tarts. He'd sneak up here to make it, knowing full well that I wanted it left open to breathe. But no, since he doesn't get night sweats, it's proper for a bed to be..." Marty's babbling paused and he whipped over to her. "Not that I'm admitting to sweating when I sleep. Or any other time. Unless it's manly sweat. Chopping down trees. Rescuing kittens. That sort of thing."

"You don't sweat—you glisten with testosterone." Brandy placed her purse on the bed between them.

"I'm practically radioactive due to all the machismo hormones pumping through me." Marty chuckled, strained his arms wide and bunched his fists closed for a manly pose. In doing so, he knocked his elbow into her purse, sending it flying to the floor.

"Crap," he called, bending over to try and help gather up her private belongings spread across his bedroom rug.

Brandy raced to beat him to it, shoving old makeup, tissue packs and so many lip balms back inside. "Ah, I think some rolled under the bed," she complained, stretching her hand under.

It was a hard position to reach, requiring her to strain her legs apart. When her knee bounced against Marty's, she turned to find him staring at her. *Way to be the least ladylike person at the party.* Slamming her legs together, Brandy sat up high on the bed and found she had a sheet of paper clutched in her excavating fingers.

That hadn't been in her purse.

She turned it around to discover a rather busty woman in a bikini which barely covered her prominent nipples. With skin of a deep bronze, her black hair wet and the high cut of the bikini bottom floss on her hip, it was rather obvious what she was.

"Really, Marty?" Brandy turned the bathing beauty on the guy shrinking deeper into himself. It was his turn to shift a bright red. "A magazine? How old are you?"

She flipped it around to find an article on how to attract a mate filling out the backside to Ms. Buxom. The man on the spot laughed and wiped the glistening testosterone off his forehead. "Yeah, about that, um, my mom was real good about monitoring internet use. Scary good. And last thing you want to do is confront her about...any of that."

"What'll my silence cost you?" Brandy asked, raising the image ripped from some late nineties sports magazine up beside her face.

Marty darted his eyes from her to the lovely lady and back. "That, that's um... What do you want from me?"

"Hm." She tapped her chin, dragging out his torture. Marty squirmed on the bed that saw a lot more than just his night sweats. An image tried to knock into her brain, of the man beside her resting here with cock in hand, but she shook it off hard.

Not...not like that.

Cursing at her damn shameful libido, Brandy said, "I've got a wall that needs painting."

"I can do that! I'm great with household tasks," Marty enthused so much she foolishly let her tongue take control.

"In only certain rooms of the house?"

Marty cupped his chin in his hand just like the senior portrait above his dresser and grinned slyly. "Why? Would you prefer I make your bed for you? Maybe wear a little maid outfit as I fluff your pillows?"

He pretended to curtsy, causing Brandy to laugh along. All in good fun. She would never picture him in next to nothing. *Because he's a friend.* "I, uh, I think the painting will be good enough."

"Then we have a deal." Marty held out his hand and she shook it. "I was hoping you'd hand over the incriminating evidence, actually."

"Oh, sorry." She passed it to him, and rather than rip or toss it, Marty folded the old wank material up into his pocket. "You don't have to help me paint. I was just kidding."

"I know," he said, knocking his shoulder into hers. "But I want to anyway. This is that yellow-brown living room, isn't it? Looks like a very bad accident during chili night occurred in there."

She agreed and had been wanting to change it for months. But somehow the energy to do it had never arrived. Curling up in her robe and watching every documentary about cute animals she could find felt like all she could manage most nights. Maybe with Marty's help, it'd finally change.

"I wanted to tell you something, so thanks for sneaking off to my bedroom."

God. She struggled to not feel even more embarrassed for her fuck-up.

Marty picked up her hands, the same ones that'd sealed their pact. "For coming out to my mom's party and giving her some fantastic cupcakes, of which I took two. Suffering my relatives and their ever-probing questions."

"They weren't so bad," Brandy assured him.

"I just wanted to say, you're welcome."

"What?" She heard a full record scratch in her head, her brain pivoting from saying that same thing to him. "Why would I...thank you?"

"You're welcome again. All that time you spend cooped up at your place. I knew you just needed a little push to get you back out into the wide world. To help you get over…you know."

He hadn't invited her to meet his family. To have fun while experiencing the traditions he grew up with. To even meet his girlfriend and tour through his old home. No, he just wanted her to stop being depressed and sad. To shake off that widow's veil and become normal.

Anger bubbled through Brandy and she yanked her hands back. Snatching up her purse, she rose and stared down at Marty. His cocksure smile flipped to a cautious frown.

He was trying. He wanted to do something good. *Just…let it go.* "I should get home. The busses…they'll have stopped running."

"I could give you a ride." Marty rose. "Janeth's about done anyway."

"No!" Brandy raised her hands as if to stop him in his tracks, but she dropped them fast. "I'll call Mel. She wanted to hang once this was over anyway."

"Okay, well, thanks for stopping by."

Brandy only nodded, her blood boiling. She knew she couldn't be around him or she wouldn't be able to stop herself. He just assumed he knew her, knew what she needed better than she did? Acted like it was a gift?

Well, maybe Brandy was tired of being the pitiable woman with a dead husband. And maybe it was finally time for her to do something about it on her terms.

Chapter Seven

Ooh. Marty's random swiping on his phone was halted by the news that Tristan Harty's Blue & Black tour would be stopping through old Philly in a few weeks. That'd land right on their one-month anniversary too. A perfect date night. Okay, he wasn't certain what kind of music Janeth was into, but who didn't like *My Half*?

After navigating to the arena's website, he found a smattering of seats available and was about to buy a pair when the price revealed itself. "Two hundred bucks!" slipped through his lips. "Sure, just let me sell my kidneys for a couple tickets. I can always grow one back."

"Are you suffering money troubles?"

Marty winced, his head turtling into his shirt at the chipper voice of his brother over the phone. He was so invested in the idea of their first couple concert together that he'd forgotten Eldon had called him. To be fair, his brother had been blathering about something unimportant.

"Only the kind due to greedy ticket companies draining the common man dry for rich CEOs."

"Martin, if you are having problems, there is a solution."

"Yeah, invest in a pitchfork. How expensive are guillotines these days? Ouch. Maybe I could make my own and save." He didn't actually scroll for prices to chop off the heads of the elite, but began to stroll down the sidewalk. The bookstore closed early for Mr. Fensin's bunion-scraping day, allowing him the freedom to wander impatiently in front of the store because he'd forgotten. He was supposed to meet Janeth for a late dinner, but if he'd remembered, they could have gotten the early bird special and saved him a few dollars.

"I was more thinking you could return to finish your degree." Eldon kept on his high horse, but Marty was used to it.

"Here it comes."

"You were only a few classes from it. I don't understand why you abandoned it to work in a shop."

Because...I didn't like it. Marty wasn't the nose in a laptop, a planner for the planner type like Eldon or their mother. But they wouldn't stop harping on him to go back to school, to cinch that degree and get a job doing business things. Eldon had always known he had an interest in chemistry and engineering, which somehow led to watching chocolate dribble out of machines onto assembly lines.

Marty had gone into college wanting to experience everything he could, which had left his parents picking his major. He'd muddled through, save the occasional class he hadn't been able to charm a pass out of. But somewhere around junior year, the minor interest he could fake had vanished.

"I like working at the shop," he said to his brother. "Today a kid came in — around Miguel's age, so he'd barely graduated to chapter books. His mom left him in the anemic kids' section and the poor guy was completely lost. But once I pulled the dinosaur books off the shelf, especially the pop up one we weren't supposed to take the plastic off, his eyes lit up."

"So you enjoy getting children books. Get your BA in business, then work to operate and own a children's store."

Marty groaned and glared at his phone. The urge to chuck it into the street like a boomerang rose, but he couldn't afford a new one. So he kept it close enough to his ear to enjoy the rest of his brother's haranguing.

"You cannot keep existing at minimum wage. That's not a livable income."

"How is that my fault? I put in my fifty hours. Fifty-five actually, and I like the job. Okay, not all. Inventory day is…ugh, and some customers I wish I could put in a woodchipper. But the rest is great."

Eldon's heavy sigh carried so loudly that people glanced across the street at him. "Whenever you do decide to behave smartly, the school funds are still in the account."

"Is now when you brag about how you barely had to touch it?"

"Martin…"

"Thirty scholarships, twenty-nine of which were academic, and the last one for the chess team."

"It was water polo, and the team disbanded two years in," Eldon said, causing Marty to laugh.

The bookstore's door opened to reveal Brandy hustling home. He tried to not leer at her whole badunkadunk popping out as she bent over to lock the front door. It was damn hard though, especially when she stared at her palm, then slapped whatever stained it on her ass.

Oh God, there was a perfect palm print across her khakis now. *Look anywhere but there. Hey, check that out, the sun. That's new. When did they add that to the sky?*

"Marty?" her breathless voice asked, directing him straight to her. "I thought you'd already left."

"Thought about it, but then I got to thinking 'Self, it's been ages since we wandered around this little treasure trove of shops. We should check out the medical equipment store. Or that proctologist's office. And we have been needing to re-felt our billiards table for some time.'"

Her face lit up at his ridiculousness and he grinned back. Absently, Brandy brushed her hair behind her ear, causing him to stare at the long line of her neck. Had it always been so straight and thin? Delicate and in need of a tender touch?

"What about you?" he gulped, realizing he was close to leering. "Do you need to have your chakras realigned?"

"No." Brandy shook her head. "But I do need to get going."

"Oh?" His passing interest suddenly skyrocketing, Marty failed to move out of the way. She blinked slowly, and he blathered, "I was wondering when you were going to cash in your chip."

"Chip?"

"Ya know, getting me to paint your apartment. Me dressed in overalls. You sipping a mai tai and telling me I missed a spot."

Her cheeks pinked at that, and Brandy's gaze drifted lower. She kept a tight grip on the strap of her purse with both hands. "You have that all planned out in your head?"

"Or I know I'm a shitty painter," he answered, wanting to get another giggle from her.

But Brandy gave him little more than a single chuckle. "I have...this thing I'm doing with Mel tonight. So, it'll have to be a raincheck."

Ah, her best friend. That would explain it. Marty stepped aside and extended his hand. "Far be it from me to keep you from your appointment." With all sincerity, he bowed at the waist. Brandy stepped past, her ponytail swishing with her walk.

"See you tomorrow, Marty," she called, continuing the long stretch down the street to wherever Mel would pick her up. And as she went, that lone black handprint undulated on her round asset.

"Martin. Martin!" Eldon's distant voice tried to scream at him. And here he'd almost forgotten he was trapped in familial hell. One of those nicer levels of hell, where it was always Thanksgiving, no one wanted to talk because they were all fuming over politics and the turkey was super dry.

"Yes, Eldon," he said, placing the phone to his ear. "I'm here to listen to you in all your babbling glory."

"Should I tell you how rude it is to ignore a phone call while in the middle of it?"

"I had to say goodbye to Brandy. She's off on some girly get-together."

To his surprise, the line went dead. Marty yanked his phone away, about to check to see if the thing had given up on life, when Eldon's patented sigh rattled through the speakers. "You know it's a date, don't you?"

"What? No. She doesn't... Why would she...? Brandy doesn't date."

"Really?"

"Yes!" he shouted at his brother. No chance. They'd talked not even fifteen minutes before closing the store. If she had a date, she'd have told him. She'd have told him if she was even thinking about dating.

"Then when I overheard her and her friend talking this morning about a double date, that was...what? Some new meme challenge where two people consume dates at the same time?"

No. She can't be. She would have told me if she was ready. That, he was dead certain of. After he'd smoothly flirted with her before noticing the ring, then learned the whole story, she'd said that she needed time. And he'd been happy to give it — as friends.

She was already dating?

"What do you care?" Eldon's pain-in-the-ass voice asked. "You have Janeth, after all."

"Yeah." Marty nodded, his stomach clenched in a knot as he stared down the street where Brandy had vanished. "Why would I care?"

* * * *

"If you'll excuse me," Brandy said, sliding out of her chair before anyone could argue. To her surprise, the man beside her stood as well. What did he want? Did he think she hoped for him to follow?

Staring at Grant like a rabbit backed into a corner, she bleated out the first thing to come to mind. "I have to pee."

The smile strained and he folded back, letting her flee to the bathrooms with crabs on the doors. If Marty was here, he'd crack some horrible joke about how unappetizing the idea of crustaceans anywhere near the lower bits was. And why was she thinking of him?

Stumbling into a stall and locking the door, Brandy sat on the toilet and clenched onto her skirt just above her knees. An ache had begun rattling in the back of her brain when Grant and Joseph discussed their app. As they switched to their gains at the gym, it had blown up into a full-on migraine, leaving Brandy silently moaning into her shrimp scampi.

With the cool scent of urinal scrubs bleaching her thoughts, she stared numbly at her fingers. Why had she agreed to this? She wasn't ready. She'd known it the second Mel had suggested this.

But she so badly wanted to be.

"Hello." Mel's voice reverberated through the blue-tiled room with fishing nets for décor. "You in here?"

"Yes," she called, rising and about to exit the stall. Then she turned, flushed the unused toilet as cover and strode out to find her friend.

"So you didn't climb out of the window?" Mel said.

Brandy hunkered over the sink and began to wash her hands. She lathered up like she was prepared to head into surgery, to buy more time.

"Why…why would you think I'd do that?"

Mel, in her flirty red dress, loomed above Brandy, arms crossed. "Who do you think you're fooling? You looked like you wanted to chew your foot off to get out of there."

"Is that a possibility?"

Mel shook her head and took up the space at the sink beside Brandy. While the mastermind behind all of this inspected her makeup, Brandy watched her fingers beginning to prune under the running tap.

"We can just leave if you want," Mel said.

For a brief second, hope burst in her heart, but as she caught the slow blink in the mirror, Brandy backed down.

"No, no, it wouldn't be... It's not polite."

"What is bothering you? You were the one who said 'Set me up.'"

"I know, I know," Brandy said, crinkling the paper towel into sections as she spoke. After the dinner party, she'd gotten home, poured herself a glass of wine and called Mel. Whether it was the running anger at being called out for her shut-in depression, or the alcohol, she couldn't say. *Probably both.*

"It's just...I didn't think it'd be so date-y. You said it was casual."

"This is. Splitting the check at a low-rent seafood place is the epitome of casual." Despite her insistence, Mel touched up her lipstick, the ruby cream speaking louder than words.

"I thought casual meant like coffee or, I don't know, bowling."

"Bowling? Who the shit goes bowling?"

She sank deeper into herself, trying to not grow more despondent at how out of her depth she was. "It's so weird. To sit beside a strange guy and act like I...like he's...like I care about him."

Her active dating life had lasted for exactly five weeks, when her cousin had tried to set her up with the brother of her boyfriend. It had been a disaster, Brandy trying to get him to talk with his face buried in his phone. Then she'd met Kevin during a football game and she hadn't thought she'd ever have to date again.

Fate was cruel when it came to absolutes.

"The truth is, I've never even, um, been with anyone else."

Mel slapped her compact closed so hard it caused Brandy to jump. "You can't be serious."

She shrugged, feeling more and more alien in her skin. Twenty-six and she had one sexual partner under her belt. One who had grown with her as she figured out her body, who she knew every button and position for. Then fate had taken him and Brandy had been left facing the unscalable mountain of figuring out more men without a single tool for how to do it.

"I haven't felt like it. I know it's been two years since he...passed, but—"

"What about before?"

"When I was fifteen?" Brandy snorted. "My parents would have suffered multiple aneurisms if I'd even looked twice at a guy." Then they'd cut her out of their lives after she married Kevin for being too young. Sometimes she wanted to laugh at their dire predicament that it wouldn't last. Though, they had been right—it was just that death had made the decision, instead of divorce.

The uncomfortable silence she'd marinated in since his funeral rose around her. Mel actively looked anywhere but the weird widow, leaving Brandy to fish for her phone. Her exhaustion at forever being the outsider walking through life was nothing compared to her terror at having to try dating.

Trying to use her phone for distraction, Brandy found her finger lingering over the Instagram button.

Was he with her again? Probably. They had the whole night, after all. A brick thudded in her stomach at the thought, but she couldn't let well enough alone. Rather than scroll through her friends' feeds, she went straight for Janeth Willows, with the fancy checkmark and everything.

Hm, no sign of Marty in the most recent pictures. There was that guy Marty had said was her editor. If someone did an image search of alpha-douche, his picture would show up. All scowls and beady eyes, but he was hot so he could get away with it. Odd that Marty wasn't wherever she was taking snaps of flowers and makeup.

Maybe he needed time to work on his next elaborate date. Because Janeth wouldn't feel like her skin was crawling when she walked hand-in-hand with a man by the river. Or like she was kicking over someone's tombstone just by sitting together on a bench and watching the sunset.

In her angry scrolling, she swiped past all the sponcon to land on the pictures from Mrs. Dashwood's party. There were filtered images of fireworks with Janeth's pretty face in the foreground. One where she placed a churro to her lips, somehow making eating look attractive. Brandy's heart stopped as she found a pic she must've missed.

Janeth was on the dance floor, the band blurry splotches in the background. And there stood Marty with one arm wrapped around her waist, another holding her hand, and the biggest smile on his face. He looked beyond happy. Joyful. Ecstatic. Like that was everything he could ever want.

"Well, I should head out there before they send a manager to fetch us," Mel said, zipping up her purse.

"Do I distract them long enough for you to run to the exit?"

She wanted to be better, to be normal. To no longer be that sad, bawling widow no one talked to, but a vivacious young woman about town. God, she sounded like her grandmother. Running back to her apartment and crawling into her sweats wouldn't help.

"No," Brandy said, silencing her phone for the evening. "I'm coming with you and doing the date right."

Chapter Eight

He didn't want to count the seconds between his knocks. Or lean close to the door to hear if there was anyone else inside. But concern had Marty tight in its grip and wouldn't let go. It barely even let him sleep, his brain constantly churning over the idea of her with someone else.

What if he was a bad dude? She lived alone, in a less than savory part of town. If anything went down, would anyone come to help her?

Lifting the bag of muffins he'd snatched up on the run out of the door, Marty raised his fist for another knock when the door blew open. "What do you...?" she began, speaking around a foamy toothbrush crammed into her mouth. As her gaze darted down to find him, her eyes opened wide and she staggered back.

"Marty? You're...oh my God, how late is it?" Brandy drifted away from the door to stare back at her microwave and he sidled closer.

Sticking a foot in, he said, "Don't worry, I'm early for once. May I...?"

"Hm?" With her fears that she was missing work answered, she whipped her head to him, then down to her pajamas. Instead of a silk slip or sexy bra, it was a set of boxy cotton pjs with sloths all over them. That brought a smile to Marty's face, until she shoved him.

"No! I mean, give me a minute. I'm not...gah!" Brandy pushed him back far enough to shut the door, then slotted the chain in. Marty's gut dropped. He was left standing alone outside in the hall, only able to catch a glimpse of her shadow. Or was there more than one in her apartment?

Was that why she needed him out? Because she wasn't alone?

"What are you doing here?" Brandy shouted, her voice bouncing from deeper in the chained-off apartment.

"I was in the area and thought I could take you to work so you didn't have to bike."

"That's...weird. You're never up this early."

I was up at four a.m. because I couldn't stop picturing you running away from a dangerous killer in your underwear. "Eldon," Marty said instead, his brother always the perfect scapegoat. "Yeah, he had another of his 'let's go over your finances and tell you why you're a disappointment to the family' meetings set up. I got tired and left."

"Oh." Her soft voice carried in a circle around the apartment. At least she didn't seem to be in any pain. Nor was she basking in an afterglow.

Okay, you don't know that. Not like you've ever seen her after... Not that he would. He was just keeping an eye on her, and feeling miffed that she hadn't come to him first. He might be short, but he could swing a tire iron with the best of 'em.

Feeling two feet tall, Marty stared at the offering he'd brought. He'd thought they might be necessary to help smooth over any tears, but the longer she stayed behind her locked door, the more he suspected it was him who needed it. First night on the dating scene and she already had some guy in her bed. *Points for efficiency and all.*

"I've got muffins."

An eye poked between the narrow crack in the door. "What kind?"

"Apple crumb and blueberry."

"Did you eat all the apple ones?" Brandy asked, far more concerned with the muffins than dragging a stranger from her bed.

"No."

"Are you sick or something? All that's ever left of the apple ones are the papers...sometimes not even that."

A frown itched across his face. He didn't always eat them. Just, on occasion. When they were in front of him and he was bored. It was no wonder she'd only called Mel about the whole dating thing. He was a shit friend.

Another jangle of the chain whipped his head up. Brandy was finishing tugging her ponytail on as she walked out to him. Catching that the collar on her polo had slid up, Marty curled a hand over to tug it down. In doing so, his finger glanced across her warm skin. She paused in wrestling with her voluminous hair to stare at him.

"Want to look professional for book slinging," Marty babbled, yanking his hand away.

"Uh." Brandy curled her hand over her neck where he'd touched her and checked the position of the collar herself. "Yeah, as you say. So, show it to me."

What? Did she leap straight from cloistered widow to red light district in twelve hours? Marty coughed, prepared to mention his girlfriend, but the flush racing from his cheeks straight to his crotch stopped him.

"The muffin," Brandy said, bringing both relief and a strange regret to him. She crossed her arms, her curvy hip jutting out so that an edge of skin appeared above her low-slung jeans. "I don't believe a word you say when it comes to baked goods."

"Here." He yanked open the bag to reveal not one but two apple crumb muffins just for her. Brandy slipped her hand inside, her mouth open in shock. She raised one to her lips and took a big bite.

"Hm, after all this time, and anticipation and years of denial," she said through thoughtful chewing, "I thought it'd be better."

Marty gulped, his legs shifting like a skittish horse. *Real shame when that thing you wanted for years doesn't live up to the hype.* Not that he'd know anything about that.

The jingle of Brandy's keys was enough of a distraction from his horny shame spiral. She slipped one into the deadlock, causing an ice floe jam in Marty's brain.

"Wait," he said, worried that she was going to leave some strange man in her apartment just to keep him from knowing.

"What?" She pocketed her keys.

"Don't you want to…isn't there some…you forgot in your place?"

As her face knit in an afghan of confusion, it struck him. There wasn't any guy inside. He'd gotten worked up over nothing. Instant relief turned his grimace into a bright smile while Brandy kept staring.

"I could get my bike, if you don't want to give me a lift back after work," she said.

"No, no," he said, his chest swelling and a tune building in his step. The urge to dance rose through his legs but Marty kept it tamped down. "I'd be more than happy to bring you home." *Unlike random Tinder guy DudeBroseph25. Ha!*

Just as he was about to give in to his euphoria and spin in a circle, he froze. "Ah, wait, I was meeting Janeth after my shift."

Brandy didn't sigh, or shout at him for dashing her hopes of a free ride in an instant. She simply ate the last of the muffin, dropped the paper into the bag and unlocked her door to fetch her bike. For the first time since he'd set out to wake her up early and see if she'd brought anyone home, Marty regretted this.

It'd been some time since she'd sat in Marty's lime-green Honda Accord. His first car ever, it boasted rust patches near the tire, a broken rear-view mirror and a duct-taped glovebox. Not that Brandy much cared, as sitting in it meant she wasn't walking, pedaling through the heat or waiting hours for bus transfers.

He'd been strangely quiet for Marty, only giving her one- or two-word answers. Though she had no idea what he was doing there anyway.

And it had to be when she'd left her laundry everywhere, especially the comfy but always despised granny panties drying over the sink. *Talk about starting the day with some serious cardio.* Her heart was going a mile a minute at the thought of Marty walking in, spotting her underwear and laughing for days.

Would he even care? Janeth probably only wore those all-lace thongs and bra sets. If any of Brandy's underwear ever matched it was by pure accident and possibly a dye spill.

As the light changed, Marty pressed on the accelerator. Brandy closed her eyes and pulled in a breath. She didn't want to be a neurotic mess this early in the morning.

"Your car?" her brain threw out from nowhere. She could feel Marty glancing at her from his peripheral vision, so she had to keep going. "It was MIA for a while there. And I noticed you never told your brother why."

"Ha. If I wanted a ten-hour lecture, I'd tell my brother something. My flossing habits can get him on his soapbox of 'dental hygiene is next to Godliness'."

It sounded as if the discussion was closed, when Marty said, "The insurance. It ran out."

"Is it still…?"

"No, all squared up. Just needed another paycheck to do it. Then there were all the fees for missing coverage which, ya know, bigger chunk gone."

She was still scraping by, thanks to the insurance policy and what little had come from selling the bakery. After only having it a year, it amounted to expenses lost, but it wasn't as if she could go hat in hand to her parents. Or the ex-in-laws. They'd made certain of that.

"Are you…you're doing okay, right?" she asked him.

"Why? Know any get-rich-quick schemes that work? Maybe a secret lamp to rub, or some rich prince who needs a new butler? I give great foot rubs."

Brandy snickered at the idea but glanced at his hands on the steering wheel. He certainly had the size for it. What they said about guys and big hands...

What are you doing?

Gripping her knees, she turned to stare out of the window just as they passed the street from her happily never after. It still had the same pale blue and pink awning he'd surprised her with, but the sign with the giant cupcake was long gone. She hadn't had the money to remove it, the landowner having done it for her. Even then, where would she have kept it? The thing was the size of her bed.

Where had her old dream wound up? A landfill? Broken into pieces and tossed onto a fire?

"You okay?" Marty asked.

Startled, Brandy swiped at her eyes out of habit. A hint of moisture clung to her fingers, but not enough to tell her she'd been crying. "Yes. Just great." Her smile was strained, but it seemed enough to placate the worried man.

Lines of cars strolled past, the morning commuters struggling to get from point A to B, everyone in a grouchy mood thanks to the rising traffic. No one glanced once at that tiny shop that two years ago had had an entirely different future ahead of it.

"It's a yoga studio now," Brandy whispered to her hands. She caught Marty looking. "The bakery I...had. They turned it into a hot yoga studio. We just went past."

"I didn't know it was along this route. I'm so sorry."

"Don't be. Hard to not take Frankford to get to the store. I went in once."

"Really?"

"Tried to. Made it as far as the door, which they'd had wide open. I can't blame them. No airflow, which is not good for a bakery. I felt like a puddle of bones every morning, thanks to the ovens all going."

She didn't talk about it, because it made everyone around her uncomfortable. She didn't think about it, because it was a needle straight to her heart. She didn't let it go, because she feared what else she'd lose in the process.

A warm hand cupped hers, pressing her fingers tighter to her knee. Marty didn't say anything, but he held her as they merged out of traffic and into the small parking lot behind the shop. As he turned off the car, the hood rattled, the engine barely cooling in the sweltering June weather. Only the loud *ping* of cheap metal reforming itself in the summer sun filled the air.

With his hand still holding hers, Marty beamed his for-once calm eyes upon her. That always wild hair scattered over his ears, Brandy aching to push it back. To touch his cheek and wipe away a hint of the muffin crumb beside his mouth. To taste the blueberry lingering on his lips and know his hands anywhere besides a friendly shoulder pat or hug.

Her face charred bright red at the thought and she tried to whip away, but she felt pinned in place. Marty snickered, the bare edge of his lip rising to reveal that one crooked tooth. Shifting in the sunken bucket seat, Brandy steadied herself. Would he kiss her?

What would she do if he did?

Marty leaned closer, his breath parting across her cheek. "I was just wondering if —"

Yes?

"Since you seemed busy last night —"

Yes.

"Did I get you out of that shell?"

What? Brandy snaked her hand from below his and twisted to stare at the back wall. There'd been a lovely rainbow mural once, but it had been painted over in rust brown. "I don't know what you mean," she said, her ego legless and bleeding on the ground. All of that was just so he could brag about 'fixing her'?

"Eldon seemed to think you went on a date. Granted, his idea of romance is sitting quietly in the same room, not talking, so he could be wildly mistaken..."

"I did," she said, turning to watch him.

Marty's face didn't crumple, he didn't rend his shirt and cry at the injustice. Scratching the ear hidden behind his hair, he said, "Oh." It popped from his lips in a single gasp of air. "Well, that's...that's nice. Very nice. Will you see him again?"

Given that she'd practically run when he'd tried to ask her back to his place for coffee, it seemed unlikely. But Brandy stared at the man who'd shown up at her apartment unannounced and bearing baked goods. "I don't know," she said.

Marty repeated how nice it all was, his expression unreadable as he picked at the mass of fast food recipes crammed into the console.

"But I will need you to take the night shift this Friday," Brandy said fast, her heart setting in stone.

"So soon? Isn't the advice to make him wait a few weeks and sweat it out?"

It was tempting to keep him dangling on that hook, but Brandy's mean streak collapsed as soon as it was born. "Mel's working a party and she asked me to help with the desserts."

"Oh!" This time, instead of a gasp from his solar plexus, Marty sat up straighter, his face glowing bright. *Not a date.* She was still as pathetic as the day before. "Well that's...that's great. My mamá can't stop raving about your cupcakes. They're great. You'll do—"

"Great?"

"Why learn a new word when repeating the same one works just great?" Marty said with a laugh, cracking open his car door. Whatever inexplicable tension had risen between them vanished in the sticky summer humidity.

"Mind helping me unhook my bike?" she asked, dropping her feet to the asphalt.

"More than happy to, my lady." He bowed deep.

She rolled her eyes at his goofing around, and both of them undid the buckles. It was Marty who hefted the bike off the bars.

As it landed on the ground, her palms wrapping around the handles on instinct, she asked, "Did your car come standard with a rack?" It was hard to see Marty going out on the trails and even less so his brother. Maybe he planned a romantic bicycling tour for his girlfriend.

"Of course not," he said, wrapping the loose straps haphazardly around the bars and locking the trunk. So it was for some magical upcoming date she could watch in near real-time over social media. Marty turned and winked at her. "I got it for you."

"What?"

"The bus system's gone to shit and you seem to be stuck riding into work through the worst weather, so I thought...be proactive for once, Marty. Get ahead of the curve. And other business terms you shout when you have no idea why the company's both sinking and on fire."

A stupid smile wrapped around her lips, Brandy gave a jingle to the bell he'd gotten her, too. 'Because sometimes she might need to scare a tourist mucking about in the middle of the street.' As they moved closer to the back door, her heart sank. "If you had other plans on Friday, with Janeth, I can tell Mel to find someone else."

"Don't be silly. The world needs to eat your cupcakes," he said with pure sincerity, before blinking like mad and turning away. "I should use that one in my next chapter of the erotic adventures of Marco Rockhard."

Brandy gulped, the same confounding tension rising, but Marty banished it in an instant. "Besides, Janeth has some influencer thing going on that night."

The cold water of his girlfriend was enough to shake Brandy from her light-headed giddiness. With her bike stowed in their break room, she followed Marty out into the store. And they were promptly met by the haggard face of Mr. Fensin.

"Took you both long enough. Don't you see how late you are?" He jabbed a finger at the clock, which showed them both to be a half hour early.

"Yeah," Marty said. "You know, it's a real shame we can't just be legally chained to the register and never allowed to leave."

Fensin snorted at the impudence and Brandy tried to hide her smile. "Lip like that is why this place is..."

She tuned out his monthly dirge about how dire the store was. Instead, she watched Marty rummaging through the cookbook section. As he pulled out a bright pink cover festooned with cupcakes, he gave her a big thumbs-up.

Chapter Nine

There's white handprints on your pants. The black pants.
Brandy winced and grabbed one of the multitude of tea towels on the stack. It was too tiny to knot around her waist, so she settled for tucking it into her jeans instead. The makeshift apron disguised the slap of flour she'd blotted across her work blacks.

In her old catering days, she'd known better than to wipe her hands off on her uniform. Even with Mel running around the tiny kitchen hotter than the sun, screaming at her two sous chefs, somehow it didn't sink in that this was a job. Brandy had breezed in and got to work making her signature tiny pies like she was back at home.

But she had to be professional. It was Mel's business on the line.

Oh crud! Brandy rolled up the edge of her towel and wiped a spilled spot of cherry juice from a white square plate. All that remained behind was one of her golden pies the size of a half-dollar. She even gave them tiny lattices and added a small pie crust cherry on top.

A great line of the dessert plates stretched along the counters, waiting for a dollop of handmade whipped cream and a sprinkle of cinnamon sugar. Mel blew back in like a hurricane and filled her arms with the entree.

"I thought this was supposed to be a laidback barbecue," Brandy said, eying the salmon dish flying out of the door.

"So did I. Forty-two, watch your ass before I break it!"

Brandy chuckled at her numbering the two useless men she'd picked up from the local college. They needed the experience, but they required a lot more breaking in than Mel had time for.

With a string of pies topped off, she picked up the sifter and added a dusting of summer snow to the desserts. The screaming she did not miss. Chefs forever at breaking point, lashing out at anyone who got too close. Smoking two to three packs a day until their hair was charred with tobacco. Cornering anyone that didn't live up to their standards and shouting them stupid for reacting.

After one too many crying matches in her car, she'd thrown in the towel. She'd felt a failure and a waste of her education, until Kevin had told her about the small bakery he'd bought her. It had been a Christmas, birthday and anniversary present in one. And she'd never wanted anything else.

"How can such skinny people eat so damn fast?" Mel bellowed, popping back in. "The desserts?"

"Ready to go out." Brandy smiled, filling her arms with the tiny plates and turning to her friend.

"Fantastic," she declared when the sound of broken china erupted from the dining room. Mel vanished but her voice increased. "Fifty-two, will you yank your head out of your ass before I shove it up there?" Her face popped back in and all the venom vanished. "Could you be a dear and hand those out? I have to go murder two waiters."

Brandy chuckled at the empty threat, but Mel could put the fear of God into anyone when her business was on the line. The party was full of people with clout and a make or break for Mel. No wonder she was in a ripping-throats-out kind of mood.

Testing to make certain she had a good grip on her tiny pies, Brandy eased out of the kitchen. She passed through the dining room where they were plating and setting up. Mel had the waiter cowering in the corner and she ordered the other to clean up.

If a broken plate was the worst thing to happen on a job, that was a miracle. But, if they were already at the dessert stage, there couldn't be much left in the service. This might work.

She'd buried herself in her work, arriving hours before everyone else to prep the multitude of pie crusts. In that routine—the familiar pull of measuring, kneading, rolling, cutting—her heart soared. She felt at home adjusting ingredients on the fly, fixing mistakes before they became problems and watching the idea in her head become art.

Locked in the overheating kitchen, her back aching from hunching over delicate work all day, was what Brandy missed about this job. As she eased out of the door, her pinkie tugging on the handle to give her access, Brandy emerged into the cacophony.

And that was the part she hated about this job. Okay, aside from the screaming.

A cavalcade of blondes and blonds in bikinis and swim trunks that cost the down payment on a car cavorted around an infinity pool. Because that wasn't enough, there was also a jacuzzi with a waterfall and rock formation which had more girls perched on it. They were all laughing and snapping pics while teeth-grating music scratched over the speakers.

Expensive plates belonging to Mel lay scattered around the pool, high heels stomping near enough to shatter them. Even the glasses were real. No plastic cups for this crowd.

Sighing, Brandy eased closer to the food table, when two men in the requisite Cayman-island tan eyed her up. One tossed a beach ball back to the girls, splattering it in the pool and spraying them in the face. Neither guy cared, both standing far too close to Brandy for comfort.

"What have you got there, dessert girl?" one asked, yanking a plate away.

"A mini cherry pie," Brandy answered. She tried to turn around and put the plates on the table, but the men wouldn't move.

The other circled closer, his hot breath darting down her neck. He stared down her shirt, not giving a shit that she knew he was doing it. Wanting to run, but trapped under the plates loaded with her hours of work, Brandy said, "Pie, sir?"

He snickered and took one while the other guy laughed. "Nothing I love more than a woman who brings me her juicy, moist pie whenever I want."

Gritting so hard to keep her smile in place that she felt something pop in her neck, Brandy spun around and started to fling the plates onto the table. It wasn't until she was nearly free of the heavy porcelain that she realized it left her ass to them. An ass that'd been a little too big to fit into her old work jeans. She squeezed her eyes tight together, afraid that one of them would grab her. And she could do nothing.

"Aiden," a voice shouted from the side. One of the many blondes appeared, wrapping her arm around the biceps of the one who thought he was funny. Or they probably both did. "Come on. We're going to take some pics in the grotto."

"Okay," he grumbled at her request but leered at Brandy the entire walk away.

She held her head up, her spine straight as a rod, until they all vanished around the corner. *Shit.* Her legs trembled, knocking her hip into the table and causing the plates to tip. That had been too close. What was she thinking?

Were all the men out here like that? Not just at the party but in the wide world? She'd been locked up behind doors of her own making for so long that maybe the entire gender had gone feral.

No, Marty wasn't like that. Not even in all the times he'd help her steady a ladder at work. He was always a gentleman about such things.

And that's why he has a perfect girlfriend while you're miserably alone.

"Whoa, girl." Mel's hand slapped onto the table, stopping the shaking. "What happened?"

Brandy opened her mouth, but as she stared at her friend, she realized that if she told the truth, it'd only enrage Mel. *Maybe make her spit fire and tear after the assholes.* And her friend needed this job to go well. Not only for the money, but the word of mouth and reviews. "Just...nerves about being back."

Mel wrapped a comforting arm around Brandy's shoulders, pulling her into a half hug. "You're doing great. The pies are incredible. Such a flaky crust on something so tiny."

Brandy crossed her arms. "I didn't think we were supposed to eat until everyone else was served."

Gulping at having incriminated herself, Mel drifted back and shook her head. "I was just trying one, for quality control. You know. Had to just make certain that it was—"

"That I was up to snuff?" Her light jab turned back on her, Brandy shuffled her feet around. She'd have shaken off those two creeps like it was nothing in the old days. Now she didn't even have the armor of 'I have a husband' to hide behind.

"Oh, no. Not like that." Mel was about to reach to comfort her again, when a loud shout for everyone to look their way echoed above the DJ.

The voice sounded familiar and, as Brandy focused, she caught the willowy body of Janeth posing next to the infinity pool. Her barely-there breasts, which practically floated on her chest, were covered in a cute bikini top of rainbows, and the bottoms had a tiny unicorn. As heads all turned to find her, she scrunched one leg up and posed like a sexy flamingo.

Phones whipped out, snapping pics of the beautiful woman. She extended her fingers out in the peace sign, laughed, then jumped into the pool. It was a sad cannonball thanks to her lack of mass, but as she re-surfaced, everyone gave a round of applause.

"I didn't think she'd be here," Brandy whispered to herself. Did that mean Marty was too? The idea that she'd have to serve him crawled across her skin and she crumpled deeper.

"*She*? Wait, is that...?" Mel pointed to the blonde star floating about the pool.

"Yeah. Janeth Willows herself. How did you not know? You're the one who follows her."

Mel shrugged. "People look different without the filters on. I knew it was a party for some fancy vodka brand—just didn't expect them to pull in influencers. Are you okay?"

That caused Brandy to scrunch her nose. She shouldn't care. Janeth was famous for being pretty and taking good pictures. Because of that she got to lounge around at parties where people like Brandy served food. It wasn't as if she wanted that life. Her selfie game was more abysmal than a cat that swiped at the screen.

"Yeah, yes. I'm good. Great," Brandy insisted, watching Janeth paddle through the water to the edge of the pool. That alpha-douche, her editor, stood by the side with a towel in his hand. As he helped Janeth out of the pool, he draped it over her shoulders because she was the sparkling talent.

There were more pies that needed to be added to the table. Brandy turned away, prepared to walk back into the kitchen, but she couldn't stop talking to Mel. "Why would I even care? Just because she's dating Marty—"

"Uh..." Mel slapped her on the arm. "Are you sure about that?"

Brandy's jaw dropped, as did Janeth's...to accommodate the tongue that alpha-douche shoved down her throat.

What the ever-loving fuck?

Chapter Ten

Oh my God!

Brandy wrapped her hands around her face and crumpled into a ball, her butt bouncing against the oven door. She'd fled straight into the kitchen, leaving Mel to watch the two inspecting each other's tonsils by the pool. Why was she overwhelmed with total embarrassment?

Her skin itched along with the flush and, every time she took her blinders away, she'd curl back in on herself. Had Janeth spotted her? Would she say something?

"Welcome back to the catering game." Mel's voice drifted through the dining room. Brandy rocketed up to her legs and tried to look busy by burying her hands in a pile of flour.

"Are they still...?" She turned to look at her friend and a tear tumbled from her eye. A floured finger was about to wipe it away, but she had enough sense to use her forearm. What was wrong with her?

"No, they finally disengaged and wandered off for more influencer brand time. You okay? I thought you'd be happier."

"Yes, I'm... I should call Marty." She fished out her phone, smearing the case with flour prints. It took almost no time to find his name, but before she pressed on the number, Brandy clicked on the picture. He'd taken it during her first week at the store. A pair of felt antlers sat on his head, tiny LEDs dancing in a pattern along the decoration.

It'd gut him to learn his 'angel' was anything but. *Flat-out rip that smiling face to shreds.* And who would he blame? Janeth for cheating on him or the person who'd told him everything, who'd revealed the rotten truth of his happily ever after? Why would he even look twice at the woman who'd ruined his perfect future?

"Can't get a signal?" Mel butted in. "I swear, something about these hills. You'd think it'd be nonstop hot spots with this many internet millionaires around."

"I was just thinking this is...something I should do in person. Try and soften the blow." Brandy slipped her phone into her pocket. She had to tell him, she knew that. He needed to know, but there was a dinner to finish serving and a kitchen to clean.

Mel loaded up their one cart with the dessert plates, leaving Brandy to stand awkwardly in the kitchen. "Don't work yourself into a knot. It might come as a relief to him. God knows it wasn't a pairing that would last. Look at her."

"Yeah." Brandy sighed and peered through the tiny window nearly eclipsed by plants. She didn't deserve him.

It wasn't until nearly one a.m. that they finished takedown, Mel pulling out all the elbow grease to leave the kitchen cleaner than they'd found it. Brandy tried to lighten her mood by talking to the other chefs about their schooling, but it'd come crashing down the second she heard Janeth's voice. The back of her skull pulsed with a hot nail named '*you have to tell Marty.*'

Mel closed the back of the truck and turned to the rest of the people who'd driven themselves. "The good thing about catering for skinny people paid to stay skinny..." She bent over and picked up paper bags overflowing with containers. "There's tons of food left over. Thing one, Thing two?"

The waiters frowned at her refusing to use their names, but were happy to take the food that'd easily provide two or three meals. "Were there any pies left?" one asked, his nose buried in the sack.

"You're more worried about those than my grilled chili salmon with lime crema?" Mel scolded, a hand on her hip. The men whose future were at her mercy gulped, but she laughed. "Yes, there's pie. Though I had to hide a few to make certain. Next time, we should have an all-dessert bar, Brandy."

"I'll..." She accepted her load, the heavenly but awkward scents of fish, asparagus, chili and cherry all rising from her arms. "I'll think about it."

Mel opened her mouth, probably about to argue, when she caught sight of the men still standing around. "Get out of here, already. I'll call you for the next job."

That was enough for the culinary students living at the whims of any locals who needed help. They dispersed, leaving Brandy to catch a ride with Mel.

"I do mean it. Next dinner, we do a full dessert spread. Really let you run wild. The pies were great—

couldn't get 'em out fast enough. But I know you can do better."

Could I? Brandy slid into the passenger seat. She made certain to buckle up and even adjusted the height on the belt so it fit her better. Mel was wilder, but at the sound of Brandy clawing her doggie bag, she too locked herself in and they were off.

Behind them, the sounds of the ultra-wealthy and young carried into the night. Despite the day winding down, they were only getting started. The fancy wine and pint glasses had been replaced with Jell-O shots and plastic cups. She only risked one last look at Janeth, watching her down a beer with the best of them. The editor-douche lingered close, but neither gave a hint that they'd swapped spit before.

Almost like it didn't even happen.

Upon reaching her apartment, Brandy thanked Mel for the opportunity and got a request for her help again. "I'll think about it," was the best she could offer. She was lucky this was a smaller gig, truth be told. Despite Mel's constant assurances, Brandy was off her game. It had taken her far too long to complete what a good chef would have done in half the time. And Brandy knew deep in her heart that if it'd been any other chef but her friend, she'd have been yelled stupid for her incompetence.

Holiday baking in the kitchen was nothing like working the line. What did it matter, anyway? She'd never have her own bakery again. Not without a miracle.

She arranged the party food in her fridge. All the containers were color coded and labeled. Even in the darkest abyss, she couldn't stop her need to date her leftovers—an organized kitchen was a godsend to a chef or baker.

Marty's fridge probably has a pet mold monster living it. He'd feed it every day. And name it Goose.

Her heart pounded harder. Brandy laid a palm over her sternum as she felt the beats shatter through her body. She had to tell him the truth. About Janeth. Tell him that he could do so much better...than a beautiful woman who made gobs of money on her beauty.

Better how, Brandy?

Some low-rent, broken ex-baker?

Why would he want chipped beef after he had steak?

It wasn't about her. It was for Marty. He needed to know before he got in too deep. Before she could back out, she pressed the Call button on his number. It rang three times, melting Brandy's spine to butter.

She was about to cancel when a groggy voice asked, "Hello?"

"Hi! I..."

"Brandy?" he asked cautiously. "Ah, says right there, Brandy. Guessing your party's done. Hoping that's the case and not that they decided to hunt you all for sport."

"What?"

"I've seen *Billionaire Hunter Island*," Marty insisted. "So, what's up?"

Tell him. Tell him that everything he thought he knew about his girlfriend was a lie.

What if he didn't believe her? What if he called her a liar and broke off their friendship? What if she did the right thing and it didn't matter? Marty stayed with Janeth and she just kept right on cheating on him behind his back because she was his one and only?

"I have leftovers," Brandy said fast. "From the party. Lots of fancy food and I was thinking you might want to help me eat them before they go bad."

A groan rolled through the phone, causing her to grip harder to keep it sealed to her ear. "I dun... What did you make?"

"Tiny cherry pies," she said.

"While I'd normally be out the door at the prospect of eating anything you made, I'm afraid one-forty-five in the morning is too late for my tender digestion."

Oh shit. She whipped her head over to find any clock. What was she doing calling him so late? Did she wake him up?

Of course you did. You woke him up to devastate him.

"Ever since I passed twenty-five, I swear. The eyesight's starting to dim, bones are all rickety and brittle. Can't eat anything after eight without turning into a—"

"I'm so sorry," Brandy shouted over Marty's blathering to try and stay awake. "I had no idea how late it was. I shouldn't have called you."

"Never apologize for offering me pie," he said, causing her to smile and blush. But a great yawn over the phone sent her gut plummeting.

"You should sleep. I should let you get back to sleep. I'm going to go."

"Thanks. Hey, did you have fun?"

"I did."

"Then it's all good," were Marty's parting words as the line went dead.

She couldn't do it. Brandy pressed her phone to her heart and sank to her knees. Her shirt smelled of salmon and limes, the fishy scent dragging her back to the party.

Why did I have to see that?

Marty was her friend — she wanted him to be happy. Janeth made him happy. So she should keep her mouth shut. Maybe they had some arrangement…

No. Not Marty. She could believe that from Eldon before Romeo Dashwood.

So tell him? Break his heart and hope that he'd finally see her as more than a…

"This isn't about you," she cursed to herself. Knocking the back of her head against the stove, she stewed deeper into how she could both help and hurt her friend at the same time.

Chapter Eleven

A knock at the door woke her from a shallow sleep. Disoriented, she didn't glance at the clock, or slip on a robe to cover her tiny camisole that did unspeakable things to her boobs. She didn't even look through the peephole, just yanked open the door and found her jaw plummeting.

"Marty?"

His hair was drenched, those puppy-dog eyes wide as he wrung a hat in his hands. Had it rained?

"You said something about leftovers," he explained with a shrug.

Brandy stepped back, letting him into her place. "They're in the fridge." She pointed to her kitchen as if he didn't know, then frowned. "But I thought it was...it's way too late for food."

His shoulder rose, turning the soaked-through white T-shirt translucent. She stared in wonder at his nearly naked body hiding below. Marty turned, revealing even more of his shirt that was so wet it suckered to every dip of his chest. Had he run through a waterfall? And why couldn't she turn away?

"Sounded like you wanted to talk too," he said, finally ripping her from his pecs.

"I, um…" *Fuck.* She wasn't ready for this. And there he stood, dripping onto the floorboards, his concern growing.

Closing her eyes tight, Brandy unleashed the bombshell. "Janeth was at the party tonight and I caught her kissing another man." She puckered her face, too terrified to look at him. Would he start pacing? Rip his hair out? Swear vengeance and challenge the man to a duel?

When nary a peep erupted from him, she risked a single peek through her lashes. Marty turned from her, leaving visible only the svelte line of his body where his cut stomach tapered into his hips. His face was hidden behind the soaked curtains of his hair.

"I am…" Brandy reached out to him, cupping his shoulder. A surprising heat blazed off the wet cotton. "I'm so sorry."

Marty whipped his head around, his eyes burning coals as he advanced. Instinctively, she pedaled back, but could only go a step before she smacked into her counter. When a hand landed on her hip, Brandy gulped. Staring at the face of the man who should be shattering into a million pieces, she frowned. It was unreadable, his expression in shadows.

But a slow growl rolled in his chest, one that shook her to the core. "Don't be," Marty said. The hand wrapped to her hip dug in to tug her from the counter, just as he curled his palm around her cheek.

Brandy could barely gasp before Marty's face filled her vision. Using the tip of his thumb, he traced the edge of her mouth. Back and forth he went across the tender skin, until it started to tickle. "I'm not," he thundered and pulled her to him.

Lips of fire pressed to hers and he tousled her hair apart. Heat pooling straight down her spine, Brandy clung to this impossible kiss. As he knotted his fist around her fallen hair, Marty tugged her head to the side and delved deeper. He played with her lip until he could coax her tongue to greet his.

She tasted his body, his being. He smelled of a heat wafting across a throbbing dance floor, of sweaty bodies twisting together in a sleeping bag. Brandy dared to wrap her hands around his waist, pulling herself deeper into his kiss.

"I was so stupid to ignore you," Marty said, his words whispering hot breath into her ear. She shivered at the touch. He puckered tender lips along the edge of her throat, each soft kiss trailing lower as he caressed his hands higher.

Marty tugged on her camisole, exposing her soft belly to his palms. Slipping a hand below her shirt, he used the tips of his fingers to glide right under her breast. "Not that I ever ignored these."

Cupping around her boobs, Marty kneaded with his thumbs as he pressed his hips tighter to Brandy. She yelped at the surprising force, but gave in to him. With each massage of her chest, he ground closer, brushing his jeans against her tiny shorts. Even through the denim she felt him hardening, his pants straining around his rising cock.

Brandy ached to run her hand over the top of it, to feel a man again. But she was frozen in place. What if she touched him wrong? What if—

Marty yanked one of his hands out from under her shirt and rolled it behind her palm. With his thumb hooked around, he guided her straight to his crotch. He nibbled on her earlobe as he let her graze her fingers against him.

"Oh." A sharp moan burst from the man licking her ear. Her long-dormant libido ordered her to touch more. Twisting her palm, she tugged his pants up and down the shaft hiding below. "Fuck," Marty gasped, his forehead crashing onto hers while he kept thrusting his hips closer.

"Let me take you," he pleaded, his gaze burning for understanding. Flitting one thumb around the waistband of her shorts, he tugged them off her hip so he could palm a bare buttock. Marty swept his other hand across the nape of her neck, holding her close as they stared deep into each other's eyes.

"Let me be with you." He kissed her, a soft touch on the lips, as sweet as pink satin. And, with his thumb, he parted the crease of her thigh. Brandy widened her stance, her body pleading with him to keep going. Suddenly, Marty stopped, right before he reached her pussy. They stood in her kitchen, his hand down her pants, hers wrapped around his cock, both breathing each other in.

"Please."

Brandy yanked on his jeans. Her fingers went for the zipper first, all of her needing him naked as fast as possible. When they refused to tug off, she remembered the button. Marty had no trouble, curling both palms around her hips to drop her panties to the floor.

Cold from the cabinets crawled across Brandy's naked back, but it didn't matter as Marty ripped off her camisole and kissed her. The heat of his touch swept over her naked breasts, raising her nipples from aroused to famished in an instant. She moaned into his kiss, his lips puckering in a smile at that before he lapped her tongue with his.

She strained to reach any part of him, to reveal his body at last, but Marty had her in flux. His touch was everywhere at once—her breasts, her ass, tugging on her hair, brushing her cheek, spreading her thighs. She couldn't keep track and hung on, her body humming with each one.

Without warning, it all retreated. Marty sidled back and stared down her body. She didn't have time to suck in her gut or do that half-turn trick to look skinner. No, he saw her in all her half-splayed, hanging-arms, chest-heaving glory. And he smiled wide.

"If you don't mind," Marty said, grabbing the neck of his shirt. Despite it being soaked to his body, he yanked it up with no fuss. It was Brandy's turn to stare in wonder. Fur as black as night ran across his pecs and straight through the hard narrows of his abs. Across his belly the forest grew, calling for Brandy's palm to rub the soft man-hair.

As she drifted her gaze lower, so too went Marty's jeans. He stood only in a pair of white boxers covered in those classic red hearts. *How long did it take him to find those?* "Ooh," he said, distracting her, "want to see a magic trick?"

"Okay?" she said slowly, growing painfully aware that she was fully naked in her kitchen with a coworker.

"Nothing up this sleeve." He pretended to show off the inside of a shirt he wasn't wearing. "Nothing up this one, either." Marty rolled his hands around his hips and, in one fell swoop, yanked his underwear off.

Holy shit!

"Ta da," he said, his jazz hands causing his maximum overload to sway hypnotically. Brandy stared in total shock at the third leg he somehow kept hidden in his pants. Curling a warm hand around her elbow, he dragged his fingernails against the skin of her forearm until he cupped the back of her hand.

Marty rustled through her hair, guiding her close by the nape of her neck as he directed her hand lower. "How do you...?" He guided her hand around his cock, a shudder rising through him as she touched it. "Find the merchandise?" Marty panted, even while finishing the joke.

Unable to help herself, Brandy struggled to cinch her hand tighter. She traversed the full length of his cock until she curled her palm around the sensitive crown. A plea dripped from Marty's lips and he pressed his forehead to hers.

Gently gliding her palm up and down his cock in a corkscrew, she whispered, "It's just what I've always wanted."

Marty gripped her waist, nibbling along her jaw. When he pressed his knee between Brandy's wobbly thighs, a moan slipped from her lips. Her under-appreciated pussy caused her to tip her hips forward and grind against the touch of skin.

God, how she wanted him. She'd been wanting him for...she didn't even know. His touch rounded back across her ass. Pressing his nails deep into her flesh, Marty lifted her. Not onto the counter, but he raised her until she hovered an inch or two off the ground.

Before gravity could yank her down, he spread her thighs with his hips, pinning her in place. His cock brushed against her soaked lips.

"Did you ever think about me pinning you beside the cash register?" Marty asked, plunging his teeth into her neck.

Brandy squirmed in his grip, not wanting to fall unless it was onto his cock. But he held it away from her. Cupping one hand to her breasts, he swept the other down her stomach. He trailed his fingers like reeds through a lake.

"Riding you behind the mass of boxes?" he asked, a smirk rising along his flushed lips.

"Oh!" Brandy moaned as he slipped first one finger, then two inside her. She tried to focus on his thrusting, but he lapped his tongue around her ear.

"How often did you want me to lock the store and take you in the front window?"

Christ! He began to swirl across her clit with his thumb and he found his way to the back door with his pinkie. A tremble consumed her body, Brandy shivering as every long-denied orgasm rose from the depths.

"Well?" Marty whispered, ramping up his efforts and nearly bringing her to confounding tears.

"Too damn often," she confessed, sounding near hysterics.

A single laugh rolled from him. In one fast move, he slipped his hand out of her and placed it over her stomach. His bony hips digging into her spread thighs, Marty gripped himself by the base as he stared at her. She tried to look away, embarrassment washing over her, but he cupped her chin and held her in place. Eye to eye, breaths matching, he plunged his cock inside her.

And it was bliss.

"Fuck," Brandy cursed, her legs rising on their own. Her toes curled as every inch of him bored deeper inside. He skated his nails down her legs and guided them up to rest on his back. Marty bent closer.

Her entire body was in flames. She kept trying to thrust down on him but could barely move. He had total control, Brandy trapped between him and the stove.

"You are..." Marty whispered, then grazed his teeth along her jaw. "So beautiful." He began to thrust, shallow and cautious, as if he feared breaking her. But she was made of sterner stuff.

Brandy grabbed his shoulders, giving herself leverage to pound onto him. This time Marty cursed, his head tossed back as he gulped in air. "Yes," he cried for her. "Yes!" He wanted only her.

She reached for him, when Marty flexed his palms under her ass. Before she could blink, he yanked her into the air. Even without leverage, he kept thrusting and nibbling across her chest.

Brandy cried out when something cool and flat struck her back. She whipped her head to the side and caught the reflected image of Marty's wild face. He'd spun her from the counter to the fridge. He slapped one hand to the stainless steel beside her face and, with the other, grabbed her wrist to tug it between them.

On instinct, she danced her fingers over her clit, and Marty locked his hand around the base of his cock. He dove his head, sucking hard on her nipple. The rumbling through her body rampaged to an aching need for release.

"My turn," Marty said. He knocked her fingers away and took up vibrating her clit while he thrust inside her. Not to be outdone, Brandy stretched and cupped his balls in her palm. "Ah, God. Your touch is... What was I thinking?"

So was his, but she couldn't voice it. Brandy dug her toes in, her legs flexing taut as she clung to the orgasm ramping through her. "This. Keep doing this," she pleaded, trying to position her hips for just the right angle.

A laugh of triumph rose from Marty, drawing pleasure from both her clit and ass. His cock filled her beyond belief, and he stopped biting along her breasts and puckered his lips. With a touch as soft as a snowflake, Marty kissed her and she was lost.

The orgasm raced through the entirety of her body. Her legs shivered and danced against his hips, her arms fell to a dead weight and the pleasure of his touch reverberated up to her eyes. Brandy gasped, sinking into the warm satiety she craved. To curl up in his arms, to lie against his chest and feel his reassuring heartbeat. To know he'd be there for her even when she woke.

A callow laugh burst from Marty, his always soft and mischievous chuckle gone. "I don't think you need that anymore," he declared and snatched the ring around her neck. With barely any force, he yanked it off, snapping the chain Kevin had given her.

"What are you...?" Brandy tried to reach for it, but she was trapped against the fridge. Marty leaned back, away from her range, with his throbbing cock still inside her.

With a cold eye, he bundled her wedding ring in his palm and crushed it. "There," he said, opening his palm to reveal nothing but pieces of glitter where her ring and necklace had been.

How...?

Marty placed his lips to his palm and blew. Diamond dust flew through the air and struck her face. Everywhere it touched, it sliced through her sharper than a scalpel. Pain sundered Brandy's cheeks and forehead. She reached to try and protect herself, but it was too late. The damage was done.

"You're over all of that trauma and bad memories," he said, his voice maniacal. "You've got me now. Forget him."

"No." Tears welled in her eyes, Brandy shaking her head so hard it bounced against the fridge. "No!" she screamed, and sat bolt upright in bed.

Oh God. She slapped at her chest, furiously hunting for the ring. Where was it? What did she...? Her head swiveled and there it sat in a small porcelain dish, as it had for the past year. Her promise to love and honor a man for the rest of her life.

Pain burned in her eyes as she raised the small diamond to her face. She protectively cupped her hand and held it close, watching the reflection of the streetlights refract through the gem. "I'm sorry. I'm so sorry. I don't know why I did that."

She felt filthy, as if she'd walked ten miles through raw sewage, literal shit clinging to her clothing and leeching into her shoes. It was a dream. That didn't count. It wasn't as if she'd —

Guilt caused her vision to focus from the diamond to the single picture on her nightstand. She hadn't had it before when he was alive. She hadn't needed it. She'd only have to roll over to watch his face in sleep.

"I wish you were here," she whispered to a piece of paper. How many nights had she cried her eyes out over that old photo? How many times had she pleaded and begged for him to come back?

How much longer could it go on?

Move on, girl. What would Kevin want?

He'd want her to be happy. She knew that in her heart. Even with his parents hating her. Even with her life in such tatters that she'd had to sell his guitar. Even with her dreaming about another guy, he'd want her to find peace.

But no one had promised that would be found with Marty.

"I wish that...that I didn't have feelings for him. That I could tell him about his girlfriend, like a friend would. Nothing more. Not expecting, not hoping. Not thinking that he'd, that we'd..."

She wanted that. For Marty to see her as more, but what was she? A broke widow working a dead-end job. A woman with no future and a past that wouldn't leave her.

Pulling in a breath sharp as diamond shards, she said, "I don't deserve anything better."

Chapter Twelve

It was not a good scone. Under the tempting bakery lights, it had looked buttery and rich. In his mouth, it tasted like kitty litter and had the texture of sand dug out of an ashtray. Marty was glaring at the baked good that had broken his heart when a shadow caused him to look up.

"Morning, sunshine," he called in a chipper voice, receiving the frown he expected.

"Hi," poor, exhausted Brandy answered with. Her usually bright eyes were shadowed, her always dewy skin ashen and dry. All clear signs of someone with a five-alarm hangover.

Marty didn't ask how she'd found him at the coffee shop, only moved his mass of shit out of the way. She collapsed into a chair, finger massaging what had to be aching temples. "They say food is supposed to help, but I think this scone would only make it worse."

"What?" Her head whipped up, her lips pursed in agony. "Make what worse?"

"Those tiny elves jackhammering on your brain," he said, swiping a finger back and forth over her serious ponytail.

The frown deepened and she turned from him. "You think I have a hangover?"

"I'd say drunk dialing me at two a.m. would lead to one. Unless you have some kind of alcohol-related superpower I'm unaware of?" Picking up his half-drained mug, he was about to take a long drink when he watched Brandy from above the rim. She was very clearly not looking at him. Oh, her head would turn in his direction, but her gaze batted around the bottles behind the counter, or the little Chinese lanterns left up all year.

What's wrong? Marty moved to place his cup down, already reaching to hold her pale, trembling hand, when it struck him. "You know I'm not mad."

"You're not?"

Funny, he'd never noticed how brown her eyes were. There were varying levels of brownness in the world. Some had the so-dull brown as to be nearly a grayish black. Others had a light brown that leaned into a terrifying yellow hazel. But Brandy's irises boasted the richest brown he'd ever seen. Brighter than milk chocolate, deeper than a river of chocolate, softer than a chocolate truffle. He should have gotten the chocolate donut instead.

Shaking off the wanderings of his stomach, he said, "I mean, if it happened to Eldon, he'd be fuming."

"How…" Brandy clasped her hands together on the table until they were folded in prayer. "How do you know?"

Marty chuckled. "How could I not? You called me, dragged me from the deepest dreams to—"

There went the crumble again and he flinched. They were always picking on each other, the way friends did. Why was this bothering her so badly? "I just wanted to say, I mean that...I didn't care. Okay, I was left lying in bed dreaming about eating your pie."

"Oh God." Brandy folded, burying her head in her hands.

"You didn't eat it all, did you?" Marty kept on poking, causing her to groan harder.

"No. That isn't...I didn't just call you for food." She lifted her head and the stricken look knotting her lips caused him to shrink back. "I need to talk to you. To tell you something..."

"What is it?" he said, wanting to rub her shoulders to worry the anxiety away. Brandy practically radiated neon-pink waves of fear and he couldn't understand it.

She winced, those deep brown eyes going everywhere but him again. "If I tell you, you'll...I don't want you to get mad."

"Me? Mad? When am I ever angry? I am as serene as one of those cheap fountains you can buy at a drugstore." Marty raised his hands and pinched both forefingers to thumbs. Gurgling noises erupted from his lips.

There it was, a momentary crack in her dour frown. But the longer she stared, not saying anything, the colder the wind blew through him. Some of that might be due to the A/C cranked to 'building a snowman' levels. Yet, he couldn't fully explain the shiver crawling up his spine.

"Brandy..." He reached out and cupped her hands with his. "You can talk to me. You know that. About anything."

She mashed her pursed lips back and forth as she seemed to chew on his offer. It wasn't until she drifted her wandering gaze away from the ceiling onto him that she opened her mouth to explain.

"It's..."

A jangle of the bell distracted him, and he sat up instantly. His hands fell from Brandy as he looked to his breakfast guest. "Hello, beautiful," he called, waving to make certain she saw him.

Janeth floated across the floor like a sea queen and rested beside his table. On instinct, Marty stood and moved to tug out her chair. He placed a quick kiss to her cheek, well aware that touching the perfectly applied purple on her lips wouldn't end well for him.

She turned to him. "You said we have a date planned?"

"Yes, and it's... Uh, could you give me a minute? I was in the middle of something with—" He jerked his chin to Brandy, but she was turtled up inside her shirt. Even her hands tugged inside the sleeves.

Janeth focused away from her phone to the woman trying to climb inside her own liver. "Do I know you?"

"What?" Brandy gasped and Marty chuckled.

"Of course you do—from the party. Remember?" He leaned closer, caressing his arm across Janeth's shoulders, but her eyes burned through Brandy.

She wasn't jealous, was she? Marty wanted to laugh at such a ludicrous thought. Brandy was a good friend, and he was always more tactile with people than the average guy. Nothing else to it. Janeth should never have to worry about him having eyes for anyone else. Turning said eyes on his girlfriend and sighing to himself at being so lucky, he said, "My mom's birthday party. With the churros."

"Ah." There was her bright smile, Janeth turning to him. "Of course. You were the girl that found his stash of porn."

"He told you that?" Brandy gasped, as if in shock that he'd share something slightly embarrassing and also funny with his girlfriend.

Shrugging, Marty said, "Why not? We don't have any secrets to hide."

"Oh my God," Brandy groaned into her hands. Was she still salty because he hadn't held up his end of the bargain? That should be rectified.

But not today. Slurping back the last of his lukewarm coffee, Marty rose to his feet. "We should get going," he said to Janeth.

She rolled her eyes. "Finally." But as she turned to Brandy, she leaned closer to whisper in his ear, "Babe." That caused Marty to grin like the town fool, his hand finding itself right at the small of Janeth's back.

"Hope you can handle the store today by yourself, seeing as how I pulled double duty yesterday."

It wasn't a groan or a grumble he got from his friend, but a slow shift of her narrowed eyes. But after staring for a second, Brandy shook it all away. "Yeah, I...I can."

"Great!" He wanted to burst in excitement for this big date, but as he went to cram his stuff into the messenger bag, Marty paused. "Oh right, that thing you wanted to tell me."

"Forget it," Brandy said, pivoting her chair to the side so she could stare out of the door.

"No. I mean, it has to be a big deal if you called me up in the middle of the night about it." As he said that, he felt Janeth's interest grow, but he was focused on Brandy. "Come on. You can tell me."

"I...I was just... Thinking about taking another catering job with Mel," Brandy spat out fast. "And I wondered if you'd be willing to take my hours again."

That was it? "Sure," Marty said, feeling magnanimous. "How soon?"

"I'll, um, have to check with her," she whispered.

He chuckled at the thought of her being so swept up in getting to bake professionally she had to call him right away. It was nice to have a happy Brandy for once. "Well, you know where to find me when you do," he said.

"Uh-huh."

With one arm wrapped around the back of Janeth's waist, Marty guided her to the door. "I have the most amazing day planned for us."

"I can't wait," she said and held his cheek. To his shock, she pecked her purple lips against him. "Babe," Janeth finished before resting her head on his shoulder.

This day was going to be one he'd never forget for the rest of his life.

* * * *

"Did you tell him?"

Brandy gritted her teeth, drumming her fingers on the counter as she tried to think of a technical not-lie to get Mel off her back. "I can't really talk now. I've got customers." Brandy peeked down the empty shelves that should have had a poetic tumbleweed rolling through them.

"Uh-huh. Is one of them a proctologist? Because you are lying out of your ass." It was a good thing there weren't any patrons, because the word 'ass' burst from her phone like a shot. "I don't get what the problem is."

"He's not here, okay? He took the day off."

"So?" Mel wouldn't give up, her metaphorical teeth latched around Brandy's leg. "Text him. 'Your girlfriend's fucking around on the side. Dump her ass.' Easy."

"No, it's not. There's a...I can't."

"Why? Two-second phone call. 'You should swab her cheeks for the EPA, 'cause them lips have been everywhere.'"

Brandy gripped the counter harder, her eyes screwed tight as the Mel-browbeating went into extra innings. Yes, she should tell him. She should have told him even with Janeth standing there, so she could've disputed whatever lie his 'princess' came up with. But her heart kept leaping about, confusing emotions pounding in her brain. Then he'd smiled, the same as how she imagined when he saw her naked, and Brandy lost all nerve.

"I can't because I dreamed about him!" she fired back fast, then slapped a hand over her mouth.

"Girl, you did what? What kind of a dream?"

"The kind where, the one in which..." She strained her neck around, making dead certain a single soul couldn't listen in. Even so, Brandy dropped her voice to a barely audible whisper to say, "A sex dream."

"I fucking knew it!" Mel shouted. "Always claiming you're only friends. As if I don't catch you staring at him when he's not looking."

"We are just..." She crushed her palm into a fist, before the memory of dream Marty doing that snapped through her. Opening it wide, she darted her fingers above the lump where her ring hid. For the first time in six months, she'd almost put it back on her finger.

"So," Mel continued stamping on, "how was he?"

"Amazing," she admitted. "He took me on the counter, and against the fridge." It was the best she'd had in, well...two years. And it wasn't real. "Then" — her heart caught in her throat, tears rising in her words as she confessed — "he ripped my ring off and crushed it in his fist."

"Are you serious?"

"Mm-hm." Brandy pawed at her face, trying to keep the professional mask on even as her body was consumed with fire. Not the good kind that her dream stoked. No, these were the flames of the bad place where they sent wayward wives. "I'm not...I'm not ready. Okay. I thought I could be. But I freaked out on the date you were way too nice to set up. And with Marty..."

Her phone gave its little 'You should look at me' noise. Half the time it was her reading app trying to get her to buy more self-help books. They'd started around the time she'd had to search for funeral information online and wouldn't stop.

Brandy was about to swipe the notification away when she read it. Janeth was streaming her date with Marty live. She shouldn't watch it. What good would it do her?

"Hm, looks like Ms. Dumpster Diving is posting right now," Mel said. "And your sexy boy toy is with her."

Fuck.

"Ooh, is he going to dump her on live stream? I have to watch this."

No, you don't. I don't. We can just let them sort it out. Figure out their lives apart from...from me.

He'd looked so happy with whatever he was planning. Downright giddy to be once again sweeping someone off her feet. As if he lived to be Casanova and Cyrano de Bergerac in one body.

With no backbone, Brandy opened the app. The video loaded almost instantly, revealing an open meadow. Too much summer had aged the grass to a streaky yellow, but that didn't lower Marty's smile.

"Okay, babe," Janeth said in her high-pitched, sing-song voice. "If you missed the post earlier, Martin here has a surprise for me."

He hates being called Martin.

The video zoomed in tighter, revealing Marty had slipped on a silk white shirt and left a few of the buttons undone. A flush rampaged through Brandy's body, her traitorous brain refusing to delete the dream. It clung to the touch, taste and sight of him, even if it was nothing more than a delusion.

"That's right," Marty said across the video.

"Is it that he's going to rip her heart out and show all her followers the cold-hearted witch she is?" Mel cut in, causing Brandy to sigh loudly. She wished that could happen.

Maybe he did know. Maybe this was all some elaborate revenge plot. Shit, that editor guy was always around Janeth. No chance of him missing that. And Janeth didn't seem the careful type.

"Close your eyes, sweetie," Marty instructed. Perhaps she did, perhaps she didn't. It was impossible to tell as the phone kept recording. Marty vanished from view, leaving only the sway of grass and wildflowers. She hoped that the calming scene would last for an hour, but Brandy could only cling to it for a minute before Marty appeared.

And with him came a long white nose covered in hair. The more Marty tugged, the more sleek hair —

bright as new-fallen snow — appeared. "You can look," he announced.

It took a moment, as if Janeth either didn't want to or didn't care. But when a squeal shredded the phone's speakers, it was Mel who shouted, "He got her a horse!"

Marty tugged on the bridle and turned the white horse's head. "I know how much you love unicorns…" As he pulled, he revealed a golden horn tied around the head of the horse and nestled between its ears. "So I thought why not take a ride together on one."

Another squeal broke from Janeth, her hand appearing from behind the camera as she rubbed the horse's flank. Its big brown eye rotated to find the strange woman touching it just as she drew her fingers up the horn. "Stars, I love it!" she shouted and the phone pivoted far enough away to show a closeup of Janeth falling into Marty's arms.

Brandy turned away, her skin prickling at this enormous gift. It was Mel shouting her commentary that drew her back. "He can ride a horse?"

"He attended an equestrian camp as a kid. Said he loved it, but Eldon got freaked out and they started going to a computer one instead," Brandy explained without pause, one of the numerous facts she knew about Marty.

The hug broke and Janeth glanced from the saddle back to her generous boyfriend. "Can you…do you know how to ride?"

Marty smiled wide. "I do believe so. Shall I help you up?" He extended his hand and, with a loud grunt, helped Janeth up into the saddle. Maybe he was just going to tug on the reins, let her play as the excited kid going for a guided walk on a horse. That was almost pathetic, really.

And he leaped up behind her. The video extended out, revealing Janeth's grinning face and Marty brushing his chin against her shoulder, his hands locked tight to her stomach as he pressed himself to her.

"Here we go," he said, picking up the reins and guiding their 'unicorn' into a trot. Janeth gasped and clung to the saddle horn, but her joy was undeniable. Marty had given her a gift that no one could ever top. It was evident even across the shitty bandwidth.

The ride passed in surprising silence. Marty made a few comments along the way, mostly in the form of horse puns, but when Janeth didn't respond, he quieted down. And all that while he held her so tight in his arms, his own smile stretched to the limits. As if…as if he was the happiest he'd ever been because he'd gotten to give a woman a unicorn.

"Let's turn here," Marty said, tugging on the reins and shifting the horse to the right. They'd been trotting along a small creek when he directed the horse directly into the water. It splashed up, Janeth crying out like it was acid.

Marty took instant offense, his face crumbling from over her shoulder. "Aren't you enjoying yourself?"

It was barely a pause before Janeth turned on her hip. "I am, babe. I just wish I'd had some warning or I wouldn't have worn these boots."

"Sorry," he apologized, as if his gift wasn't living up to her high standards. *It's a freaking unicorn!*

Leaning close, Janeth puckered up and placed a sloppy kiss to Marty's lips. Maybe she'd realized she was being too harsh. Maybe she knew her judgmental fans were watching. Or maybe she really did care for him and whatever had happened at the party had been a fluke.

Maybe it was a good thing Brandy had stayed quiet after all.

The horse, at the behest of Marty, walked them under a willow tree. For a moment, the phone went dark as the lens struggled to adjust to the low light. But as it rose, so too did a mess of twinkling lights positioned all around the bowing branches. It looked like fairies dancing in the leaves.

"This revenge plot is taking forever," Mel whined, somehow still involved in this.

After sliding off the horse, Marty turned and once again held his hand out to her. "May I help you down?"

She giggled, fully giving in to his little princess play. To act like having a man answer to her every whim, assist her in small inconveniences, pamper her relentlessly was a good thing. *How sad.*

Marty tugged the two of them closer to the trunk of the tree, which was when the camera panned away from Janeth's beautiful face. There, perched instead of carved on the trunk was a bright red heart sign with the initials *JW* and *MD* on it.

Oh no. Brandy tried to close out the app, to shut off her phone and hurl it to the ground. But her limbs went numb and she couldn't move, only watch helplessly as Marty brushed back the silver-blond hair that fell across Janeth's face.

"You are the most beautiful, arresting woman I've ever met," he said. "And I've been dreaming of telling you here in this little slice of fantasy with a unicorn as a steed that…"

No. Shit. Damn it.

"I love you."

He'd said it. He'd put his heart in his hands and she'd broadcast it to the entire world. What would happen? Maybe she'd realize she couldn't keep lying. Or that she didn't care that deeply for Marty. Or...

"I love you too, babe!" Janeth cried and wrapped her hands around him. As the two fell to kissing, which Brandy averted her eyes from, she spotted the comments on the side blowing up.

OMG! They said the L-Word!

This is the most romantic thing ever!

I'm so jealous right now.

Get in line. No. She wasn't jealous, she couldn't be. She was heartbroken...for her friend. To be that deep into a woman who not even a day before had made out with another man?

"So you really didn't tell him," Mel whispered, sounding as stricken as Brandy felt.

"He's..." Despite Mel not being there, Brandy gestured to the phone. The two lovebirds were chirping more platitudes at each other, then Janeth began giving her 'please like and subscribe' spiel to the camera. It'd grind her teeth, but there was Marty in the background grinning through it all like a loon. He didn't care that she was more engrossed with her phone than him. He had his one true love at last.

"He's happy," Brandy admitted. "And I can't crush him. Not now. Not when he's so... It's not my place."

The line fell silent as the video finally snapped to black. Somehow that made her feel worse. What were they up to without two thousand people watching? A flash of dream Marty hoisting her up in his arms flooded Brandy's body. She wanted to sink to her knees and cry, but she couldn't afford to.

A jangle of the shop bell drew her away from the whole mess. Lucky for her, the customer barely glanced up as he shuffled back for a book. *Get it together, Brandy. He's one guy.*

"I've got to go," she said, straightening up and tugging on her drooping ponytail.

"Girl...there's other fish in the — "

"Save it, okay. I'm not ready. It's...I'm not," Brandy snapped.

"Okay." Mel sounded hurt, causing Brandy to feel even worse than before. "But you're gonna have to choose to leap back in or lose him forever."

No, she wouldn't, because he'd already made that choice for her.

Chapter Thirteen

He'd never been happier. The sun beamed a bright hello. Birds sang their beautiful songs everywhere he stepped. And he was in love with a beautiful woman. Nothing could ruin the heavenly mood that Marty'd been in for the past week.

"We should talk."

Nothing except his brother.

Marty's jolly holiday crashed to the ground at the pinched cheeks of one Eldon Dashwood. He always wanted to add an *esquire* at the end, just to mess with him. But that'd end in Eldon pointing out how he wasn't a barrister, thereby ruining the joke.

"Hi. Nice to see you. How's your day going? Other normal platitudes people use upon running into each other," Marty said to him.

That caused the polished man in a full suit, despite the fact it was both ten thousand degrees out *and* a Saturday, to stumble. "Yes, Martin. Your day, it's... well?"

"Fabulous, Eldy, thanks for asking."

Eldon's jaw grinding at the use of the old nickname could be heard above the roar of traffic skipping out to the start of the Fourth of July parade and picnics. Normally, Marty'd be right there with them, sparklers in hand. But he had plans to spend the holiday with Janeth. *Hopefully somewhere flameproof.*

He'd only wanted to stop by for a quick donut and coffee before rounding back to pick up the massive pile of mostly legal fireworks. As long as he fired them away from any neighborhoods, no one should care. When he'd told Janeth about his plans for the holiday, she'd hemmed and hawed until he'd mentioned all the dramatic shots she could get. The thought of kissing her under the spray of red and gold crackles in the sky was keeping him running against the heat.

Speaking of which, Eldon looked like he was about to hit the sidewalk and crack his stupid glasses. "Shall we adjourn to the recycled air of the comestible store?" Marty asked, jabbing a hand behind Eldon to the bakery.

The glare told him that someone had already pissed in Eldon's oatmeal that morning, but even his brother gave in to that smattering of common sense. "Yes, that sounds like a wise idea."

While Eldon claimed a table, which wasn't too hard to get in the place, Marty sidled up and placed his brother's usual order as well as one for the biggest iced coffee they had. After his long night, he wanted one in a Big Gulp cup, but had to settle for twenty ounces. Still, it would all be worth it once the sun went down.

"Would you like anything else, sir?" their friendly neighborhood barista asked.

His stomach grumbled in response and he peered through the glass. Soft fairy lights highlighted a cracking array of scones, but he knew better this time. "How about a chocolate donut? With those stars and stripes sprinkles, please."

"Coming right up."

Armed with donut and frozen coffee in one hand and a steaming hot mug in the other, Marty waded through the tables to find Eldon. Instead of burying his face in a newspaper, he drummed his fingers arrhythmically. Placing the hot mug down, Marty said, "I don't know how you can drink this stuff."

"Consumption of too much sugar is bad for you."

"I meant drinking boiling hot water when you could bake a cake on the sidewalk outside." Marty stumbled into the chair beside his brother and hefted the donut to his lips. The chocolate frosting was good, a little too sweet, but as he bit down, he shuddered. "This damn thing's stale. Who makes the food here, anyway?"

"They have it brought in," Eldon said before sucking in his piping hot coffee. He was a total slurper, always making that 'wet vacuum hoovering up Jell-O' noise when eating hot liquids.

"Do you know where, 'cause I think someone needs to put that bakery out of its misery?"

Eldon shook his head, placed down his cup and drove straight to business. "I got into the schooling funds earlier."

Shit. "What? Why?" *Don't spit your coffee out. Drink it slowly and think.* "Going for a double PhD?"

His brother's eyes narrowed to slits. "No."

"Then…what were you even doing in there? It's only for schooling, remember. And if you aren't going to school…"

Eldon became flustered, a hand rising to hide away his cheeks. The man was the worst liar, which was why Marty had taught him how to play poker the second he'd watched a tutorial on YouTube. "That isn't the... It's not that I had any intentions to remove the money. I merely look after it. Renew any CDs, maintain the stock investments."

"You're playing the stock market with that money?" Marty slammed his cup down and glared at his brother.

"Mutual funds are hardly 'playing the stock market.' Keeping that much money liquid can be a recipe for disaster. It's best to..." His apologizing gussied up as explaining snapped away. "When I went to inspect the money, I noticed nearly ten percent had vanished."

"Maybe it was a rounding error," Marty said with a shrug.

Eldon practically seethed in his chair. And since he was already a swamp ass from his suit, steam rose off his head. "I thought you knew better than to take our parents' and grandparents' investment and waste it living outside your means."

Goddamn it. Here it comes again. "I am not living outside my means. Do you see any fancy watches on my wrist?" He twisted it around to reveal their grandfather's old watch from El Salvador that he'd once again forgotten to wind. *Crud.* Marty started to turn the dial while trying to defend himself with grade-A distraction bullshit. "Or a new car? Maybe shiny specs? Nothing's changed."

Crossing his arms, Eldon raised his snooty nose even higher. "Then where has the money vanished to?"

"It's, um..." Marty placed the cup to his lips and tried to speak and drink simultaneously. Gurgling bubbles sloshed over the side, but Eldon wouldn't abandon his new crusade.

"Martin Cruz Dashwood—"

"Oh, that is low. Using my middle name like you're Mamá."

"You should be so lucky it's me who spotted this and not her. She'd tan your hide for a month!"

A ray of hope rose in Marty's chest. "Then you haven't told them?"

"Not yet." Eldon kept thrashing at him with the stick, but Marty was focused on the carrot. "What's happened? Did you lose your job?"

"No. I'm good. It's good. Everything in my life is good."

His brother managed to say 'if that were so, you wouldn't be withdrawing so much money' in a single glare. Their entire family could write stories with a quirk of an eyebrow or a sneer on the lips.

"There's just some...credit card debt I'm trying to get out of. Okay?"

"Debt from what?"

Jesus Christ, he wouldn't give up. Marty was tempted to slam his coffee down and flee into the street when his phone buzzed. It didn't matter if it was a scammer offering to pay cash for a house he didn't own—anything would be a great distraction.

Burying his head in his phone, Marty's drowning spirits lifted at Janeth's beautiful face. He read her text and his momentary reprieve dropped.

Can't make it tonight. Sorry. Something came up.

Pain twirled through his chest as Marty wanted to tell her that he'd spent a lot to make this special. That he'd given up on a Dashwood picnic for her. But instead he texted back.

What is it? Anything serious?

No. Something I've wanted to do.

If you knew you'd be doing it, why didn't you tell me the day before?

His fingers froze right before he pressed Send and slowly Marty deleted every accusatory word. While he struggled to think of a response that wasn't crammed full of anger, Janeth responded.

It'll help grow my brand.

Oh. It was a job. That...that made sense.

Love you, babe.

All the pain of her ditching him at only a few hours' notice vanished at that single word. Dewey-eyed, he turned up to find his killjoy of a brother still seated across from him. "Martin, there's another matter I wanted to talk to you about."

"Is it my lack of flossing?"

"No, though you really should. Dentists recommend..."

Marty groaned and dropped the phone with the incriminating texts on the table. For a brief second, Eldon's gaze drifted to it, but he didn't read what was on there. "This woman you're dating."

"I knew this was coming. You're jealous. I'm sorry if I got myself a hot model, but—"

"As if Elena couldn't be if she wasn't busy being a brilliant neurosurgeon," Eldon shot back. That defensiveness struck Marty. It wasn't that his brother wouldn't defend his long-time girlfriend—it was just that he only did it in a mealy-mouthed 'she's a nice person' way. This attack had real teeth.

"Trouble in bland-adise?" Marty asked, earning another scowl from Eldon. Oh yeah, something was in his craw and he was taking it out on his younger brother instead. Suddenly it all made sense.

"Ms. Willows. I only wonder if...is she a good fit with you?"

"No complaints on her end," Marty said with a jab of his elbow.

Eldon coughed, his pale cheeks turning bright red. "Mother doesn't like her."

"Mamá doesn't want to lose her baby boy."

To his surprise, Eldon scoffed. "Lose? You think your relationship is anything... You do. You think this is potentially permanent?"

Marty winced at the laugh in Eldon's voice. "You know, you could turn a beautiful sonnet into instructions on tire inflation."

"But she's..."

"Beautiful, well cultured, beloved by thousands." He could keep going, but that had to be enough.

With no more ammo left in his belt, Eldon stared at his hands. No grease under the chocolate man's nails, because he always wore gloves. Absently, Marty licked at the leftover donut frosting clinging to his.

"What does she know about you? What does she care?"

"Plenty. We've been together for…nearly a month already. Shit, I should get her something for that anniversary."

"Anniversary implies yearly, as in annual and —" Eldon silenced his yapping and sighed once again. "She kept saying our mother was from Mexico."

Internally, Marty winced at that massive slight against their parentage. But he couldn't entirely blame her. She'd only met their parents that one night, and there'd been that massive distracting party. With the blue and white bunting of the El Salvador flag. And the food had been every favorite from his mamá's childhood. Still… Janeth was originally a pretty white girl from Ohio. It wasn't fair to expect her to know the intricacies of every Latin American country.

"So it slipped her mind. Or didn't sink in. She'll have lots of time to figure it out," he said, trying to assure himself as much as Eldon. "Look, I've got to go."

Go where?

It didn't matter. He'd figure something out.

Marty rose from the table, prepared to leave his barely eaten donut to his nosy brother. To think, he'd been on cloud nine before. Now it felt like a worm had wiggled into his brain and kept whispering cruel comments to wick away his confidence. He wanted to tug on his ear until the vile bug fell free.

At least he knew that Janeth loved him. *Hard to challenge that, Mr. 'Potentially permanent.'*

Grabbing his coffee, because he wasn't going to abandon a caffeine fix even in the middle of a fit, Marty turned to stomp away. He got as far as the door before Eldon piped up again.

"Does she laugh at your jokes?"

"What?"

"Your jokes. Your little japes and pranks. Does she find them funny? Does she join in or is she just waiting for you to stop talking?"

"Of course she does," Marty said, fully certain that Janeth was in stitches whenever he made one. He just couldn't remember an exact moment. *What about when...?* No, that was Brandy. *Or there was the time I put that...?* Brandy again.

"You can't ruin this, Eldon. Your deep hatred of anything romantic won't infest me!" Marty shouted at his brother and stepped back into the sweltering heat. But the worm kept whispering in his ear, *"She doesn't play along with you. Will she ever?"*

Chapter Fourteen

Are you doing anything?

That one text, and the fact that his girlfriend was flying out to Las Vegas on some makeup brand's dime, left Marty awaiting a long night of manual labor. Somehow it seemed like his own doing.

Another text from his brother lit up his phone, but he ignored it and knocked on Brandy's door. As it opened, Marty yanked out the paintbrush he'd bought. "Your handy..."

The rest of his witty saying drained to gurgling as he stared in utter shock at the woman standing in Brandy's apartment. That sometimes frizzy and always pulled-back hair sleekly caressed her shoulders. It shone bright as onyx all the way down to the softly curled ends.

Her face looked brighter than he'd ever seen. The endless brown of her irises drew him in and her pink lips glistened. And, most confounding of all, she wasn't in their requisite boxy polo shirt and khakis uniform. A white tank top with straps thinner than a pencil hugged around her pair of...

Nope. Shouldn't look at those. Even with the decree to keep his eyesight level with the horizon, he couldn't stop glancing just at the edge of where her lady bits smooshed together. That deep, dark canyon of mystery kicked off a fire in his brain.

"You okay?" this stranger asked breezily and she placed a hand to her hip.

As if the shirt wasn't tight enough, the black jeans amped it up. They swept around her curves, making Brandy look more like an exaggerated lady silhouette from truck stops.

Marty tried to laugh at himself. *Hell.* Why was his head so hot? He moved to swipe away the hair clinging to his sweaty forehead and smacked the paintbrush into it. The damn thing fumbled out of his hand to clatter on the ground. "Uh, yeah," he said, bending over to pick up the damn brush.

What is your problem? It's just Brandy.

"You startled me."

"It's my place," she said, gliding back. Her jeans' hems drifted over her feet, nearly hiding away the entire naked foot save the tips of her toes. Why did he find that detail adorable?

Mentally pinching himself to get back into shape, Marty stared at his friend. And he made certain to keep his gaze high above to keep things G-rated. "You're never out of that green polo. I mean, except when showering. Probably."

Jesus, you're making it worse.

"And when I saw you all fancied up, I thought you might be a well-dressed robber."

Brandy didn't blush at his compliment. Instead, she stared down at her outfit and sneered. "This is hardly... Wait, I was at your mother's birthday party. In a dress."

Okay, true. And she'd looked nice in it. But this was...different. A small frown burrowed along the back of Marty's brain courtesy of his damn brother's doubt. "Were you? Who can remember?" he said to excuse himself out of this mess.

Brandy didn't challenge him, but her smile faltered and she glanced away. *Slightly dick move to save on pain later. Nothing more.*

He didn't want to keep dragging out this torture, so Marty put on his most serious voice. "Now, madam. I believe I was hired to do a job for you."

The laugh warmed his heart. Brandy pointed to the wall beside a tarp-covered floor. "There it is, in all its ugly vomit-yellow glory. I asked my super if I could paint it when I moved in and never found the time."

Marty slapped his hands together, pinching his puny paintbrush in the process. It looked like she had a roller, at least. *Nice to know there's one person with a brain in this situation.* He was about to take a step forward when a heavenly scent drifted under his nose.

"Is that...?" *Yes. Cheese, tomatoes, doughy crust.* "Did you get a pizza for your most trusted painter?"

He eased around the kitchen counter to find a golden and glorious pan filled to the brim with the cheesy, pepperoni-festooned goodness. Abandoning the paintbrush in the sink, Marty dug through her drawers to find the cutter.

"Get? Are you sure you're really Marty Dashwood?"

"The jury's still out," he said, slicing through the bubbling crust of mozzarella and cheddar. "My brother is dead certain there was a mix-up at the hospital and I was some changeling baby left behind."

Brandy laughed at the thought and he lifted the oversized slice. As the piping hot sauce struck his tongue, Marty hissed in pain. But burning his mouth was worth it as the fresh, homemade pizza, crafted with a skilled touch, slid down his throat.

"This is so good," he moaned around his bite. Not greasy, not stale, not cold. Everything his usual takeout menu wasn't. In a word, perfect.

"Uh-huh." Brandy slipped into the kitchen and took the cutter from him. "Food is for after you finish your job."

"But it'll be cold then," he whined, wanting to devour the whole pie in one go.

Her lips quirked up into a half-smile, half-smirk. Were they always so sculpted? *Definite shapeage going on, especially with her cupid's bow.* "I could always call your mother and tell her about your extracurricular activities."

"Ha. My mission to perfect that was why I didn't have time for any after-school groups," Marty said, about to cut another slice off with her chef's knife. Then he caught Brandy fishing her phone out of her pants' pocket. How did it even fit in there? Did her phone curve to make room for her... "Wait! Okay. Your personal rent-boy is off to work."

Releasing a beleaguered sigh so she'd know how in pain he was, Marty dropped the last of his crust onto the pan and stomped off for his painting job. A gallon of minty green paint glimmered beside the clean tray, as well as one fluffy paint roller. Everything was ready to be slathered in green. She'd even taped up the sides and removed the outlet plates.

A strange gurgle of regret rolled through him. That had to have taken time to set up, and he'd texted her while bored and still angry at being abandoned. The trunk of his car was crammed full of fireworks that wouldn't see the light of night. How long had she been waiting for him to come hang out?

"I don't hear painting," Brandy said as she sat on her couch. With her back turned to him, she booted up various streaming services and began to hunt for something to watch.

At least she wasn't going to hover over his shoulder and critique his every move. Though, it was hard to see Brandy being anything but encouraging, unless they were kidding around.

Guilt sprang up inside him, but this tasted different. Instead of the unsettling acid of knowing he was lavishly courting a woman beyond his means, he felt sad at... *Nah, it was probably just gas from the pizza.*

Hefting up the gallon can, Marty spread his feet wide, waddled over to the tray and dumped. "Oh shit!" he shouted, watching a tidal wave of fresh-breath green slop up the side and nearly escape out of the front.

"Crap, crap, crap!" He lashed the roller out, holding it before the cresting paint like the last dam fighting off a hurricane.

As the paint settled back, most of it remaining in the container, all he heard was the slow click of the channel. "That's why I put down plastic," Brandy said, causing him to break out into laughter.

* * * *

A lovely minty shade covered almost half the wall while Marty and Brandy sat on the couch. She chewed delicately on her pizza slice and he couldn't help but wolf down a fourth. When she drifted her super-brown eyes over to him, he smiled. "Sorry, but I worked up quite the appetite."

"Am I going to have to make another pizza to get you to finish?" she asked, as if she hadn't been the one to tell him to take a break and eat dinner with her. The TV played through a loop of random fireworks displays, which they'd been mostly ignoring.

Marty shrugged and leaned back into her couch. "The night is young," he said before tipping back his beer and having nothing dribble out. "And the well's run dry." Hopping to his weary feet, he made a beeline for the fridge before asking, "Do you want a refill?"

"Yes, please," Brandy called.

After fishing out two more IPAs from a local microbrewery, Marty drifted back to the couch to spot a string of cheese clinging to her face. She seemed unaware of it, extending her hand out for a beer. But rather than hand it over, Marty leaned down and cupped his thumb to her chin.

A soft breath caught in Brandy's throat and he looked up into her eyes. His hand didn't shift from the simple cheese-removal, but he felt his thumb caressing her cheek.

"Marty…?"

"Sorry, you had a bit of—" He yanked his hand off to show her the cheese string. Brandy's cheeks turned a ripe pink and, for the first time since he'd sat down, she turned to face the TV.

Feeling weird for feeling weird, Marty was about to crack open his beer, but as he watched Brandy wipe all around her mouth, he put on a snooty accent and bowed. "Would the young lady care for bottle service?"

She laughed at that, as he'd hoped, shaking away the weirdness. "If you'd be so kind, good gentleman." As she held her hand out, Marty raised the hem of his T-shirt and wrenched off the screw-cap.

"Only the classiest of techniques, I see," Brandy said, accepting her second beer of the night.

He was on his third. *Wait...* Cracking the beer open, he got onto his third. It had to be his imagination, but this was tasting a lot less like grass clippings yanked from the inside of a lawn mower and left to ferment in ditch water for a month.

A chuckle rolled through his memory and out of his mouth. Clutching the bottle in his hand, he collapsed back to the couch. "I was thinking about the first beer I ever had."

"Oh?"

"Would you believe I was only fourteen?" he asked with his lips pressed around the glass.

Brandy snickered. "Yes."

As the refreshing beverage that was so not getting him drunk passed down his throat, Marty wiped off his mouth. "Would you also believe it was Eldon who got it for me?"

"No! No way. Your brother...?"

"Yup. He managed to sneak off with an entire six-pack when our dad wasn't looking. I thought it tasted like pissed-on bread. Hasn't really improved much, truth be told."

"Eldon Dashwood?" Brandy repeated his brother's name as if they had to have another that lived in the attic and killed every full moon. "Your brother... committed underage drinking?"

Marty laughed so hard at the shock in her voice. "Don't let him fool you with his uptight act. He could get into deep shit when he wanted. Just usually made sure I was around to siphon off some of the blame. And it always worked, now that I think about it."

"What happened? With the beer. Did you get away with it?" She sat on the edge of her seat, enraptured with his tale of teenage malfeasance.

"Of course not. My parents caught us before we even finished the first one. Ooh, it was the apocalypse after that. Real wrath of God, rain of fire. I was grounded for... Come to think of it, I think I'm still grounded."

"Then," Brandy said, reaching over and yanking his beer away, "I'll have to confiscate this from you. Law breaker."

"Please, no. I'm just a misguided youth who was led astray by cruel hooligans. Take pity upon this lost soul, kind lady," Marty cried in pure telenovela drama fashion. He even clasped his hands together and prayed to her.

She gave him another laugh, one of hundreds of the night, and handed the beer back. "I had my first beer after prom. We all snuck out to a field and sat in the back of Kevin's truck." Her voice tapered at the end and she stared off into the distance.

There was that ghost again, always butting in whenever Brandy dared to let herself have a bit of fun. Marty didn't say anything, but he cursed the dead a little for wrecking the living's life. "No way was I touching alcohol for prom. My mom actually got a real breathalyzer from some cop and she threatened to test me every hour. If anything came up, I wouldn't be seen for a year."

"She did not." Sweet, naive Brandy defended the woman who ruled her children like a lioness — proud, brave and liable to crush their skulls in her jaws if they ever acted out.

"I didn't mind. I was far too busy to care about breaking the rules, what with the magical night I had planned."

She licked her lips, Marty watching with more interest than usual. "Knowing you, there must have been a lot."

"Corsage, serious tux with tails and a top hat. A lobster dinner at a real restaurant, because it just wasn't prom without lobster."

"Was there a limo?"

"Took me two summers to save up enough," Marty said, remembering the massive thorns that had burrowed into his flesh from all the yard work. "And I got her friends to swap the songs on her phone so it'd only play the one I wrote to ask her out. As well as a little poem I wrote comparing her beauty to a summer's day. May have cribbed from the Bard for that, but I was young and a delinquent."

"Wow," she said shaking her head and staring at her hands. "You must have really cared for that girl."

"I…" He had liked her enough, liked her even more when she'd said yes. But it hadn't grown to anything like he'd hoped. "I wanted to make prom special."

He felt a great disturbance in the universe and turned to find Brandy's face telling him to rethink what he'd said.

"Oh God, no. Not like that kind of special. If you think my mom would kill me over a beer, I can't even imagine what she'd do if I'd been a teenage father. Seriously, I don't think a punishment has been invented yet that would fit."

She patted her knee as if trying to stomp out more confounding awkwardness. They didn't talk about sex, but they didn't not joke about it either. There was always some risqué innuendo between them. *How is this anything new?*

"Can I ask you something?" Her voice was soft and tempered, as if she was prepared to pull back if he said no.

"If it's about my first time, I'd describe it as awkward, messy and narrated by David Attenborough."

"It's not that. I don't…" There went her lip again, all wet and glistening. "You put in so much work. Far more work than any other man I've known, and I'm always amazed at it. With girls. With dating."

"Maybe I love romance," Marty announced to the world. "Maybe my heart beats for love and all I crave is to have it returned in kind."

"Yeah, but you can still be loved without having to go all out and rent yourself a uni— A limo."

He heard the unspoken unicorn in her sentence, Eldon's damn ear worm burrowing deeper into his psyche. But Marty shook it off. Brandy had no idea what seed his brother was sowing—she didn't mean anything by this.

Dropping his half-empty beer onto the coffee table, Marty tried to chew on her thoughts. "Can I, though?" slipped from his lips. He heard a soft gasp, as if Brandy was about to launch into a long list of his becoming traits. Any other day, any other mood, he'd have let her. But the combination of exhaustion and alcohol tweaked his tongue enough that he let the deepest buried truths free.

"I'm not an idiot. I figured out real quick that most girls, when drawing up their Prince Charming, don't want a short brown boy with wild hair and giant feet. Didn't help either that there was Eldon, already six feet tall when he was only fifteen. Skinny as shit, but then he had to go and pick up a sport too."

He scratched at his nose, certain that the sniffle was just a bit of an allergy and nothing more. "Eldon gets to be the whitest damn Latino, and I'm trying to not get called a drug dealer while cruising around on the playground in my Big Wheel." *And what does he do with all his perfect gifts from God? Locks himself in his room with books for friends. If it weren't for Elena all but dragging him out on a date, it was doubtful Eldon would even glance at a woman.*

"So you're romantic to...to beat your brother?" Brandy asked.

"Nah. I had Eldon beat when I was the most adorable baby ever born. It just...it's nice, ya know, romancing someone. Watching her eyes light up, her mouth quiver, her breath gasp as she realizes all my hard work. As I sweep her off her feet and she knows she can trust that I'll always be her prince."

It was how he'd survived college, the Don Juan of the dorms. Always dropping off long-stemmed roses to girls who'd had a bad time. Leaving little notes of encouragement before tests. Waiting for her to see him for what he was. But everyone's relationships had seemed to be in a confounding state of flux. There'd been more than a few fights with jealous boyfriends who'd wanted to rearrange his nose for him. Most he'd talked himself out of, but it had cooled his 'romance fishing' technique.

"Is it so wrong to want to be loved?" he sighed to himself and hoisted the beer back into his hand. While he drenched his sorrows, Brandy watched.

"Janeth, I...I hope she knows what she's got with you."

Odd. He'd been more than happy to take every opportunity to name-drop his girlfriend, but in the oasis of Brandy's apartment, he didn't want to hear it. Didn't want to think about her. But he put on a smile. "I'm sure she does."

Brandy's face shifted, but not to anything he could understand. Her emotions faded in and out so fast he couldn't keep track. What nearly sent Marty reeling was the guilt in her eyes.

Because she'd lost her one true love.

She has to sit here on her couch listening to you blather on about how amazing romance is with a broken heart. Probably forever.

"I'm so—" Marty began.

Brandy finished with, "...sorry."

They both laughed at the synchronicity, leaning their foreheads closer together. He felt the heat of her body nearly against his and watched her eyes soften to a heartfelt smile. Raising his hand in the air, Marty could almost feel it being tugged to her cheek. To hold her safe in his hand and take those struggling lips in a...

"That wall isn't going to paint itself," he declared, leaping to his feet. *Whoa!* Said minty green wall spun around him, but he got a good grip on his head. The sudden rise in vertigo required his full attention, and not the idea that he'd nearly... Nah, he didn't. He'd just been going to wipe more sauce off her face. With his lips.

Fuck.

Brandy, unaware of what he'd nearly done, rose. She placed her quarter-finished beer on the table. "I supposed I'd better help."

"Have no faith in me?"

"If it's all the same, I don't think you want to stay the night."

A hot flush crawled across his body. Thank God for his natural deep tan to help mitigate it. Still, he couldn't escape the pinching in his chest as he watched Brandy—his good friend—smile at him. Laugh with him.

Marty shook his head, trying to clear away whatever fog kept creeping back in. "I dunno, I'm great at slumber parties. Know the best scary stories and can braid better than any ten-year-old."

Chuckling, Brandy slapped a hand around his shoulder and twisted him to the wall. "I'll be sure to hide your bra in the freezer then."

Chapter Fifteen

She'd feared her tongue would slip the second Marty came over, and unload everything about Janeth on him. For a brief second, Brandy had almost dismissed his request to paint the wall with the excuse that she'd already done it. But, thank God, she was a terrible liar, to the point of not even bothering.

This was...nice.

Marty took command of the remote, flipping through potential background movies until he switched to one of the few music stations. Motown piped through her little apartment, causing her hips to sway as she worked the roller up and down the wall. Marty stood beside her, attempting to put his tiny brush to work and only covering a tenth of what she could.

"I'm going to beat you," Brandy declared.

"Only because you stole that," he complained, pausing in his artistic swipes at a flat wall. With paintbrush perched on his hip, he pointed at the roller that was constantly splattering paint back at her. Fat drops landed in her hair, but Marty somehow avoided all the spray. Maybe he was just that lucky.

Brandy dipped the roller through the paint tray. "I can't steal what I bought. Not my fault you brought a tiny tool for a big job."

"Ouch," Marty scoffed. "I'll have you know it's not the size of the tool but the consistency and rhythm of the strokes that matters." He cracked a smile at her and heat burned across her face. Had to be her damn apartment and the shitty air conditioning.

So much exercise in a tight space with two bodies…it was no wonder she felt flushed. Struggling to reach the ceiling, Brandy pushed harder against the wall. A large swipe of gross yellow lingered above their heads. "Damn it!" she gasped, straining on her toes and making no progress.

Her blackmailed man paused in his delicate strokes to watch her. The flush returned again, causing her to break out in fully flustered sweats. Uncertain what to do, Brandy kept trying to reach what she couldn't get.

"Here," Marty said. "Trade?" He passed her the small brush and took the roller for himself. Starting where she'd already greened up the wall, Marty began to inch the paint higher. A slick roll scattered over the yellow, but the line was light and left a two-inch gap above their heads.

He gritted his teeth and took a step closer, straining his hand far above his head. Out of ideas, Brandy stepped back and watched Marty. It was obvious he couldn't get any farther past what she'd done, but he didn't seem to want to give up.

She'd never thought of him as short. Okay, compared to the average guy, he was smaller. But it didn't matter, not to be her friend. Not to be her…not to work in the shop. He never seemed to have that little-Napoleon complex, like a chihuahua trying to bite a Great Dane's ankles. To think it bothered him to the point he felt like he had to prove himself with a cheating…

And there you go, thinking it's your job to fix his relationship.

What? You'll slot into the place where Janeth was kicked out of? Like you're ready for that.

Too much pizza and alcohol sloshed about inside her, unsettling her stomach. Brandy reached to touch it, when she caught the paint-soaked brush in her hands. That would have been quite the mess —

"Ah!" Marty cried, and his straining tiptoes collapsed. He splattered right onto the wall that was coated in wet paint.

"Oh no." Brandy dashed to his side, but it was too late. A great smear of mint green covered the entire front of his black T-shirt. Marty held up his hands, showing one stained palm too. The other clung to the roller and he stared in shock at the mess he'd made.

A strange smile rose on his lips and he took a step closer. "Brandy, come here."

"What?"

"Give me a big hug!" he said, flailing both hands.

She took a step back and knocked right into the damn stool she'd moved so they could reach the ceiling in the first place. Movement in her peripheral vision caused her to turn back to find Marty advancing.

"Don't you dare," she warned, shaking the brush at him.

He snickered at the empty threat. "Come on. It's tradition."

"No, it's not," she shouted, laughter escaping. Marty lunged for her, but Brandy was quicker and ducked under his arms. He spun around but kept lumbering toward her like a reanimated corpse.

"Of course it is. The Fourth of July hug."

"Stop!" She full-on giggled, running for her kitchen. Marty was quick on her heels, his entire torso glistening from the wet paint.

What was she doing in here? The stove and counters trapped her in place, pinning her between escape and Marty. He winked and — in his smoldering voice — said, "Don't you want to be wrapped up in these arms?"

Yes.

And she hated herself for it.

"Here." Yanking a towel off the stove, she wiped at Marty's hand. That seemed to slow the charging beast. His minty-green belly showed, but it stopped the attack. Instead, he stood silent as she wet the towel and kept cleaning him off.

"So you don't..." Brandy glanced away from his nearly spotless palm up into his face. A breath rolled between his barely parted lips and his Adam's apple dropped.

Shaking off the rise in her body, she said, "So you don't make a mess of my place."

"Too late for my shirt," Marty said with an accepting sigh. "Well, don't want to be a poor guest." And, before she could get another towel to sponge off the paint, he gripped the neck of his shirt and yanked it off.

Holy crap. Shame tried to direct her to look anywhere but at the half-naked man attempting to rinse off the paint. But she couldn't escape the pull. Instead of the nearly full spread of man fur of her dream, he only had a light smattering that was a softer brown than his head hair. It dashed halfway across his rounded pecs, then pointed straight down his flat stomach. Even with a giant pizza sitting in there, she could make out a hint of a four-pack flush to his half-moon belly button. And it was sexier than anything she could have dreamed.

"You, uh..." Marty swallowed hard, his voice tenuous as he stared at her. "Find anything?"

Shit. He caught me. "That scar on your...um." She pointed to his side, because even acknowledging that he had a set of lats twisted her tongue into knots.

"Oh, that." He laughed, drawing a thumb down the stark white line amongst a sea of brown. "You wouldn't believe how I got it."

"Eldon's doing?"

"No, this was all me. I..." Marty paused in caressing his old memory and turned to her. The friend, the confidant, the widowed coworker staring at his half-naked body. "I'll tell you about it some other time. For now, there is a wall to subdue!"

Brandy smiled, all laughs as he jumped to the paint and this time used the stool to climb up near the ceiling. *So he's shirtless. It was an accident.*

"Are you coming to help, or do you intend to sit in a chair watching me work up a sweat while you sip wine?"

A nice deck chair, Marty in low-slung jeans holding a rake. No, by the pool and he'd just emerged from the water. Droplets shimmering on his skin and he wore a tiny pair of...

"As if. You need me to keep you from messing it all up," Brandy said, getting a laugh from him. Shaking off her foolish fantasy, she moved to join him. But before she left the kitchen, she shut off the water on his soaking shirt.

Rather than dive back into painting, Marty stood above a pint can, glaring down as if it'd wronged him. Brandy paused from lifting her backup brush to watch him point at the smaller can, then to the half-used gallon. "What's this baby for? So the mama doesn't get lonely?"

Brandy laughed and, with her screwdriver, cracked open the can. Brown the hue and vibrancy of melted milk chocolate rested inside. "It's for the accents," she said, pointing to the various edges where the walls connected. "Something I saw online, to give the room an old-world feel."

"And you didn't trust me to do it?" Marty gasped as if she'd wounded him.

She dipped the brush into the brown paint, barely soaking it into the bristles before she rose. Marty watched, his dignity on the line. Twisting the brush in her hand, Brandy stepped closer. Her hand glanced against his, about to pass over the brush, when she said, "No."

"Traitor!" Marty cried in faux indignity. He reached for the brush, but she wasn't having it. Laughing, Brandy tried to leap back from his range, only for Marty to swipe against the bristles.

Drops of brown splattered off the brush onto her body. She froze, her arms locking in place as cold paint clung to her face, chest and arms. Oh, and her tank top. Of course.

She expected Marty to break into laughter, but he wore a slightly concerned look. "Let me help," he said, and excised a white handkerchief from his jeans.

The only thing that surprised her about Marty carrying an old-fashioned kerchief around was the fact that she hadn't seen it before. He swiped at her upper arm, smearing the brown paint in a line to connect her freckles. "Damn it," Marty cursed, trying again.

"Here, you have to dab it." She tried to reach for it to do it herself, but Marty clung to his white linen.

"Please, let me." He blotted now, pulling more paint free, and Brandy tried to stand perfectly still. It wasn't easy as Marty moved from her arms across her chest.

The stained kerchief drifted against the top of her breast, his fingers pressing and swiping into the start of her padding. "That, uh…" Marty stuttered, shifting on his toes.

She felt the same secondhand embarrassment rising and tried to slide away. But he raised his head and the handkerchief. Rolling it to a clean spot, Marty pressed the surprisingly soft fabric to her cheek. His thumb and the kerchief dipped into her smile line. The rubbing gave way to a gentle swish of his finger back and forth, Marty's gaze locked on hers.

Somehow his fingers curled around her chin, holding Brandy, propping her up. Keeping her mouth in line with his. She swallowed deep, instinctively licking her lips and finding a dab of paint on them as well.

But there was no time to worry as he wrapped his fingers around the small of her back. No, they didn't just hold, they pulsed against her skin. Marty guided her closer, a serene smile on the lips about to press to hers.

"Marty," Brandy breathed, her mind at war. One faction wanted to give in, to let him dab and wash every inch of her body. Another kept screaming that he had a girlfriend, one she couldn't find the courage to tell him was a cheater.

A wet chill crawled up her spine and she frowned. "Did you get paint on your other hand?"

He whipped free the palm that'd worked its way under the back of her tank top and, sure enough, brown streaks were smeared over the fingertips. Marty stared at it in shock while she tried to tug up her shirt to keep it free of the paint. Not too high, maybe an inch or two, but whatever moment they'd almost had evaporated. Now it was just awkwardness and uncertainty.

"Would you mind..." Brandy spun around to show him her smudged back. "Fixing this?"

"Um, sure. No problem," he said and wiped the handkerchief against the small of her back. This time there was no accidental slip down to the curvy part of her ass, no warm palm cupped against her stomach to keep her in place. It was hard and industrious scrubbing. Nothing more.

What was she thinking? Of course it wouldn't be anything more. They were friends. And even if she started to feel differently, he never would. Not about her.

"I'm starting to think you're right," Marty said, causing Brandy to gulp in shock. She glanced over her shoulder at him, pain drawn across her face. But his goofy smile lessened it. "I can't be trusted to do delicate work."

"Yep. Told you so," Brandy said.

"Hm." The scrubbing increased ten-fold, causing her to gasp.

"Ow. Are you trying to set my skin on fire?"

"There's a drop here that isn't... Wait." Marty leaned closer, his face nearly flush with her naked skin. "Did you know you have a mole back here?"

"I do?" Brandy asked and tried to turn in a circle to see. It didn't work, but it spun her around to face Marty, who kept his gaze level with where her back had been.

"Pretty big too. Like size of my pinkie."

"What, are you going to tell me it's got a hair coming out of it too?" she said and the buried pain snapped free.

That caught him, Marty staring at her as she struggled through a thousand emotions at once. It didn't matter that he could have kissed her. He didn't. And he wouldn't. That was obvious.

"Just, you might want to get it looked at. You never know," he said softly. Then in his boisterous voice, he shouted, "I don't want anything bad to happen to you. Who would I have to talk to every day?"

She knew it was a joke, a little laugh to lighten the dark turn. But Marty's eyes didn't hold the smile. He darted them around her body as if he was weighing the idea of her vanishing off the earth.

Brandy shivered at the focus, letting her tank top drop. "I think that's enough painting for one night. I still have that horror collection..."

"Ooh. Does that have the 1970's version of El Silbón? Did you know they used a real heart for that scene?"

And with that, they slammed back on the friendship wall thanks to a whistling demon. Marty hunted through her DVDs and Brandy touched the edge of her lips. A single drop of chocolate paint stained her finger and she frowned.

Chapter Sixteen

"Did you see there's another one?" Marty asked, scanning the price of a book box set for *Dinosaur Men on Pluto*.

The mom holding the credit card sighed. She looked the type to want her precious baby to only read Proust, but the kid's eyes lit up at the thought. "Mom, did you hear…?"

"Yes. We'll just take this, then see what you want to get."

Marty knew better than to argue with the customer, because it usually ended in him bleeding from his ears. But as he ran her card and waited for the slow internet to add the money into their till, he reached under the counter. "I just so happen to have a *Sabertooth Man from Neptune* bookmark," he said and dropped the piece of PR buzz from the publisher into the bag.

He ignored the mother angrily stuffing her wallet back into her purse and handed it all to the kid about to explode. Just as she gripped the bag, Marty said, "That one has a Mammoth princess in it."

"Mom, Mom, did you hear...?"

"Yes. Let's go. We have to get you to piano lessons."

The kid deflated in an instant, clearly preferring to fly around in space riding triceratops over playing Chopin. But that was the extent of the influence Marty could have on the people who walked into the shop. When the bell jangled for their exit, he called out, "Have a nice..." and didn't bother to finish. They never heard the last part anyway.

Humming to himself, he heard a special phone chime, and a smile wrapped around his lips. There was his lovely princess, her hair ethereal and skin pore-less. His heart soared while opening up her text.

Hey, Babe, was a full orchestral symphony to his eyes. If eyes could hear, at least. Either way, he flexed his fingers and began to tell her about how he couldn't wait for their next special date. She'd only got in the day before, but needed a full twenty-four hours to overcome the jet lag. It had left Marty scheming in lover's pain until he could see her again.

She responded with *Sounds great.* Then two heart-eyes emojis.

Another bell, the evil one, interrupted his text romance. Marty didn't glance up, only raised his hand and said, "I'll be with you in one minute."

"Take all the time you need."

His head shot up and he found Brandy standing awkwardly by the 'redecorating your life' display. Dropping his phone in his pocket, he danced around the counter to her. "How did it...are you...?" It had taken her a week to even get in to see a doctor and, judging by the look on her face, it wasn't good.

She scratched at her arm, most of which was hidden by the elbow-length sleeves of their terrible work polos. *Is there a bandage under it? Did they take blood? Or give her an IV? That's serious, right? IVs?*

"They said that it is potentially serious and I should have it removed for biopsy. So I'm going to a dermatologist."

"When will they fit you in? Christmas?" Marty asked.

"Wednesday, actually. There was a cancellation," she said with a strained smile on her face. He knew she was faking it, the worry clear in her pale skin and watering eyes. "At least I won't have to wonder for long. Probably. Only twenty-six and I might have... That doesn't help."

"Do you need anything? Should I get you a glass of water? Some hot towels?"

Brandy glanced up at him, her lips twisted in an almost smile. "Do you think I'm preg—"

His phone buzzed loud enough in his pocket to jangle his keys, interrupting her. Certain it was Janeth, he took a quick peek. Instead of his angel, another gushing approval of his last date appeared.

Marty sighed while liking the comment and responding. "Sorry about that. It's been doing that all day."

"What?"

"Blowing up with people liking things of mine, commenting on things of mine. Following me like I won't lead them into the sewers."

She snickered. "You have a, what, Instagram account now?"

"Also Facechat, Tweetsnap, Gootube, and whatever that music thing is." Marty adored having attention lavished on him, but he preferred it in a more one-on-one setting. And preferably where pants weren't required. The lack of an instant response to tell him if he was straddling the line of bad taste kept him off social media, save for a small account he'd made to pick on Eldon.

To be fair, somehow his brother had wound up running the Twitter account of a local bread bakery. It hadn't lasted long. Only Eldon could make bread epically boring.

"What are you even doing on it? They didn't give your brother the chocolate factory to watch over, did they?" Brandy asked, causing Marty to laugh.

"Sadly no, though that would be fun. I could make so many 'candy bar in the pool' jokes if he did," Marty crowed at the idea, bringing a bright smile to Brandy's face. Then he turned back to his phone and said from the side of his mouth, "Janeth requested it. Said it'd help her out, so... There, all caught up."

The scratching increased, Brandy clawing along her shoulder. *Did they douse her in itching powder at the doctor's?* She worked her nails past the shirt and onto her poor skin. In a matter of seconds, dark red lines appeared.

Marty reached out and was about to grab her hand. At the same time, Brandy began to drop it, as if she realized the damage she was doing. That left his hand, still on a heat seeking course for hers, heading straight to her, um, *chest region. Very unmanlike chest region.*

Which he couldn't stop noticing now. Despite his earlier thoughts, the polo didn't really hide her overflowing bounty, so to speak. It didn't do her justice by any means, but there they were. Existing all this time. And he'd somehow kept missing them.

Until he'd gone to her place late at night, stripped to his pants, and almost... It had been the beer, of which there'd been a lot. So much consumed that he'd had to come back the next day to get his car. Drinking always made him extra friendly, which had birthed the idea of pressing his lips to hers...in a greeting of friendship. To caress the small of her back, which *holy macaroni does it swoop out in a serious ass. Missed that too.*

Not helping, Marty. The trick was to not think about it and wait for it all to go away. Which left them dancing around each other as if they'd actually fucked.

"Hey, you know what we should do?" he shouted, as much to distract Brandy from her potential health problem as to shut up his libido. *Who gave that damn thing a bullhorn?* Blindly, Marty snatched at the first two books he could find. "Excerpt time!"

Brandy accepted what looked like a nonfiction book about Iraq and he thumbed through one on English gardening. This would go well. She too seemed to stare at him with incredulity. *But in for a penny and all that.*

"You get to start first this time," he said and licked down his finger in anticipation of flipping fast.

This was probably a bad idea. He always picked lighthearted affairs. *Not affairs. Stories. Books. Things that don't have anything to do with cheating.*

He needed an intervention. Maybe if he dunked his head in holy water during mass? It'd solve the problem, because his mother would kill him.

"Okay," she said, shaking him from his panic. "Forty."

Marty cracked open the book. "'Before you can expect a vibrant garden, it is vital to prepare the soil lest you waste your seed.' Oh, I'm sorry. I think I grabbed the gardening erotica by mistake. I wonder how much plowing is in here?"

She laughed at his madness and raised her head. "Your turn."

"How about...?" There went the damn phone. He whistled exasperation through his teeth and pulled it out.

While scanning through the giddy girls all wishing he could be their boyfriend, Marty glanced over to find Brandy wilting. "How about fifty-three?"

She nodded, trying to force on her smile, and opened the book. Even as he did his boyfriend duty, Marty watched her with lowered lashes, her lips a juicy pink as she said, "'Within the confines of history, both everything and nothing is true. When the winner dictates truth, it must be viewed as a lie.'"

"Morbid," Marty said. "I'm sticking with my sexy English retirees getting horny with the gardener in their housecoat, thank you very much." He clasped the book tight to his chest as if he adored learning about daisies and azaleas. Eldon had tried to give him a house plant once. Marty had thought it was plastic until his brother had yelled at him. *Surely the wilting yellow leaves are all part of the experience to make it look authentic.*

"All right, what shall we learn next between preparing soil and ignoring history?" he asked, squaring his shoulders for more hot troweling action, when his phone went off again. "Sorry, just give me another..."

"You know, if you're..." Brandy placed her book back on the stand. Her endless brown eyes drifted to him and his pit of despair opened wide. Marty flinched, prepared to take the knocks of 'terrible friend,' but

Brandy shook her head. "I should get back to work. My appointment ran over and you know Mr. Fensin."

"He threw such a fit about you asking for time off, I stuck a coat on a chair and balanced a basketball wearing a wig on top."

She snickered at the bald-faced lie, but walked past him, leaving Marty alone to deal with the work of having a girlfriend. He wished he knew what to say to make everything go back to how it was. But as he watched her jeans cupped tight to her buttery buns sashaying away, the devil on his shoulder laughed at him.

Chapter Seventeen

Living with Eczema. When It's More Than a Rash. This Ringworm Is No Diamond.

Coping with Cancer.

Brandy's finger lingered over the shiny brochure with an image of a late-fifties woman staring at a sunrise. She looked at peace with her life, accepting whatever was to come — no doubt the long litany contained inside the three-fold paper and in bullet points. It looked as if that woman already saw the best of her past and was ready to face an uncertain future.

"Do you have a grandparent, dear?" a kindly voice asked from behind her shoulder.

She whipped her head around to find a roughly seventy-year-old woman watching her like a hawk. "Yes?" Brandy answered, confused why a stranger would care.

"It's always hard to deal with losing them to the big C," she said, freezing Brandy's heart cold. Her hand paused in tugging out the brochure as she stared in shock at the old lady. "But if they lived a good life, then it's God's will."

A flush burned across her cheeks. Brandy abandoned the pamphlet and scuttled back to the plastic chair she'd been relegated to for the past fifteen minutes. What was she going to do if it was cancer? She couldn't exactly bike her way back and forth to treatments. And the money was…

God, just thinking about dealing with insurance had twisted her stomach into so many knots she hadn't been able to eat for a day. It was already awful, with a deductible that'd require a third job just to meet the minimum. She'd survived with it thanks to being young, healthy and having no dependents to take care of. It could all come crashing down in one fell swoop.

What had she done wrong?

Okay, so maybe she wasn't religious about using sunscreen. And there was that one summer in high school when she'd gone white water rafting and burned her back to a crisp. But she ate well. Well enough. It wasn't all junk. She gave to charity when she could. And she tried to be friendly.

Did none of that matter? Was it another cursed twist of fate, just like losing her husband?

The lump in her throat expanded and sank deeper into her chest. Two years after the worst day of her life, here she was back on the brink again. And who could she call on?

Would her parents even answer the phone? Her in-laws sure as shit wouldn't. Mel had her own busy life and the same empty pockets as everyone else. There was no husband to hold Brandy's hand, to bring her soup when she was sick, to brush back her patchy hair and tell her she looked good bald.

Loneliness never grew sharper than when death stalked outside the door. Worst of all, it was her fault. All of it. If she hadn't gotten that sunburn, she wouldn't have grown a weird mole. If she hadn't been trapped in the familiar but empty trap of mourning for two years, she might have had someone here to help.

If she hadn't been driving that day, he'd be here.

That doesn't help, Brandy.

"Excuse me, miss?" the receptionist called from the desk.

Brandy shot to her feet and, stiff-legged, walked over. Was she prepared for this? Did she have a choice? "Yes?"

"I'm afraid the doctor is running late and it'll be another half hour."

"Oh." She should be angry, or at least annoyed, but Brandy felt numb. "Okay."

Her adult life had seemed to have started so early. *Married young. Owned a tiny bakery at twenty-two. Widowed by twenty-four. Dying from cancer by twenty-six.* She'd hoped that at the end of the dark tunnel of grief, the light wouldn't be an oncoming train.

And who would care in the end? Who would even come to her funeral? Or plan one for her? It had been maddening trying to pick what was best for Kevin with a thousand vendors hounding her for answers. No random friend or estranged relative could be expected to handle all that stress and cost for her.

Would they just toss her body into a ditch and let the wildlife chew it to bones?

Light bounced off the shiny front doors as another soul walked into the dermatologist's office, which sat next to a pizza parlor in the strip mall. She winced at the assault, prepared to shrink back into her green polo's collar, when a familiar smile replaced the glare.

"Marty?" she whispered, moving to rise.

He gave a little wave, then darted to sit in the chair beside her.

"What are you…?" She wanted to ask him why he was there, but in that moment, she was too joyful to care.

"I thought you could use someone to wait with you. Sit here and do the magazine mazes or watch your purse. Doctor offices are the worst. Never know who's hoping to steal your stash of tissues." He made threatening eyes at the kind old lady with cancer opinions. It was only a moment when she glanced up from her knitting, but the look of indignance brought a chuckle to Brandy.

"Excuse me, sir. Do you have an appointment?" the receptionist butted in on his kind gift. At least if he was kicked out, there was a dojo he could visit next to the pizza shop. It wouldn't be a total loss.

"No, but I'm here as a support animal," Marty said as he locked his fingers around Brandy's. He slapped his hand over hers, pinning her safely in his grasp. "Think of me as that hairless cat that looks like Yoda got into the hot wax."

The receptionist sighed, clearly not in the mood to deal with his nonsense. But Brandy stared in awe at him giving up his lunch hour to sit in a stuffy doctor's office just for her. "Thank you," she said.

"It's no big deal," Marty said and he wrapped his arm around her shoulder. "I'm here for you, no matter what happens."

For the first time in days, she wanted to cry tears of happiness. But Brandy blinked them away, her smile rising as she laid her head on Marty's shoulder. The fear of not knowing what could happen lingered deep inside, but at least she wouldn't be alone facing it.

"If you're here, who's watching the store?" she asked.

"Oh, I left the basketball in charge. It's already made employee of the month."

* * * *

Two days of her trying to ignore her phone, to religiously check every spam call and voicemail to see if it was news. To sit on the edge of her seat and chew apart her cuticles until a nail salon would throw holy water on her.

At least Marty was providing some distraction. He rolled into work with his usual bag stuffed to the gills. "All for the new display. With the Fourth over, I was thinking we should add a little spice between fireworks, ooh, ahh. And back to school, womp womp."

So she left him with a drill—always terrifying—and a two by four he claimed to have found. The loud power tool noises had Brandy concerned she might miss the call, so she slipped off to the back. It was much quieter, leaving only the rattling of worry in her brain to keep her company.

They'd said it'd probably take a while, that the lab was always backed up. How long was a while? Three days? A month? Two years? Would she already be dead before they got the results in?

Not helping. To her continued surprise, when she'd had a massive welt on her back to take care of, Marty had arrived at her door. He'd brought soup, because somehow that was supposed to fix everything. As it was proper tortilla soup, she wasn't going to argue, even if the temperature outside was hotter than the food.

With Marty at his most jovial, yanking every joke out of the ether he could, she should have told him. Talked to him. Explained that he deserved better, and that she was...

She was tired of waiting for the answer. For some angel to descend from on high and tell her, *"Brandy, you are ready to date again. To love again."*

"Hey!" The drilling stopped, and Marty shouted even louder, "Can you get the screwdriver out of my bag? I think I stripped this."

Brandy chuckled to herself. He'd once helped her to put up bookshelves. *Rather simple project, just follow the instructions.* Until the shelves had been put in at a slant and her books had kept trying to rush for the floor. She'd wound up laying a rolled-up towel in front to keep them in place.

"Have you found it yet?" he shouted.

"No," she called back, scattering a random assortment of books, boxes and empty bags from his donut place on the table. "This thing is a mess. Did you have putty in here?"

"Oh dear, it's breeched containment!" Marty called with a laugh. "Wait, I bet it's in the pocket. Eldon gave it to me and he sure loves his organized pockets."

Laughing at his brother, who probably put labels on every one of his tools, Brandy unzipped the front pocket and reached inside. A hard box the size of her palm bounced against her fingers. Curious, she tugged it out and stopped dead.

Square, it nestled perfectly in her hand the way a ring box would. Black as a tuxedo, it bore the sign of a hinged lid...exactly like the box one would use when making a large, life-changing request. Blood thundering in her ears, she tugged back the top and a massive sparkler smashed through her heart. Simple, brilliant and of the knuckle-crushing variety — it was a diamond ring. An engagement ring.

He'd had to leave her place early — something to do with Janeth. Brandy hadn't said anything at the time. She'd just let him go and waste God only knew how much on this? *Fuck!* She had to stop this, to intervene before he ruined his life chasing after...

"Brandy?"

Slapping the box shut, she stuffed her hand into the bag's pocket and yanked on the zipper. In her panic, she forgot to move her skin, catching it between metal teeth. *Damn it!*

"Hm?" she gritted through the pain, trying to wipe away both the fear for Marty and her heart shattering into a million pieces.

"The thing I use to put in screws? I believe it's colloquially known as a fingamajig."

What would happen if he proposed to Janeth and she turned him down? It'd kill Marty. What if she didn't turn him down? What if she just kept on cheating on him behind his back while they were engaged? While she was walking down the aisle? While they were married and living happily ever after?

"I, uh, I couldn't find it. But you know what would be fun?"

"Watching a very unstable table shatter through the door?" Marty said, darting his focus to whatever he was building.

"Ha." She laughed at his joke and ran out into the store. Grabbing the first two books she could, she spun around and said, "Playing our game."

Marty dug the battery pack of the drill into his palm in thought. "You know I'm usually down for this, but..."

Brandy rammed the book into his gut, not taking no for an answer. She had to do this. She had to be the one to break his heart before it could get so much worse.

"If it means that much to you," he said, laying the drill on the ground then rifling through the pages. "Why not?"

How could she hurt him? Break him into a million pieces just so that...so that he might look at her differently. He certainly would now.

That damn ring, a symbol of pain and joy, of strife and love, floated through her mind urging her on.

"Why don't—?"

"You go first!" Brandy interrupted him, holding the book she had no intention of reading.

"Uh, sure. Page twelve. Always a good number there."

She pretended to shuffle through the book, not caring what was in the mass of paragraphs and sentences. "I have to tell you something you're not going to like."

Marty snickered. "Already so dour. We're off to a rousing success. Your—"

"Ten," Brandy threw out fast, needing to get this done. Blood pounded so hard through her ears she barely heard Marty's reading. Instead, she watched his lips. *Always so soft and sweet, saying far too kind things.*

He glanced up from the book and said, "How about thirty-four?"

Brandy nodded, her teeth clamping together like the bars of a jail. They didn't want the truth to get free, to ruin whatever they had between them, but she didn't have a choice. "She's cheating on you, your girlfriend. I saw it at the party."

Only the briefest flit of her gaze drifted up to Marty, but he looked entertained and not bowled over by her truth. Oh God, he had no idea.

"Well, that is a morbid tale of..." He peered at the cover and for the first time his frown rose. "...puppy training."

Come clean, Brandy. Tell him everything. Finally rip that damn Band-Aid off and face him.

"Marty, I—"

"Ah." He held up a hand and dug into his phone. "Sorry, looks like one of my 'fans' sent me something that I just have to see. It's weird that I have fans, isn't it? I'll never get used to it."

He pressed Play on whatever video the follower had forwarded. Tinny sounds of shitty house music rose from his phone. At first, Marty wore the same wry grin as usual. Brandy gripped her book harder, cursing herself for not picking something from the literary fiction section. But as she turned around, Marty's happy look crumpled. First it transformed into a puckered frown, then his eyes lit up in an emotion she'd never seen on him in the year and a half she'd known him — rage.

"I have to go," he said, his voice as cold as the grave. He didn't slip his phone away, only kept it tight in his palm while picking up his bag.

Brandy must have failed at repacking, as a pair of shorts and flip-flops tumbled free. She raced to put them back in, but Marty was already marching out of the store with a dark cloud trailing him.

"What if Mr. Fensin…?" Brandy called to him.

Marty paused in front of the door, his bent back straightening in a heartbeat. "I don't give a fuck about Fensin," he thundered and ripped open the door to vanish into the parking lot.

Brandy clung to the book in her hands, her eyes shut tight. She had no idea what was on that video, but she hoped it'd fix all of this. Somehow.

Chapter Eighteen

Even while he glared at the traffic lights, the video wouldn't vanish from his brain. Two grainy bodies grinding together on a deck chair with only the shrubbery to provide a hint of cover. They didn't care who caught them. They didn't care that someone would record her and share it with her boyfriend.

"Aaaah!" Marty unleashed the feral roar that'd been building in his throat since he'd watched the woman in the video turn around. Sadly, it was aimed directly at the old woman pushing a cart across the street in front of him. She glared as if putting a curse on his next one hundred generations, causing Marty to hunch deep into his shoulders.

It could be a trick. There were computers that'd put faces on other people's bodies, even in video. And the footage was so terrible that it had to be even easier to fake. Or the date, the only proof that it'd happened last weekend. That could be fabricated easily. Even he knew how to do that.

Janeth would clear it up. No problem. Marty's knee, bouncing since he'd got into the car, finally struck the console. It hit in just the wrong spot, sending shockwaves of pain shooting up his thigh. But even as he gritted through the pain, he assured himself that it was all a big misunderstanding.

She'd said she loved him. How could his princess cheat?

It didn't take much work to find her, Janeth always leaving a digital crumb trail. She'd been near the ship docked at Penn's Landing that had been turned into a restaurant. Far too fancy for the likes of him, but probably something she expected.

In too much of a confounding rage to find good parking, Marty picked the first place that didn't cost him a literal kidney. Jogging up the gangplank, and trying to not imagine someone was holding him at sword point, Marty glanced across the massive ship. Four masts towered above him, American flags whipping in the wind.

How many engagements, anniversaries, baby announcements and birthdays shared with a loved one had those flags seen? How many promises had been made atop the planks of that ship?

To think he'd been planning on…

No, give her a chance to explain. It could be a lie from one of her online haters.

His first challenge was the gatekeeper, a host dressed not in old-timey sailor garb but the white shirt and black slacks that fancy restaurants required. He gave one slow look at Marty's barely tucked-in electronic store cast-off uniform and all but slammed the door shut.

"I'm looking for a woman," Marty said.

"Unsurprised," the little shit sniped. "But I'm afraid we can't supply that here."

The place wasn't packed, but he couldn't find hide nor hair of Janeth. Snickering to himself, Marty pulled up his phone and called her. With one eye on the galley, he watched until a slender hand emerged from the dessert tray that'd obscured her.

"There she is," he said, rebounding around the man before he had a chance to respond. Despite his shorter stature, Marty hauled ass. No doubt the host was calling for all manner of pirates to descend and hurl him into the briny deep. But he was talking to Janeth, no matter what.

Barely out of breath, Marty paused in front of the woman just placing the phone to her ear. She had two silver jewels adhered right under her eyes, which glittered in the mood-setting candlelight on the ship. "Martin?" she gasped, as if surprised to find him.

Her white-blue gaze drifted to the retinue of waiters he pulled with him. As they all came to realize she knew him, and wasn't about to panic, they sheepishly turned to walk away. At any other time, he'd have known better than to pull what he had. Brown guy attempting to get anywhere *they* didn't want tended to end in him being shot. But he was so frustrated that he didn't care.

"I didn't know you would be joining...me for lunch," Janeth said as she gestured him to a chair already tugged back.

He didn't realize that until he'd already sat down and pulled out his phone. "Is this you?" Marty demanded, needing the proof that he wasn't wrong. That he hadn't placed all his dreams on a woman who'd cheat on him without a second thought.

The easygoing smile on Janeth's face hardened to stone. She watched as the two people on his phone got down to business fast. In a snarl, she damned herself by asking, "Where did you get that?"

"Is. It. You?"

Her snort cut straight to his marrow. Leaning back so that she nearly elbowed a passing waiter, Janeth said, "What if it is?"

"What?" Marty flipped his phone back, drowning himself in the obvious misery of her wrongdoing, just to make certain he hadn't invented it all. "You're...you're cheating on me!"

His voice carried over the ring of buoys and diners, heads swiveling over to them. Janeth seemed to realize what trouble she was in, not from breaking his heart but the outsiders judging her. Dropping her voice, she reached for his hand. "It was a...a momentary lapse. I was alone and drunk. I always act out when deep into drink."

"It happened three days ago!" he shouted, not buying her excuses. She wasn't pleading with him, begging for him to forgive her. There were no tears in her eyes, no wobbling of her lips. A hard, stern look glazed across her face and a shark emerged from his angel.

"What of it? What right do you have to decide what I can and cannot do when you're not around?"

"Excuse me? I'm your boyfriend. That tends to come with some unbreakable terms and conditions."

Her cold laugh rattled through his bones, sharper than any winter chill. "No, you're not."

"I'm not what?" He reared back in confusion. They'd agreed to start dating during the picnic. It'd been going on for a month.

"You can't honestly believe someone like me" — she waved a hand down her body — "would date a man such as you? For fuck's sake, I'm a head taller than you without heels. It's goddamn hilarious if I stand anywhere close to you when I'm in them."

A crack burst through his ears, causing all sound to fade to a loud whine. Pain ripped through his chest, stamping his breathing to little gasps of air. "No," Marty croaked, struggling to fight through the crushing reality. "No, you...why would you keep me around if you think I'm such an embarrassment?"

Janeth shrugged. "The clicks. You get amazing ROI with my fans. They adore seeing what dates you'll come up with next."

That was all he was to her? An investment? A way to grow her brand? All those people fawning over him, pretending to call them the cutest couple in the universe? It was a lie? She didn't want him because of who he was, of how he made her feel, but because he kept spending all his money, time and heart on her. An ache ran up his jaw as he ground his teeth harder and harder. Through it, he forced out, "But you said...you loved me?"

"Of course I did — there were cameras on me."

"Your cameras! I never wanted a fucking thing to do with—" Despite Janeth starting the cursing, Marty felt disapproving eyes swing only upon him from the people who could unleash the police. He struggled to drop his voice, but he could barely hear it over the sloshing in his ears. "Was it all a lie? You just picked up some ugly little Latino to keep your viewers happy for a month?"

To his surprise, she frowned at that. Was there more there after all? She just struggled to see what they had beyond her influencer sphere? He could help her break free, to come into the light and really love him.

Hope rose in Marty's soul as Janeth picked up the proverbial knife and jammed it into his heart. "You weren't the worst person I've had to spend time with."

"Are you fucking serious?" he screamed, slamming so hard into the table that the silverware made a break for it. Out of habit, he caught a butter knife about to hit the floor.

"Look, it's nothing personal, okay? It's just—"

"Don't you finish that," Marty said. The hand holding a harmless butter knife began to wave.

"Listen, pal," a voice thundered in his ear as a massive hand landed on his shoulder. Marty might not have had the size, but he was a single strip of sinew. All of that flipped him directly into the face of the man caught on tape screwing his girlfriend.

Ex-girlfriend.

Aiden blinked slowly, no doubt needing a minute to register what had happened. But he tried to reach for the butter knife in Marty's hand and Marty was in no mood for anyone to touch him. He yanked his hand away and tossed the knife to his left.

"Don't do anything funny, man," Aiden said in his low rumble.

All that time, Marty had shaken off how close Aiden was to Janeth. They were friends, he was her employee, she needed him around for unexpected photoshoots. All that time Marty had wanted to believe a woman like her could look twice at a guy like him.

"You'll know when I'm doing something funny," Marty snarled as he spun the knife down and slammed it onto the table. "Because you won't understand it. As for you…"

She was acting. He could see it now, Janeth widening her eyes beyond anything normal, her hands helplessly clutched to her breast. She had to appear completely terrified of the scary boyfriend. Sorry, the scary brown boyfriend who'd come to tell her off. Nothing could be her fault as long as he was angry. Hot- blooded Latino and all.

Worst of all, Marty was steam-piping angry, but all he wanted to do was crawl into a small box and wail. And the whole time, the restaurant glared at him. Made him into the bad guy. As if he hadn't invested his life, his future, his everything into the woman who'd used him for likes.

The suits were closing in. Waiters held their trays like shields, the hosts speaking hurriedly into phones. He had to leave or risk a night in jail for Janeth. She wasn't worth it. She wasn't worth anything to him.

"You have no idea what you've lost," he said. Aiden tried to grab his arm again, but Marty shook it off. "Fuck you, fuck both of you. I hope all your precious followers learn what really happened between you and your unicorn boyfriend."

There was the first sign of real distress. Janeth's mouth fell open and she hunched over her phone. If the fan had sent the video to him, then others knew. And, judging by the pinch in her forehead and furious typing, they were spreading it.

His heart was crushed, his head bowed, but Marty walked out of the restaurant and her life on his own two feet.

* * * *

Get here, ASAP!

Brandy prayed she'd typed that right, as her phone was trapped behind her back. The tell-tale glare of the manager burned through her and she stood up straight. But that wasn't enough as Mr. Fensin circled her, knowing she must be up to no good. Brandy released her phone onto the chair behind her and stepped forward.

The bell jangled, raising her hopes, but it was only a customer. That at least distracted Mr. Fensin, who greeted the lady with a gruff, "Welcome to the store."

A regular, the woman glanced warily at Brandy, who shrugged but tried to act peak professional. *Come on, Marty. Where are you?*

"Where is he?" Fensin growled, both claws and teeth out and eyeing up a pink slip. He stared daggers at the front door, then spun to Brandy.

"He, he's out to lunch."

"It's two-thirty."

"A late lunch. We were swamped earlier and Marty didn't have time." God, she was a terrible liar. She could feel her face cracking with each glare from their overlord. If Marty had given a hint of what had sent him running, she could've made up a better story for the boss. *Oh, he's out tracking down some inventory or chasing a shoplifter.* Anything better than 'he suddenly had to eat at two in the afternoon or pass out.'

"How long's he been out?" Fensin huffed.

"Not very," Brandy pipped up instantly. *Come on, make it sound realistic.* "Ten minutes, maybe?"

Her boss snorted. "Thought you only had five."

Real capitalist Scrooge she worked for. The only reason the job was livable was thanks to him never being around, and the fact that she had savings to survive on. Otherwise it'd probably be nothing but cat food dinners.

Mr. Fensin turned away from glaring out of the window as if he hated every person on the planet. "You aren't protecting him, are you?"

"What? Why would I do that?"

He answered with a snort. "Like I don't know what kids get up to on their 'smoke breaks'."

Brandy bristled at not only the idea of her being a kid, but that he'd ever allot them smoke breaks. She tried to ignore the other sticky innuendo hanging in the air. *'I don't see Marty that way.' 'He's just a friend.' 'We would never...'* God, every one sounded like a pathetic lie.

But they weren't. He'd never so much as kissed her. He clearly thought they were only friends. And she...well, she was an idiot. That was all.

Fensin loomed closer, his caterpillar eyebrows arching until his pupils contracted to pinpricks. It sent Brandy shrinking, her natural instincts to run and hide from any confrontation kicking in.

"What'd you want?"

Oh, thank God! Brandy glanced up and her praise to whichever saint was in charge of texts faded. It looked like someone had run over Marty in the parking lot. His head lolled at the base of his neck as if he couldn't lift it. That always vibrant smile was a dry frown, his skin crackling like a Victorian with consumption. As he risked a single look at Brandy, she saw not only heartbreak but endless betrayal lurking in his eyes.

"Finally," Fensin snapped between them, looming over the broken man. "Where were you?"

Brandy tried to get Marty's attention and somehow tell him what to say, but he wouldn't look up. "I was tracking down a special order," Marty said smoothly.

"Hmph, she said lunch," their boss spat and jabbed a shaky thumb at Brandy.

Marty didn't flinch, didn't falter. "I grabbed a sandwich along the way. Beef and cheddar if you're curious. Off a cart down by—"

"I don't give a shit," Fensin interrupted, causing the one who worked retail to almost shush her boss for cursing. "I've gone over the books, proper this time." He waggled a finger at them as if they were pulling some long con with the finances. "And it's come to my attention that we don't need two employees."

"What?" Brandy gasped.

"You've got to be bleeping kidding me." Marty muted his own curse and tipped his head back to the ceiling.

"So I'm cutting both your hours," Fensin continued, snapping them away from the impossible choice of who should go. "You" —he jabbed a finger at Brandy— "work Monday, Tuesday, Saturday. And you" —now it was Marty's turn— "take Wednesday, Thursday and Friday."

"What about Sunday?" Marty responded in an instant, as if it was all a joke.

"I'll flip a coin," Fensin said, causing Marty to chuckle.

Didn't he realize what that meant? Their hours were being cut in half. They wouldn't be full time. There wouldn't even be the hint of benefits…including health insurance. *Fuck.* When would it run out? Right away?

What would she do if she had to pay out of pocket for chemo?

Die. That was it. The choice was die slowly from the cancer or quicker from starvation and exposure.

Panic seized her arms. Brandy tried to wrap them around herself as she stared dumbstruck at the two men glaring at each other. How could she do this? Could she get another job and deal with cancer treatments? But that'd have to be part time too? *No health insurance. No help.*

She was alone and not even her friend holding her hand at a doctor's appointment would fix it.

Through the terror swarming from her brain to her heart, she watched Marty switch his stance. It went from broken and fragile to sturdier, as if he was prepared to do something stupid.

"Since it's Tuesday," Fensin said, "you head home." He prodded a fingertip into Marty's shoulder. It barely moved him, Marty crossing his arms.

"So that's it then? I just go home for the day and you cut my paycheck in half?"

"Yeah. It's called being the boss, son. You'd do well to learn your place."

Shit. The hair on the back of her neck stood on end. Fensin's venomous response rang through the bookstore. Marty shook his head less like a man clearing his thoughts and more like a bull about to charge. She caught his fists clenching and unclenching.

No. She didn't want this. Even if his quitting, or attacking their boss and being fired, might let her keep her job, it wasn't right.

Marty's gaze drifted from the sneering visage of their boss back to Brandy standing behind the counter begging for him to stop. To her relief, his fists unclenched and his hands fell limply to his sides.

"If that's how it has to be," Marty whispered, more to himself than their boss.

Fensin all but clapped over his victory. The smug bastard didn't give a shit about this place the rest of the time, but now he was high king of the shop. Browbeaten, Marty slipped to the counter beside her. He picked up his bag, the one holding the small box Brandy was doing her best to not think about.

As he drew close, she held on to his shoulder. "What happened?"

He blinked rapidly and swung to her as if he was surprised she was standing in his corner. A warm hand caressed hers. "I broke it."

Broke what?

She couldn't ask as he'd already moved to the door, away from her. Just before he shoved the glass open, Marty turned to her and in a bittersweet voice said, "Bye, Brandy."

As the door swung shut, his form slipping away into the steaming heat of July, it struck her. She wasn't just losing her health insurance, her stability, her livable paycheck. She'd never get to work with her best friend ever again.

Damn it.

Chapter Nineteen

Darkness. Cruel, oblivious, unforgiving darkness leeched from every pore of his body. The light extinguished when his heart crumbled to dust, only a shadow remaining between his lungs. It was the darkness that sustained him, kept his body alive and clinging to this now heartless earth.

What was he but a lost shadow with the other half of his soul wrenched from his body? Doomed to wander the city streets, seen by nobody and touched by none. Not until the cloud of darkness beating inside of his concave chest gave its last, pathetic thump.

Another knock on his door caused Marty to roll over. Rather than bother rising from his couch to answer it, he hit Repeat on his phone. The loudest, sharpest music he could find blared from the speakers directly into his ears. Girls used breakup songs and ice cream. He had heavy metal and a sea of flaming-hot Cheetos. The end was the same though.

"Martin!" the would-be reaper at his door called. "Open up."

"Go away," he shouted back to his brother, and began the laborious task of rolling over to stare at the back of the couch. There were a lot more red handprints all over the navy upholstery than he remembered. Not that it mattered. Nothing did, or ever would.

He was worse than cursed—he was unloved. A pointless wretch of flesh and bone, knitted together by a callow God and set adrift in—

Eldon burst through the door. The sound of the real world shattering his cocoon caused Marty to sit up. His brother stood on the threshold, scanning the mountain of takeaway boxes and bags of trash Marty hadn't found the energy to toss.

"Did you break my door?" he shouted, a brief burst of anger shaking away the doldrums of heartache.

"You gave me a key," Eldon responded, dangling the single key on a cheap ring that he'd marked with Marty's name. *Of course he'd label it.*

With the mystery solved, and no threat of possible eviction, Marty flopped back to the couch and his groove. He'd been working on it for a week—morning, noon and night, only leaving for bathroom visits or when he'd stumble into work, glower at anyone even venturing near the romance section and return to the groove.

"You cannot keep doing this," Eldon buzzed above him like the obstinate horsefly he always was.

Marty waved a hand at his brother and cuddled closer to the cushion. "Leave me alone. I'm dying."

"You're not dying."

"My heart was ripped out of my chest. Not many people can survive that," he harrumphed before digging deeper into his couch. Why did he ever give his brother a key? Their mom had probably made him.

Eldon, in true robot form, sighed. "Can you not turn the melodrama down? And that racket? How have the neighbors not complained?"

"They have. Often." Marty fished for his phone, which had slipped under the couch, and increased the volume.

"No." Eldon bent down and stole the phone. In an instant, the screeching of a banshee upon the lovelorn's door died. "This won't stand."

"I didn't ask you," Marty said, spinning around and facing his brother. His incredibly tall brother. Eldon's head cut off somewhere in the clouds, leaving Marty to stare at his tie. It was gray. 'Boring, bland, wouldn't know romance if it walked up and socked him in the heart' Eldon Dashwood. But he was tall. And that was all that mattered.

"Go home, Eldon. Leave me to my misery."

"For fuck's sake, Martin. I'd expected better from you."

It was less the admonishment and more the fact that his brother had cursed that caused Marty to focus on him. The suit was stiff, the buttons polished, the glasses cleaned, but wear showed on his brother. No one knew how to find it better than the brother that usually caused it, but it was there. Was he really worried about him?

Too bad.

"Sorry for not rising to your expectations of how to deal with having your entire life turn to complete shit overnight."

"She is hardly…" Eldon began, leaning closer, when he paused. His bland face yanked away and he gasped. "When did you last shower?"

That required too much time away from his groove. Here was comfort. The couch would never abandon him. It needed him as much as he needed it.

With Eldon's attempt at brotherly bonding over, Marty slumped back to his cushions. "Leave me to my grief already," he ordered, flapping a hand at his brother. Marty dug his chin deeper into the couch, wondering if he could smother himself from grief. Not on purpose, more if his body would become so tired of this pointless existence that his lungs would just deflate like a balloon and refuse to work.

Martin Cruz Dashwood. Died twenty-five years young from a lack of love. He was too beautiful for this world.

He brushed his cheek over the cushion, prepared to chase sleep, when hands locked around his stomach. *What the…?*

Marty flailed his arms and legs, trying to kick away, but that diet of Cheetos and misery had left him weak. He couldn't do anything but wretchedly wave his limbs as Eldon plucked him into the air.

"What are you doing? Put me down!"

Eldon's bony fingers dug into Marty's stained shirt as he marched his brother away from the living room and down the hall. "This isn't funny, Eldon. We're not kids anymore! You can't do this!"

Still his brother wouldn't say anything. No, the *bastardo* just carried Marty like he was a babysitter again, charged with getting his younger brother washed up before bed. *What?* Did Eldon think if he just locked him in there, he'd have to take a shower?

Well, too bad. The pain in his heart couldn't be relieved by a single drenching of water or scrubbing of soap. It would never leave, no matter what his brother did.

Marty's ass struck the bottom of the shower stall and he swung his head up in anger at the brother who'd put him there. Old, mildewy water seeped up his pajama pants. He'd have to change them or be faced with...

"Ah!" he cried as Eldon flipped on the damn tap. Cold water sprayed Marty's head and chest, his skin erupting in goosebumps as he whipped soggy hair from his face. Before he could lash out in rage, Eldon had already walked away.

"We'll talk when you're done washing up," he said, and slammed the bathroom door.

Marty slumped over, his back bent so the cold water could only hit what it'd already damaged. The shivers trembling up his body were the first thing he'd felt since that woman had broken his heart. Shattered it. Kicked the pieces into the waves. Then laughed at his crumpled form.

He should reach over and shut off the tap, but the longer Marty sat there, the warmer the water became. It didn't feel so bad after all.

* * * *

He wasn't better, even if he had scrubbed himself clean and put on a real shirt and pants. That, Marty intended to make abundantly clear as he strode back into his living room.

Funny, he'd expected to find that Eldon had vacuumed and cleaned his place. But no, there was his

'I know a close Thai place' mountain. And 'it's not alcoholism after a breakup' beer can Stonehenge.

No, his brother was in the kitchen, hovering over the coffee pot, making...

"Tea?" Marty spat as he spotted the familiar string dangling from Eldon's mug—which he'd no doubt bleached before using. "You come into my place and make tea?"

"What of it?" his brother asked, taking a careful sip. Probably worried about catching the plague or something.

Marty hefted his massive plastic jug of coffee grounds, dug a spoon in and chewed down. The full-punch of bitter caffeine was worth it for the sour look he got from his brother. "Well," he said, splattering some of the grounds. Wiping it off, he began again. "I'm here. Alive. Clean."

"More or less," Eldon said.

"Forgive me for not putting on tails and spats, your majesty," he responded with a deep bow. "Unless you were going to clean up my place..." He watched Eldon's full-body twitch, as if he lived in fear of the very idea. "...then I'd say you can leave."

"Hardly. Martin, you've been locked away bemoaning your state as if you've suffered the gravest injustice in the world."

"I. Was. Dumped!"

"And? You're hardly the first person."

"She..." She'd made a fool out of him. Used him, tricked him into her web of lies until he was punch-drunk happy to dance to her every whim. He wasn't certain what he hated more—that she'd turned him into a chump in front of millions of strangers...or that he'd really fallen for her.

Marty stumbled into the chair, his chin nearly striking the table as it grew too heavy to lift. "I loved her."

His brother sighed and placed the steaming mug of weak-ass tea beside Marty's chin. "You barely knew her."

"So what? Doesn't change how I feel. Which you'd know if you weren't nothing but a series of ones and zeros cooked up in a lab."

"What?" Eldon blinked.

"Binary. You know, the numbers to make computer programs… I'm saying you're a robot!" *God.* Wasn't his brother supposed to be the smart one?

Eldon groaned and leaned against the table. He never sat when he visited Marty, always hovering around on his feet. Eldon Dashwood was important. He had very vital places to be. Wasting his time with that foolish younger brother was beneath him.

"Martin…"

"Would it kill you to not call me that?" he asked, glaring at the tea instead. "Like actual strike by lightning, you fall down dead?"

All he got was the Eldon sigh. "Why are you twisting this month-long romance into something special?"

"Because it was! I thought…she was the one. My other half."

"Who never laughed with you. Who didn't seem to share any of your interests. Who only tolerated you for views."

Marty shivered in his wet clothes. "We were fated. I mean, how much better of a meet-cute do you get than 'I saved her from a mugging while on a bicycle?' It's perfect."

"It doesn't matter," Eldon said.

"To you."

"To anyone! Do they hear your story of how you met before handing you a marriage license? No. Do they require you to pass a certain level of 'aww' before letting you sign a lease together? Martin...Marty, it's all in your head."

He thudded his knuckles against the table, listening to each bone rat-tat-tat as they rolled. "You don't get it. You never did. You don't have to, you've got..." He paused at Eldon's look and restarted. "I just want that rush of butterflies and urge to skip singing down the sidewalk. To have someone I can sweep off her feet into my arms and watch her eyes light up whenever she sees me across the room."

But he hadn't had that with Janeth. He could pretend, sure, and boy had he ever. She'd loved the gifts, the attention he'd given her. The dates that had fed back into her bank account thanks to AdSense tagging along. But had she ever looked at him when she didn't have to?

"What do you know about love?" Marty moaned as he crashed his cheek to his table. "It's all data files to you."

"You're such a fool." Eldon kept on being his usual self. He was right. Marty was foolish for trying to explain anything to his robotic brother. The man avoided romance like a rash, and look where that had got him. Two fools trapped in a quagmire of their own making.

"I need to get back to work," Eldon said, checking his phone. Marty was curious what time it was and moved to swing his watch around, only to find it had stopped dead. *Damn it, not again.*

Eldon rose to his full height. "I will check on you again to make certain you've cleaned this biohazard up."

"Because Mom told you to?" Marty fired back. As his brother's eyebrows shot up, he knew he was right.

Tugging on his suit coat, Eldon turned to leave, but before he did, he gestured to a new container he must have left behind. "You're a fool for missing what's right in front of you," he said, and slipped back out of the door he hadn't broken down.

Marty twisted around the nearly opaque white plastic container until he found a blue latch on the bottom. As he popped it open, a tray of cupcakes with verdant green frosting greeted him. They could only have come from one person, but he tasted one anyway to be sure.

"Oh God, that's good," he groaned, falling into the perfect marriage of buttercream, amaretto, sponge cake and a hint of pear. Brandy must have been by to leave this for him. Had she knocked on his door and he was too deep into the cups of misery to answer?

A new ache rose through his heart. Work was a fog, made all the worse because he could never talk to her. See her. He didn't realize how much he missed her until she wasn't there.

Marty absently poked a finger into the second cupcake's frosting.

At least I can rectify that pain.

Chapter Twenty

He took the time to not only put on an ironed shirt —
hunter green to better match his color, and unstained
pants — but even shaved. Not that Marty had much in
the way of facial hair. Like a chihuahua had fallen into
barber clippings, as he liked to joke. It didn't matter —
the freshly clean look suited him best.

The strong odor of Wildcat Mountain lingered
around him as he raised his fist to knock. Okay, maybe
he'd overdone it on the cologne. But after Eldon's
performance, the last thing he wanted was to still carry
a smell that would put her off. While tossing the boxes
and giving a halfhearted scrub of his kitchen, Marty put
in a lot of time thinking.

Thinking beyond how thinking hurt every nerve in
his body. And while he couldn't escape the red burning
behind his eyes if he let his mind wander, one fact kept
bobbing to the surface. He owed it to her to try one last
time.

He knocked again, about to go a third time, when a voice shouted from inside. "Yes, I'm coming! Just had a pot on the..."

The door swung open to reveal her deep eyes glistening in shock. Wisps of black hair dangled around her face as the always-there ponytail started to slide to its demise.

"Marty?"

"Hey, Brandy," he said with a small wave, as if he'd spotted her across the street on their way to work.

"What are you...?" She whipped her head around behind him, as if expecting to find someone forcing him to be there.

"I wanted to thank you for these." Hoisting up the cupcake container by way of explanation, he opened the lid to reveal all the treats were gone.

Her soft cheeks brightened pink and Brandy slid back. "Come in. Probably silly of me. I mean, I just...I dropped them off and, for all I knew, you weren't even home. But I kept thinking that, wondering..."

As he stepped inside and she shut the door, her wandering sentences all focused to a single beam. "How are you doing?"

He twisted on a smile and focused on her. "Getting better. Do I want to know how you found out?"

Wincing, Brandy grabbed the container from him and hustled off to whatever dinner she'd been working on. "It's, um, Mel."

"I should have known."

"Saw it all go down on, ya know, the 'gram," she said. "Do people even use that? 'Gram? Never mind."

Absently, Marty's gaze swung away from the woman vanishing behind her counter to the now minty fresh wall. Brown accents divided it up, making it look like it belonged in an old-fashioned Tudor home. Or at least some quaint village cottage. She'd known what she was doing all along.

"Let me guess, I'm the big bad in her story."

"Actually, they've been ripping her apart in the comments. I mean, not all, but a lot of them are behind you one hundred percent. Think that what Janeth did..."

Her jolly reporting faded as Marty made a low grinding sound at the name. He'd be a happy man if he never had to hear it again.

"Sorry the, uh, the place is a mess." More banging of the pots broke from the kitchen before Brandy emerged. She swiped the back of her hand across her forehead, causing her hair wisps to scatter. Marty watched them all fall haphazardly, practically crying out for someone to help.

Brandy glanced down at her requisite green polo and she blanched. "I am a mess."

"You look..." *Stunning.* Sweet lips that whispered jokes in his ears. Rich eyes that sparkled with mirth whenever he walked to her. A wholesome face that'd never lash wicked malice against him. And her body was...banging. The polo didn't matter. The loose khakis with the worst pleats couldn't hide her. Every soft curve made itself known in an instant. He stared at her like one of those eye puzzles where at first there was only garish wallpaper, then suddenly a sailboat.

Where once there was a friend, I saw...

"Good," Marty whispered. "Very good."

"Ha," she said with a scoff, but her blush increased and she began to comb back her hair. "Work is the worst now. All day back and forth, moving inventory, keeping an eye on the front. On the back. I swear I'm running ten miles a day just to look out for shoplifters and…"

Brandy's complaint faded as she stared at him. Silly Marty. That goof who'd build castles out of cardboard boxes. Who'd once asked her to dance to a children's nursery songs album. First because he'd thought it was funny, but as the music continued, because he didn't want to let go.

"It's not the same without you there."

"You mean Mr. Fensin didn't calculate the cost of having one person doing two jobs? I am flabbergasted!" Marty responded and flapped a palm to his face as if he was about to faint.

Her luscious lips with the perfect little bow on top quirked into a smile. But as they parted, her smile faded. "I've missed you," she released into the world between them. The truth he couldn't escape, no matter how hard he might try.

It was one thing for Janeth to crush his heart, but to not see Brandy six days of the week? To not slip up front to be closer, share a sandwich with her, talk about anything and everything—that gutted him. And he hadn't realized how much he needed her until he'd seen that little cupcake container to remind him that she cared.

She'd always cared.

Marty took a step closer and a knot clenched in his stomach. *Strange.* In all his years playing the part of Romeo, not once had he gotten knock-kneed, sweated from his palms or felt like his belly would burst. If he got this wrong, he could ruin everything between them.

If he got it right…? That was just as scary.

"I've—" he started, when Brandy's phone rang.

At first she didn't react, her gaze only on him. But as the phone ran through its second verse of *My Half*, she snapped away. When she pressed it to her ear, all the color drained from her face.

"Brandy?"

"It's...it's the doctor's office. Finally. Oh, God." Tears welled in her eyes, striking deep into Marty's heart. She shook her head as if she couldn't do it. He rubbed her shoulder, trying to will any strength she might need.

Brandy smiled and answered the call. "Hello. Yes, this is Brandy Benson."

She walked away to listen to the news that could be doom. As she slipped from his grasp, a cold terror swept through him. He tried to read her body language, but she'd fully turned from him. Only her back was visible, her free hand hanging by her side.

It felt as if decades passed before she said, "Thank you," and hung up. Marty held his breath, watching on tenterhooks as she turned back to him. Tears glistened at the top of her cheeks.

No.

It didn't matter. He wasn't losing her now. Striding forward, he opened his arms to pull her safe, when a smile appeared. "It's not malignant!"

"What?" Shock ripped away Marty's vocabulary until he could only handle the *See Spot Run* words. "Is that...what does it...?"

"I don't have cancer," she shouted, happy tears tumbling from her eyes like a cleansing rain.

Elated beyond all reasoning, Marty wrapped his arms around her. They leaped up and down, laughing together. "Oh God," Brandy kept whispering, her lips beside his ear. "God, oh God. I thought…And it's not. All that worry over nothing. I couldn't stop thinking."

"Me too. The idea of—" He paused and shifted in her safe embrace to fall into her sweet soul.

I could have lost you. Not for a day, or a week, but forever.

Marty pulled her to him, those petal-soft, honey-sweet lips pressing to his. In a flash, the knot he'd been carrying around burst into a stream of electricity zapping through his body. Heat coursed from her touch into him not only by her tender mouth, puckering gently to his for a deeper kiss. His hands, cradling her resilient body against him, felt each rising charge.

Somehow, his palm found its way up to her hair and he did what he'd wanted to do for a year and half. Brandy gasped as he tugged her ponytail band down through her silky dark locks. As her freed hair tumbled to the small of her back, Marty ran his fingers against the fallen tips.

All his life, he'd prided himself on being the man with a thousand lines to sweep any girl off her feet. But in that moment, he was completely speechless.

A soft breath curled across her cheek, Marty's flushed lips parting as a second, uncertain laugh escaped. Brandy felt her knees could go any second, her body hanging upon the fingertips she had pressed around his waist.

He'd kissed her.

Really. Truly. Taken her chin in his palm, pressed his lips to hers and changed everything.

Was she ready?

Her heart's once tepid beats kicked to a pounding rhythm as she watched Marty's hand. Wide, tan, the pads holding calluses from all the boxes he'd carried for her, but the tips...perfect for caressing.

"Marty," she whispered, her eyes closed tight as if she was wishing on a star. The cliff's edge hung before her, a million fears circling below and waiting to pull her under. A barely evident gasp caused her to look at him. "Be with me."

"Tonight?" he said with a gulp.

"For..." she began when he surged forward. The gentle kiss of a summer's rain transformed into a famished typhoon. Heat rose from her belly, causing Brandy to clasp him. To touch the stomach she'd seen naked what felt years ago, to reach up and tousle through his hair. To cling to Marty as he swept his palms over the back of her shirt.

Even through the thick polyester she could feel those palms pressing and kneading, bringing a flush through the part of her she'd thought dead. She wanted more. She needed it, him. To have not just any man but Marty himself hold her body and bring it to such blissful heights...

Brandy snatched at his shirt, fumbling to undo the buttons. She walked closer to him, their hips glancing off one another as she pulled and tugged at his impossible shirt. Marty chuckled at her force, his laugh caressing her ear before he lapped along the shell. A shiver danced down her spine, Brandy finally undoing enough of the shirt that she could graze her palm over his chest...only for Marty to stumble back.

"Whoa!" he cried as first he, then she, stumbled onto the couch. His hands remained locked around her waist, pulling her on top so he had to take the brunt. A reassuring laugh rose from Marty, whose shirt dangled to the sides of his chest. Brandy was trapped, her hands pinned on the cushions and her breasts pressed over his acreage of warm, naked skin.

Marty smiled wide and caressed her back. "If I knew you were that strong, I'd have let you bring in the stock," he said. A burn rose in her stomach from her wondering if she had already messed everything up, when Marty's touch rifled its way under the back of her polo.

"Oh God," she gasped, biting on her lip at the warmth radiating across her spine. Two years since she'd known that touch, since she'd wanted anyone to caress even the small of her back. Her body hummed from only the sweep of his palm against her skin.

Marty drew his nose along the side of her throat, raising her chin with the tip as she trembled above him. "Hey," he said, "you're stealing my thunder." He brushed hot lips against the thin skin on her neck, the pecks gentle and soft, until Brandy began to grind against him. They landed so his hips rested right above hers, but she felt a hardness rising from his pants and pressing ever tighter to her lower belly.

"Holy shit," Marty sputtered, a moan rising from his throat as he glided his hips back against her.

She knew what was there, but in that moment, Brandy needed proof. To see it, to feel it, to hold it in her hand, to thrust down upon it until he begged only for her. She snatched the zipper, when Marty grabbed her hand.

"Wait." He released his grip in an instant and cupped both his hands around her face. "I want to do this right," he said, and kissed her on the lips.

Right how? Even confused, Brandy moved to resume the kissing, but Marty was already rising off the couch. She stumbled with him. He was still in his shoes, leaving him a half an inch taller than her. An odd feeling, to have to look up in order to fall into his sweet face.

Marty brushed through her hair, softly combing the locks back until they lay on her shoulder. Was that it? He didn't want to take it any further right now? He tumbled his combing fingers from her hair down the line of her arm. One touch after another set off goosebumps across her body. As he reached her wrist, he circled the rest of his fingers around and reached for her hand.

Without another word, he pulled on her hand to lead them to the bedroom. Panic tried to take hold. What was she doing? Did she even remember how to do this? Oh fuck, how messy was her room?

But at the reassuring smile on Marty's tender lips, the panic faded. He shoved the open door, walked into the bedroom then promptly turned and filled his arms with her. Only the blue light of her fish tank shone upon them, not that Brandy noticed. Her eyes were tight as she savored every touch of his certain hands.

The coy and careful lover from the couch snapped to a man who hoisted the cursed polo straight off her. His palm cupped along her bare stomach, causing the breath to catch in her throat. "Purple," Marty said, causing her to stare at him.

Purple what? Had her stomach gone purple? She glanced down and got her answer.

"I've always wondered, and somehow always knew," he said and swept his palms straight up her purple bra.

God almighty! His gentle touch, soft through the padding of the cups, sent her reeling. Marty answered by taking her lips in a kiss. As he swirled his fingers over her nipples, coaxing them through the petals that were meant to hide them, he delved his tongue into her mouth. She wanted it. Needed it, too.

Greedy, Brandy parted her lips and drank Marty's nutty and sweet taste. He was amaretto sours, peanut butter ice cream, salty and sugary and masculine too. Every roll of his tongue with hers, every assured flex of it rippling along her lip made her legs tremble in anticipation. She wanted more, all he had to offer for as long as he could.

Marty picked up her hand and placed it on his waistband. Then the other. She clung to the pleated fabric where a belt could go and stared in wonder at him. Did he really want that? Want her to...?

A soft chuckle rumbled from his throat. He cupped her chin and brushed across her lips. Brandy chased it with her tongue, rolling along his thumb and causing a sputter of breath to escape from him. He pressed tight to her back, holding her close so he could breathe the same pant of hunger down her ear.

For a brief second, a cruel urge to torture him rose through her. To watch Marty squirm as she teased him with all he could take until he screamed for her. But that would require her to not be begging for him now.

Hooking her hands in place, she unzipped his pants. She expected him to wiggle free himself, but Marty whispered in the hollow below her ear, "Take 'em off."

Slowly, she tugged on the hips of his trousers. Boxers? Briefs? Hearts on them either way? They didn't have to fall far before she realized the truth.

Commando.

A tan cock, with a head as red as his blushing cheeks, rose into her palm. She circled her thumb along the foreskin, causing Marty to buck his hips. "I always knew," she said, widening her hand and gliding it down the full length of his shaft.

Then Romeo became putty, especially as she cupped his balls and nestled her palm in the burrow of black hair.

"Knew...knew what?" he gulped.

Brandy smiled and raised her torturous hand higher to once again circle the crown. "That you were packing heat." She was about to laugh at her stupid pun, when a breeze brushed against the part of her spine that'd been covered by her bra.

"Wait until you see what it can do in the wild," he whispered, and guided her fingers to hold him tighter. One-handed, Marty tugged the straps of her bra off her shoulders, freeing her breasts. She had to release him to toss it aside and expected Marty to put her hand right back.

But he stared in wonder at her chest, his cock twitching as it hardened. "*Me luces tan bella*," he cried and swept his palms over her naked breasts. A thousand feelings swept through Brandy at once. Joy at him finally touching her, regret at how long it had taken, pain for the loss she could never escape, fear that it could all go wrong...and, overpowering it all, happiness. A strange, unending giddiness lightened her body until she'd swear it was floating.

"Are you laughing?" he whispered as he released her breasts and cupped his hands down her stomach to the khakis remaining in the way.

Brandy tried to shake it off, but another giggle escaped. "I'm sorry," she sputtered. "It's not you, it's..." She couldn't explain it, and, afraid that Marty might grab his balls and go home, she kissed him hard. The joyful laughs subsided as he fumbled with her pants. Unaware of the inside button, Marty tried to tug them aside.

They slipped a few inches down and Brandy was about to help, when he shook his head. "I will uncover the secrets below," he declared. First, he placed her hands on his hips and crooked his fingers down inside her waistband.

Brandy strained higher, sucking in to try and help. The button was right there. He had to have felt it. But Marty moved lower, the edge of his nails scraping down the front of her panties. With his tongue, he lapped her bottom lip into his mouth. With his hand, he reached into her pants until he could draw a slow trail straight down her pussy.

"God," she gasped into his mouth, feeling Marty smile at her response. His exploring finger worked its way around the elastic of her underwear and pleas dripped from Brandy's lips.

But he started to slip away, as if afraid she wasn't ready. *To hell with that.* She reached out and cupped his cock. Giving a steady jerk to the pliant skin, she watched Marty's smirk of satisfaction collapse into awe.

He ransacked his finger through her panties, pulling as hard as he could on the edge until...

"You're so wet." Marty groaned at the same moment she did. Taking his time, he swirled through her entrance, softly caressing the lips aching for something harder to cup. She didn't stop her impromptu hand job, her confidence rising the harder his cock plumped in her grip.

From inside her depths, his finger emerged and flicked against her clit. As he did so, he thrust his hips, leaving Brandy panting in time with him. Fuck, it was so…perfect.

Brandy wanted more. She tried to tug off her pants with one hand, yanking down on the waistband, only to have them snag. *What…?*

The button.

She paused in her jerking, which caused Marty to slow as well. *I want you.* Brandy reached for her pants. *I hope you want me too.* Undoing the infernal button, she tugged off the jeans, leaving herself in only a pair of black panties.

"Please," Marty shouted so suddenly that she nearly jumped. After picking up her hand, he let her knuckles graze his lips as he whispered, "Please let me inside you."

As Brandy nodded, Marty leaped onto the bed. He tugged on their handhold and patted the mattress beside him. Giddy, she clambered up. Marty swept his hands along her breasts and her belly, before flexing against her ass.

With both hands wrapped around her buttocks, he flipped Brandy onto her back. Legs flew everywhere, leaving her terrified she might kick him in the nose. But Marty avoided all manner of limb threats and pinched the hips of her underwear.

She gave another nod, this time having to bite her lip to keep from squealing. To be certain this wasn't a dream. Marty smiled in response and bent over her.

"Beautiful," he said and kissed right above her belly button. Shifting, he tugged her panties an inch lower. "Enchanting." Another kiss was placed below. "Gorgeous." Each word invited a touch of his lips ever farther down her body. So too went her panties, leaving Brandy clenching her toes in anticipation.

At her knees, Marty abandoned stripping her fully. He rested on his stomach, caressing one hand with up the side of her thigh, and the other... Barely the tips of his fingers fluttered across her labia, the touch so slight she wasn't certain if she'd imagined it. Then another.

Each return of his gentle caress sent a stronger throb pulsing through her body. She gnashed on her lips, her limbs locking in place to keep herself from thrusting onto Marty's fingers. If it weren't for her panties locked around her knees, she'd have splayed herself wide open for him.

Fuck, the ache riding clear across her lower belly was only getting worse. His soft, tender strokes were setting her up higher and higher, but she couldn't see the end. Even as he slipped his way to her clit, teasing the full hood until Brandy began to whimper, she feared dying before coming, as if her body wasn't strong enough to survive this long torture of pleasure.

"I need you," Brandy sputtered, concerned tears might rise in her voice.

"You have me ensnared," he said, scraping his nails up the outside of her thigh and around to the bottom of her ass.

Oh God. She shuddered, tempted to lie back and let him continue until her heart gave out. *No.* Hooking an elbow under her, Brandy stared into Marty's illuminating eyes. "Not all of you," she said.

His smile burned bright and he scrambled on top of her. When he needed his hand to strum her nipple, he'd tug on her panties with the other. When her hair had to be brushed back, he fumbled to toss away her underwear with his foot. Marty gave his all to get her naked, easing her panties nearly off until they hung upon a single ankle.

But it didn't matter as he rose above her, pressing his arms astride her head and deeper into the mattress, brushing her inner thighs farther apart with his legs, and resting his cock right above her soaked pussy.

"Marty, I don't..." She gulped, realizing that she hadn't been on birth control for over a year. "I'm not protected."

He smirked and reached down for his jeans that had somehow tumbled to the side of the bed. "Good thing I'm always prepared," he said, easing a silver condom onto his cock.

"Since when?" Brandy laughed. In the two years she'd known him, Marty had been many things, but a boy scout was not one of them.

"Since it came to you," he whispered and guided the tip of his cock to her.

God, yes! Brandy hooked her leg around his hip, pulling Marty deeper inside. Her sparkly pink dildo was no comparison to the full breadth of a man stretching her beyond belief. A sharp cry almost escaped from her, but it quickly subsided thanks to a rush of pleasure.

Looking up, she stared deep into Marty's gaze, lost in his passionate eyes. Locked together, he began to thrust. Every brush of his hips against her thigh was answered by her pushing herself onto him. She wanted him so deep he was gasping for air.

Marty picked her hand up off his back. He bundled it in his and they stretched higher together. As he did so, his pumping body pressed against nearly all of her.

Fuck! His pubic bone found her clit. Brandy wanted to cry in euphoria, Marty finding her G-spot, and his glorious pelvis... A warm kiss, sweet as honey, took her. Marty kissed her again, as soft as the way he thrilled her pussy with his fingers. All the while, his cock rammed through her. Fingers threaded together in an innocent handhold, lips offered tender kisses of promise, and her body burned to a cinder from how he rode her.

"Oh God!" Brandy cried against his mouth, her body succumbing to the orgasm that trilled through her veins. It washed across her in cacophonous waves, each pulse bringing more pleasure that wouldn't ebb. She clung to it like a hoarder, fear rising that this could be the last one she'd ever know.

"Brandy." Her name whispered through the air. She watched his lip quiver with the B, his mouth parting into a smile. Raising his head higher, Marty cried out, "Brandy," once more and collapsed onto her.

His dark hair nestled across her breasts. Their slick bodies pooled together as they both struggled to breathe. Even as he drifted in and out through his orgasm, Marty held her hand.

She'd gotten it wrong with her dream. All demanding and tense. This was the real Marty. Romantic, passionate, sweet and surprisingly sensible. This was the better Marty.

Chapter Twenty-One

An arm lay across hers, masculine with its sharper lines and wider wrist. Brandy was entranced by a mole that, at the angle they lay, folded into a heart. An entire naked man pressed to her back, his thighs cradling her buttocks, his lips whiffling in sleep against the nape of her neck. But all she could focus on was that arm.

How foreign it felt to have another resting on top of her, limp fingers shielding hers as if he should hold her hand at a moment's notice. How familiar it was, to be cupped entirely by someone she trusted and cared for.

A bright smile on her lips, Brandy snuggled deeper into Marty's slumbering embrace. As she did so, she must have brushed against him enough to cause his slow breath to spurt as he woke. The slumbering fingers locked around her hand for a moment before he curled his palm over her stomach.

Hot words brushed across her throat. "Morning."

"It's still dark out," she said.

"So?" Marty tugged on her, flipping her around until she stared deep into his mischievous gaze. "It must be after midnight."

"You're sure of that?"

He cracked into a smile, the other half buried in her pillow. "I'd say my performance required the full allotted hour." Slowly, he drew his hand up her side, dipping the heel of his palm down to brush against her nipple. Leaning closer, Marty whispered, "And another half-hour for encores."

"Is this your way of asking how I found it?" she said, then kissed him.

The shrug seemed to say, 'I care not' but she knew Marty. Knew the way his eyes darted from the side, how he kept reassuringly petting her. He was worried.

"It was...you're wonderful," Brandy said and dove down for a proper kiss. The knit blanket slipped from her shoulders, exposing her naked body to the glow of the streetlights. The blanket tumbled around her hip like those old Renaissance paintings, and she felt Marty reaching for it. Did he intend to cover them both up? Return to a light sleep?

She got her answer in the form of his hand curling around her ass. He tried to rise above her, but she had the high ground now. Precariously balanced on her hand, Brandy brought her body flush to his, to find that his cock had decided it was morning for both of them. A low moan escaped from the lips cradling hers and she tried to move in sync with it.

Pain swarmed up her wrist, which was stretched to breaking point thanks to all her weight on it. She tried to ignore it and swept her free hand through Marty's soft belly fur. Brandy made her way down the treasure trail pointing to his hardening dick, when a great rumble broke below.

Even Marty blinked in surprise at how loud his stomach cried out for food. An awkward moment, to be sure, between two people sharing their bodies for the first time. But Brandy didn't fluster or try to charge past it. She smiled. "If you wanted breakfast, you could have just asked."

With a laugh, he answered, "Guess I shouldn't have skipped dinner...or lunch."

Sighing, she rolled to the side and onto her feet. "That won't do." Brandy reached for her robe, but paused and picked up Marty's shirt instead. Slinging that around her body, she watched him stare with rapt attention as she slowly buttoned away her breasts. "How does eggs benedict sound?"

"Treasonous," Marty said as he chuckled. "And far too much work."

"Mm, I'd say you're worth it," she responded.

"Am I now? Oh, or you mean... So, for reference's sake, what would you say is worthy of a cheesecake? Or those rum balls you made last Christmas?"

Brandy brushed her palm under his jaw. "You'll have to figure it out."

"I intend to," he declared and kissed her with the same sexual heat that had tugged her into bed.

As his lips slipped to the corner of her mouth, her heart seized control. "I love you," she whispered. A sentiment she'd once shared as easily as breathing, it now locked around her tongue like barbed wire. *Deny it, hide from it, refuse to contemplate it, but there it is out in the open.*

Marty stared in surprise and the confident woman shrank to the old terrified Brandy. "Eggs!" she shouted before he could speak. "I was going to make eggs. I will make eggs. Maybe pancakes too. I forget if I have any milk. Silly me, I always have milk. Never know when there might be a baking emergency!"

With that pathetic display, she dashed for the kitchen, leaving Marty alone in her bedroom. It wasn't until the pot was on the stove, butter melting away to a fine layer of tasty fat, that the full ramifications struck her.

She'd never told another man that before. Because she'd never loved another man besides her ex-husband. Not ex, dead. Somehow, him being an ex seemed easier. To abandon the relationship instead of having it cut off by fate until only tattered edges sliced through her life.

"Come on, stupid shame. I know you're coming for me." She'd felt it in every damn thing she did since the day Kevin had died. The first time she'd had to open a piece of mail with his name on it. Stopping by the store and walking past the pack of gum he always bought. Not making cherry-filled donuts on his birthday because no one was there to celebrate.

And here she was, sleeping with another man. Making eggs for him dressed in his shirt. Loving him. Really, truly, so deeply in her heart it stung every second to be without him, loving him.

Absently, she wound her hand around her neck. There was no necklace holding a ring. Brandy had stopped wearing it days back. But it didn't mean that Kevin had left her heart too. All their years together, their struggles, their joys — she didn't want to lose them.

But it was time for her to have more. To grow her heart to fit more. To find new adventures. New highs, no doubt new struggles and a love that was both familiar and very different.

Brandy glanced over her shoulder to find the picture of Kevin from when they'd first opened the bakery. "You'd like him. He's hilarious and...sweet."

Oh crap. She'd forgotten to ask Marty how he took his eggs. Despite every silly moment they'd shared at the bookstore, that one had never come up. Turning down the heat, she dashed back to her room and froze as a familiar voice rose from her bed.

"I was wrong and I...I need you back. Please, let's give this another go. Call me soon, babe."

Love?

He hadn't imagined it, right? She'd said it before slipping off to make him breakfast. Why did that make him sound like some secretary-chasing 1950s troglodyte?

Her ass did look great, though. His shirt barely reached around what she had going on, leaving two perfect little eclipses below.

Focus, man. Okay, one more thought on her bubble butt straining from below the linen. And her tits...

Love? Really?

Right after sex. No peacocks and violin symphony required?

Shaking his head, Marty did the only thing that made sense in the world and put on his pants. He needed something to do. Sure, Brandy was...and he had...they had...boy, had they ever! But there was a lot of baggage in her past.

His too, come to think of it.

Frowning, he fished out his phone under the pretense of checking the time. And not because he wanted to play the latest version of Sheep Wars, which added a vengeful goose in an eyepatch. In doing so, he spotted three missed calls...from her.

"And a voicemail," Marty whispered to himself. Without a second thought, he pressed play and Janeth's voice filled Brandy's bedroom.

"Martin."

He gritted his teeth at that despised version of his name.

"I know that you are having trouble forgiving me. You have every right to be angry, even if I never said anything to the contrary about our being exclusive."

"Because when one says 'I wanna be your boyfriend' they really mean 'but you can fuck whoever you want. It's cool.'"

Janeth coughed over the recording, as if she'd realized she'd overstepped her bounds. The sweet voice he heard more when the camera was on than off took over. "I was wrong and I...I need you back. Please, let's give this another go. Call me soon, babe."

She wanted him back? Just like that. *Forget everything that had happened with Aiden and try again?* Marty glared at his phone, both of his thumbs hooked over the screen as if the tiny devil ordered him to call her and the angel warned him off. Or maybe it was the other way around.

"You can't."

He whipped his head up to find Brandy standing right outside her door. *Did she...?* The stern flat lips and pale face told him before he needed to ask.

When he didn't answer, she spoke for him. "Marty, seriously. She's cheating on you."

"Cheated. Once." His brain, in an emotional frenzy, found its way back to the pedantic quackery that Eldon thrived in. Too bad it had never worked for him.

Her face flushed bright red, Brandy looking about to say something. But she shook it off, and instead came back with, "That makes it okay? What? You're offering a three-strikes deal?"

"I didn't say that."

"What do you mean? Huh? You just...you come here, you..." Brandy gestured to the bed they'd rolled around on until her blankets had wadded up on the floor. Damn. If he'd known that all of *that* would have happened, he never would have come to her apartment.

Right?

She snorted and cast her eyes to the ceiling. Oh, that wasn't good. "You cry that she broke your heart. Acted like you were on your death bed. Vanished for weeks, wouldn't even answer a text and, what? One call from her, one voicemail and you'll run right back to her?"

"I don't know."

He knew he'd said the absolutely worst thing possible, but he couldn't stop himself. She did that to him. Stripped away the artifice of charm and left him just as himself. No skill, no talent. A short Latino with half a degree and the inability to change a tire.

The warble in her voice slammed a dagger through his heart. "Why did you come here? Why did you...?"

"Because I-I wanted to see you. I missed talking to you." And he meant it. He tried to get closer, to find some way to convince her that it wasn't a slight against her. But Brandy wasn't easily swayed, and she dodged him. That small movement, her actively avoiding him, added a pinprick to the already wedged-in dagger.

Silence thundered through the room, shaking the windows and rattling the floorboards with its massive volume of nothing. The sonic boom of her silent tears could shatter a small town, and the shaking of her lip to hold back the sobs opened a pit to hell under his feet. "But not enough to choose me over a cheater, a fake…"

"Hey, Janeth is…"

"She was using you, and— Why am I even arguing this with you? Why can't you see what is— Why can't you just goddamn be with me?"

There was no stopping the tears now, streams drenching her cheeks as she glared murder at him. He became all of two feet tall, his stomach churning into a thousand knots. "It isn't that simple."

"Who says?"

"Your husband," he shot back, causing her snarl to snap into a gasp of pain. "Your first love. Your… How can I possibly compete with that?"

Incapable of watching her crumble into the agony of remembering her husband, Marty did the cowardly thing and stared at the wall. A small plate with an etching from the Grand Canyon hung on it . *Did she get it on a vacation with him? Their honeymoon?* Another reminder that she'd already walked through the steps of love he's barely started down.

"You selfish asshole," she spat. "If all you want is that perfect meet-cute, flawless courting and happily ever after, then why did you sleep with me? Why did you even let me think for two fucking seconds that I…that you could be with me?"

You know why.

I was weak. I was exhausted. I missed her beyond counting. I wanted to make her happy. I need her. I…

"I don't know." He stumbled, the back of his neck burning hot from her fiery glare. She knew he was lying, but Marty couldn't explain his chunked-up brain. One part of him knew that being with Brandy was pointless. She was his friend, the one he talked about dates with, not the one he whisked off on a three-day vacation to Paris.

But another part of his soul banged around inside his chest. It seemed to have something it needed to tell him, but it couldn't be heard over the years that had told him how romance worked. *You don't fall in love with your best friend.* Everyone knew that.

"Get out." Her icy words shattered through Marty's wall, finally whipping his head over. Brandy tossed his shirt at his feet and she wrapped herself up in whatever she grabbed. Even feeling two inches tall while picking up his shirt, he watched her naked body wrathfully vanish beneath a robe.

A familiar stirring ran through him, but as she glared at his inaction, Marty shook it off. "I should have known when I saw the ring," she said, like a lamentation to herself.

Ring? What ring?

He'd barely looped the shirt onto his arms before Brandy jabbed a finger to the door. "Get out of here, now. I can't…"

Taking the first few steps out of her bedroom, Marty turned and tried to beg. "Brandy, please. It was—"

"Don't. Don't talk to me. Don't try to act like it was nothing. Don't wish it all away!" Her voice cracked as she ripped straight to the heart of him. "I can't talk to you. I can't look at you. I need you to leave."

His head tumbled down, the chin striking his naked chest as he didn't have the energy or time to button his shirt. With laborious steps, he worked his way to the door. *You're going to leave it like that? You may never talk to her again!*

But it's Brandy. She forgives me. We argue sometimes, I do something stupid…okay, this is epically stupid, then we get over it.

Are you sure it'll happen this time?

Gulping, he ran his hand along the outside of the door. His body remained half in and half out. Before she could order him once more, Marty whispered, "I was afraid. I came over here because I thought that I might never see you again. I could lose you…forever."

Tears welled in his eyes, washing away the woman he missed whole-heartedly. She locked her arms around her chest, her hands digging in so tightly that her knuckles turned white. "And so you did," she said and walked away from him.

Broken, Marty slipped through the crack in the door and fell into an abyss of his own making.

Chapter Twenty-Two

"…and two chocolate donuts." Marty tried to keep on a smile while putting in his order, but his face refused to obey. He'd known he'd fucked up the second he'd stranded himself outside her apartment, trying to figure out how to get home without his shoes. But, even with each potentially glass-infested step, he couldn't say why. And Brandy didn't seem in the mood to help him understand anything.

Numb from the eyebrows down, he watched the friendly barista shimmy one donut out with tiny tongs. It had gold and silver stars embedded into the chocolate frosting. A special donut. One that she'd certainly like.

"Wait," he said, pausing the barista from reaching for a second. The look stared down the man who always got two, rain or shine. Because he always had someone to share with. And now… Marty winced and apologized, "Sorry. I only need one."

"Okay." It was no matter to the woman bundling his small order into a bag and ringing it up at the counter. He'd skipped his usual fluffy cotton candy coffee for a cup as black as his heart. And two sugars, because Marty wasn't a masochist.

Digging open his wallet, he sighed to himself. The one good thing about his removal from Janeth's online world was that he had more disposable income. It was in the 'we can get two pizzas for dinner' range, but preferable to before.

"There you are," a voice called to him.

Marty groaned, wishing it'd been anyone else who said that. Wished it'd been one in particular. He glanced over his shoulder to find Eldon sliding in behind. "You know there's a line," Marty said, pointing behind two other people.

"I'm not here for drinks." Instead of the usual prim and uptight countenance that came naturally to Eldon, he looked like someone had dropped him in a wind turbine and he'd hit every wall on the way down. Running a hand over his splattered hair, Eldon insisted, "I need the ring."

"What ring?" *Why is everyone on about a ring?*

That struck a sour chord deep into Eldon, who loomed above his brother. He looked about ten seconds from grabbing Marty by the collar and throwing him through the window. "Oh," Marty groaned, the pieces slotting into place. "That ring."

"You'd better not have lost it...or worse."

Marty snickered and yanked open his bag. "Think I have a gambling problem? Betting on the ponies to see who's got an ace up their...hoof?" It didn't take him long to fish out the box Eldon had strangely left in his keeping for reasons that he hadn't gone into.

For a moment, it seemed as if Eldon would simply take the box and be on his way. But, sure enough, his brother took a quick peek to make certain Marty hadn't absconded with the sparkler for Elena.

"Do you have a plan?"

"Yes. No. I'm not... I don't have time for this. She could be..." Eldon, the man of steel—in that he was rigid, flat, and gray as concrete—whipped his head around wildly. This was probably one of those brotherly things Marty should inquire about and offer advice, but after his last couple of weeks, it seemed like asking a bear how to drive stick.

In his mad glaring and lack of explaining, Eldon stared at the small bag passed to Marty. "Only one?"

Marty shrugged. "Since we're not working the same shift anymore..." He tried to keep it breezy, uninterested in the comings and goings of a woman he worked with. But his heart crumbled to dust at the thought of trying to distance himself so far from Brandy.

A warm hand cupped his shoulder, shaking the piping-hot coffee in the process. Marty glared at the unsteady liquid then turned toward his brother's surprisingly concerned eyes. "Martin, what did you do?"

"Nothing. I...I didn't mean to hurt her. I would never, but you wouldn't understand."

Eldon crossed his arms, his very important date forgotten in order to butt into his brother's life.

"She's already been taken." Marty reared back at the words escaping his lips. "Wow, that sounds bad. I mean, what do I do, just accept being second best for the rest of my life? Being the other guy because the first didn't make it to the forever part?"

As the words left his mouth, Marty braced himself for an Eldon foghorn lecture. Not only because he knew it'd be coming, but because he deserved it.

But Eldon sighed, and in a gentle voice, said, "You romantic fool."

"You emotionless robot," Marty cut back, his hackles sizzling at how quickly his brother cut him down.

"Perhaps what you need is a cold bucket of sense dropped on your head."

"And what you need is a fire lit under your ass. Yes, I know what's up with you and Elena. Mom's been talking."

That caught his brother fully by surprise. The calculating look was wiped away to leave behind genuine pain. *Damn it.* Why did that seem to be Marty's legacy lately? Everywhere Martin Dashwood went, misery appeared like mushrooms after an acid rain.

Eldon dug through his pockets as if he'd left something important in there, but didn't pull it out. "Then let me tell you, not as your brother, but someone too proud to admit what my heart wanted—you're wrong. Your ideals, your…your childish dream of being some woman's only happily ever after is wrong."

There it was. Every time they tried to talk girls, it always devolved to Eldon pulling out an actuary sheet for his best possible mate. Romance never factored in and love was a cheap ploy invented to sell chocolate. He'd never understand.

"I don't know why I talk to you," Marty fumed, spinning on his heels and marching out of the door. He was so tired of people chastising him for his passion.

"Marty," Eldon whispered and the name froze him in his tracks. "What is more important? The cute story you write in a wedding article or the hand that holds yours for fifty years? The sweeping date you took her on to propose, or how she makes your heart throb every time you find her sitting beside you on the couch?"

A cute smile with blue frosting caught in her teeth flashed through his mind. Her knee bouncing into his on accident as they debated Japanese rubber suit monsters. How she'd appear out of nowhere, a thermos of soup in hand, if he so much as complained about a scratchy throat. That he'd buy two umbrellas if rain was forecast, because she always forgot one.

"Love isn't...it's not just romance. That's a brick in the foundation, one I'm realizing I should have focused on. But there's so much more to it. And maybe your castle isn't perfect. Maybe the turrets don't match and the bunting is tattered."

Marty stared at his brother as the strained metaphor snapped in half. Eldon seemed to sense it too, and he shook his head. "My point, don't throw away a relationship you've built for years with laughter, kindness and love just because it's not shiny enough."

What had he done?

Reaching a hand out, Marty took his brother's and the two gave a hearty shake. Maybe it wasn't what he'd envisioned when donning his Romeo tights. Maybe it wasn't a sweeping fairy tale romance sung by bards to look at his best friend and one day see more. But, for the first time in his life, he wanted what Eldon was blessed with. Not a girlfriend, but a partner in every sense of the word.

"Oh shit," Eldon cursed. He grabbed Marty's watch and spun it around. "Is that the time? I have to go!"

Eldon bolted for the door, but before he vanished, Marty called out, "Good luck with Elena."

"And don't you muck it up with Brandy. Mamá adores her," were Eldon's parting words.

All this time, everyone around him had known. His mother, his father, even his robot brother wanted them together, but Marty'd been too starry-eyed to see the moon in his life. *Never again.* He needed a plan, he needed to apologize, he needed...

"Wait, I need a second donut after all!"

He had no plan, no idea what to say, or if she'd even listen to him, but for the first time in weeks Marty wanted to sing. It felt like a slab of concrete named 'foolish expectations' had fallen off his shoulders, leaving him able to float above the sidewalk.

Dashing as fast as his legs could carry him, he ran for the bookshop, donut bag in hand. It could at least serve as an ice breaker and peace offering while he tried to drum up the right words to explain how he felt. Why he was the way he was.

Okay, that might take a few years and a therapist.

But the idea was solid.

Running through the door, setting the bell jangling to gift another angel its wings, Marty called out, "Brandy?" No one was at the counter, but he dropped his half-finished coffee cup in place. "Hello? I am a very frail old lady and require help getting a book down from the top shelf."

"Oh, okay," a strange and unwanted voice piped up from the mystery section. Still hopeful, Marty turned to find a green polo and khaki pants strapped to an unknown kid somewhere in the late teenage to early college age. "Sorry? Where's the old woman?" he asked in full-on naiveté.

"Who are you?" Marty demanded, his hackles raising.

"I'm Peter, the new guy. Mr. Fensin knows my grandmother through — "

Marty waved the babble away. "Brandy? The woman who works today. Where is she?"

"Oh, the one that quit."

"What?" *She quit?*

"Yeah, just said she wasn't coming back anymore. Got another job, I guess. I dunno. I was told to show up today and someone would train me. Wait, are you the *M* guy? He said it was like…Marvin? Are you Marvin?"

She was gone? *No.* No, he couldn't lose her.

Not while there was still time. Not when he'd finally realized why he was so damn stupid and wanted to fix it.

"Sure, I'm Marvin. Any chance you know where she went?"

"Who?"

For God's sake, the youth today! "The woman whose job you took."

"One of the other bookstores, I think. The big one. You know."

No. But it didn't matter. He'd do whatever it took to find her. Walk the floors of every bookstore in the city. Ask everyone he met for a sign of her. Beg for someone to help him find that other half of his heart he'd let be ripped from his body.

But first… Marty dashed around the store's shelves, grabbing up books as a plan formed in his head. Yes. That had to work. For once, his photographic memory might actually be of service to him.

"Um," Peter mumbled, watching wide-eyed as Marty filled his backpack with books for research. Fairly certain he had a good start to make amends,

Marty dashed for the door and swung in a circle to scoop up his coffee along the way.

"Aren't you going to train me?" the new kid shouted just as Marty stepped out onto the street.

He turned around and gave him a thumbs-up. "You're doing a bang-up job, kid. Keep at it and one day you might make manager."

"Really? Thanks!" the guy, unaware that they were *all* managers, chirped back.

Clinging tooth and nail to the last string of hope in his life, Marty ran down the street with his hands wrapped around an arsenal of romance.

Chapter Twenty-Three

A haze rose from the multitude of lights running along the track in the ceiling. It lit up the desolate black parking lot like a lighthouse crashing into the sea. Brandy sighed, staring across the darkness of five a.m. whispering through the suburban wasteland.

"New Meat," her manager, a man barely older than her, called.

She spun in place, trapped behind a cash register as she waited for the doors to open to a stream of bleary-eyed customers. No doubt they'd head for the in-house café and only buy a book if it got in the way, but that didn't seem to matter to the corporate overlords.

"What are you doing?" he asked, eyeing up the uniform she'd be paying for with her first check.

Her eyes darted to the half-finished cup of coffee left on the counter and she raced to hide it. But that didn't seem to be the answer as her manager hoisted over a broom and said, "If you have time to lean, you have time to clean."

Seriously? She twisted her lips into a smile, as if that was the wittiest thing she'd ever heard. Without a single complaint, she dropped the broom to the polished floor and pushed a few specks of dust around. Placating the masses had never seemed so monotonous.

The whole time, the manager stood over her watching. She tried to shake it off, in no mood for any man paying her attention, but she couldn't exactly tell him off in her first week.

"Surprised you're not complaining about the hours. I know how those little shops operate."

Brandy snickered. "This is nothing. I had to be up at four, sometimes even three in the morning."

"What the hell for?"

"I…" She paused. "I used to be a baker."

He chuckled at that. "And I can see why you quit." His assumption on her life faded as he turned to stare out through the giant, polished windows. There were no local band posters taped to them, no lost dog signs, no fading PR from indie publishers. It was all scrubbed clean, save the two giant signs advertising their big sales and the latest bestseller tied in with a new movie.

"Excuse me," he shouted, his hand waving at someone outside. "The store doesn't open yet."

She heard such a banging on the window it sounded like someone desperately needed respite from a storm. But the weather was calm, if not too balmy, so more than likely the person was drunk instead. It wasn't until the voice struck her that the broom slipped from her hands.

"I'm looking for someone. Do you have an employee called…?"

Marty's plea faded as she rose to stare at him. He looked red-eyed, with bags piling up under his lids, but that could be due to allergies as much as anything else. "Brandy," he whispered so softly she couldn't hear. Only the formation of his lips revealed that he spoke her name. She used to feel happy at the thought. Now it shivered through her.

"Please," Marty shouted louder, knocking twice as hard on the door. "Please, let me talk to you!"

"Sir. You cannot enter the building until official opening hours. Store policy," her manager said.

Marty's face fell. He darted his eyes from her to the man hovering close. But he stopped trying to break the glass with his fist, at least. That seemed to be enough for her manager, who gave a little tip of his head. "I'll head to the break room. If he becomes a problem, please come and get me."

A problem? Her heart thundered at the thought of Marty being anything but a blessing. Then the reality crashed down around her and she nodded to her manager. "Thanks."

He seemed to take it with a smug smile, spinning on his heels and marching to where he could no doubt lean to his heart's content. But before he vanished, he said, "And you're not allowed to unlock the door."

"Understood," she said, even as her eyes lingered where the mass of keys were crammed into the two locks on the ceiling and floor. It was an instinctive response. Why would she even want to talk to Marty?

After what he did. Said. Left me alone and broken.

Why should she even want him?

"I'm not supposed to talk. I have work to do," she said as loudly as possible in the hope he'd leave her alone.

Brandy slipped behind the counter, her back straight as she faced the sea of books before her. She was so focused on being the best employee that when the glass knocked directly over her shoulder, she leaped into the air. Spinning around, she spotted Marty holding an open notebook flush to the glass. On it he'd written *Daisies For Summer page a hundred and twenty-seven.*

Her eyes narrowed, trying to tell him that this was her job, her brand-new job that she didn't have time to play at. Not like anyone here would get or appreciate their game. They were all too busy cleaning. Or rearranging. Or just keeping themselves important to the algorithm at all times so they wouldn't get fired.

Brandy shook her head. She didn't owe him anything.

When he tugged back the notebook, she expected that to be the end of it. For Marty to wander back to his car and speed away into the night. She'd probably never see him again. One chance and done.

The notebook flipped back around with the word *PLEASE* added in giant block letters. He'd even drawn a few hearts around it, like this was junior high study hall. And, as foolish as it sounded, a part of Brandy started to melt.

Well, at least the book was right near the front. And if she did it, he might go away. Less chance of her manager firing her because of him hanging around.

With those flimsy excuses in her mind, she picked up *Daises for Summer* and thumbed through to find the right page. "'I'm sorry,'" Brandy read aloud, then she stared through the window. "Is this from you or me?"

Marty didn't answer and flipped the page. The number *Forty-five* was written this time. "You're not playing the game right," she said. They always worked forward through the book to build up the plot. As her sight graced the page, she clung tighter to the book. "'There are none in this world stupider than I.'"

Through the heavy glass, his face half-hidden by the harsh reflection, Marty mouthed along with her. His head hung lower, his hand placed on the window as if to reach for her. So he was apologizing. That...that was a start, at least.

Just as she was about to shout at him to wait until after her shift, he showed another page. This one bore a new book, *Wings of Flame*, and three numbers. Brandy tried to think where that would be. Sci-fi and Fantasy, or Romance? Laying *Daises* on the counter, she dashed into the shelves. Despite the store being the size of a small aircraft hangar, she spotted the familiar fiery bird feather cover and ran back to Marty.

A strange smile wound about her lips at finding him, as if she'd hoped to see him again. Pausing behind the counter, she tugged the book open. "'It has taken me a lifetime to understand what was obvious.'"

Marty banged on the window and jabbed at the next page for her. Flipping fast, she landed on fifty-seven and read aloud, "'I love you, Daniel.' *Daniel*?"

He pointed at his notebook, where *Ignore the Daniel part* was written. "Wait." Brandy inched closer to the window. "Are you serious?"

After yanking out a marker, he caught the cap in his teeth and added a new number below the others. She thumbed quickly to find it. "'Beyond the heavens and the stars, greater than the mountain's peaks and valleys, deeper than the ocean's crypts.'" Brandy pulled in a breath even as her hands rattled the book. The black letters danced across her vision and her brain tried to piece together what he was saying.

She knew the words, the sentiment, but she didn't understand. "Why? Why now? Why are you...why are you telling me this here instead of —" *Instead of choosing to walk out of the door on me.*

Pulling in a deep breath, Marty raised his head and flipped to the last written page on his notebook. A new book was shown with orders for her to read an entire poem. *Where do they keep the poetry in this place?* Holding *Wings of Flame* tight in her arms, Brandy dashed deeper into the stacks.

Past the manga, the cookbooks and the sheet music, she found it. The cover was nothing more than a simple pastel green color and the title, *Songs of My Heart*. For a moment, she froze, wanting to read the poem to herself before she confronted Marty. What if it didn't explain anything? What if it was all an excuse? What if he didn't really want to be with her, but wanted to tell her she could be loved?

Dread sloshed in her stomach, keeping the book locked shut as she walked back to him. Marty still hadn't vanished, both of his hands pressed to the glass as he waited for her to arrive and read his explanation. Standing below the halo light above the stack of bestsellers, Brandy opened the pages of *Songs* and dove in.

"'My eye slipped past your supple face,
My hand missed all your subtle grace,
My mind ignored your sumpt'us thoughts,
But my heart, oh, it missed you naught.

For though it have no sight nor voice,
To my heart there was but one choice.
My brain may dream of castles in the sky,

My eyes flitter to glints of a magpie,
My ears caress songs beyond the sea,
But my heart, sweet heart, belongs only to thee.

Time that it needs to grow strong,
To whisper in my ear, to find the song,
To shower my eyes with what is true,
To tell my mind it's always been you.'"

Tears washed across the words, wiping away the work of a poet Marty must have scrounged through hundreds of books to find. As she stared at that confounding man, her hand clasped to her mouth, he began to shrink back, his hands wadded in his pockets, the notebook fluttering to the ground. He mouthed something, but she couldn't make it out.

Without a second's pause, Brandy marched to the front door and cracked open the first lock. No rain of hellfire burned her skin, no flock of reapers came for her soul, so she unlocked the second and walked out into the night.

Marty, the man she'd always pictured with floppy hair and a cheeky grin, stood in the dark alone. "I'm so sorry. What I did. How stupid I am to get caught up in... That it took me this long to figure it out," he said as she walked to him. "I keep thinking over and over how if I'd just—"

Her lips silenced his pleading apology, Brandy pouring her heart into the kiss. It was sweet, a touch naïve, and praying for him to finally realize what he had in front of him. Hands cupped her cheeks, Marty's thumbs wiping away the tears dripping from her eyes while he deepened the kiss.

"I love you," he whispered as if awestruck. Then the familiar smile returned and Marty shouted, "God, it feels so...right to say that. Did you hear that, world? I love her!"

His cry rung through the parking lot, pinging off streetlamps and employee cars. And straight to her heart. From his pocket, he tugged out a paper bag and passed it to Brandy. Her confusion melted to understanding at the dented and cold donut inside.

"I swear to whichever God you want me to," Marty said, causing her to smile. He cupped his hands around the nape of her neck, pulling her to him until their foreheads crested together. Running his nose against her cheek, he finished, "I will never forget what my heart knew all along."

As Brandy kissed him, praying it to be so, the indigo of night gave way to the vibrant pinks and rose of a new dawn. She looked up, about to point it out to her hopeless romantic, but Marty took her for another kiss instead.

Chapter Twenty-Four

Seventeen months later

The ball of mistletoe dancing in the breeze kept him distracted from the sea of books spread across the table. Not the *ding* of the cash register as hungry pilgrims from far and wide made the trek to the holy reliquary of caffeine and sugar. Nor the slow glare of his brother from across the table, eyebrows perked in their 'I have something serious to share' way.

It was all that damn mistletoe, and — worst of all — Marty had no one to blame but himself. He'd insisted on it and the owner had humored him.

"This archival system will be the death of me. Turn a corner to find my body splattered to the ground, and there, with a bloody knife in its hand, stands EAS ready to finish the job."

Eldon chuckled, causing Marty to stare in terror at his brother. He might still be the same stick-up-his-bum Eldon Dashwood, but the hard edges had smoothed down from their razor-edge finish. God save him, but his brother had even left his scarf slightly unknotted inside the bakery.

"I'm proud of you. Already working on your master's."

"You sound like Mom," Marty sighed, trying to hide the blush of family acceptance. It was no doctor or lawyer, but they seemed to approve of 'I think I want to be a librarian.' Which meant endless schoolwork for his foreseeable future.

"Here you go," a voice called from behind his ear, and a jelly donut covered with powdered sugar landed before him.

"There's a mistake," he said, spinning in his chair. "I ordered two."

Even with her cheeks dusted in sugar, Brandy smiled wide. Her fingers, probably coated in flour, ruffled through his hair. "I already ate mine."

She moved to rush back—hungry customers and all—but Marty wrapped his fingers through hers. Before she could slip away, he tugged her close. "Mistletoe," he whispered and kissed her less-than-chastely on the lips. It'd be a downright obscene, ladies-fainting-in-the-aisles kiss if there weren't people watching.

Sadly, he had the whole of the morning to wait until he could hold her in his arms again. Releasing her back to her throngs of famished worshippers, Marty watched Brandy resume her place at the counter. That apron knotted tight at her waist certainly did wonders for her sugar-dusted booty.

The sound of shuffling papers redirected his attention to his brother, unfortunately. "Hey," Marty shouted, yanking back his homework. "No cheating off me."

Eldon scoffed at the outlandish idea. But, as he stirred his tea using one of Brandy's legendary biscotti, he said, "I am amazed you're working so diligently this early in the morning."

A laugh broke from Marty and he scratched at the nape of his neck with a pencil. "This is late. I've been up since four."

"You? Four a.m.? What in the world for?"

With a sigh, he turned to watch his beautiful baker. Her entire face lit up in joy as she passed over a bag of beignets to the cherubic businessmen. He'd suffer a thousand early mornings in exchange for waking to find her in his arms, to kiss her goodbye before they had to abandon their cozy cocoon and return to the world outside. Even if he now required a gallon of coffee to make it to ten.

To his foolish, romantic heart's surprise, Eldon gave a knowing smile and slipped back into his chair. "I understand. Mamá was wondering about Christmas."

"I will be eating my weight in tamales, yes."

The snort from his brother told tales of the year Marty really had tried to beat the record. "This is regarding the seating arrangements and..."

Rising from his chair, Marty said, "Hold that thought. I have to do something." His brother grumbled at being interrupted, but he didn't care. Gliding across the small, new bakery opened just in time for the Christmas rush, Marty approached the woman at the counter.

"Hey," he said, to pull her from the racks of tasty treats waiting to be frosted.

With the back of her hand, Brandy swiped up a stray tendril of hair and faced him. "Hello yourself."

"There's something I've been wanting to know, and I hope you have the answer." From his pocket, he pulled out a small wooden puzzle box and pushed on the mechanism. Three cracks formed along the box, each edge pulling and folding down to reveal the treasure inside. A small gold ring with a bright emerald twirled in place. "Would you marry me?"

Brandy smiled brighter than the sun, her fingers trailing above the spinning promise that he wanted no one but her for his life. Giggling, she nodded, wiped at her cheeks and said, "Yes."

Without pause, Marty leaped over the counter, sending her business cards splattering to the floor. All around them, people clapped at the happy news as Marty scooped his bride-to-be into his arms. She laughed with him. He couldn't spin with glee in the tight space, so Marty danced with her in his arms. Slowly, he pulled her forehead to his, both lost in each other's eyes while he slipped his *abuela*'s ring onto her finger.

"Congratulations," Eldon said, rising from his chair and adding to the applause. "I must say, I'm rather shocked at the subdued proposal."

Marty stared at the ceiling and said, "Ah, about that..."

"Last night he took me out on the river in a rented boat he covered in roses," his fiancée said.

"Not covered. You could still get to the wheel, if you stood on one leg and hopped."

"And, as night crested across the surface of the river, bright letters rose from the water. A dozen floating glow sticks asked me to marry him." Brandy turned and planted her lips to his cheek, wiping away the sting of shame and leaving only a lovesick fool in its place.

He didn't even listen to the sigh of exhaustion from his brother. Marty was too busy being enraptured with not just the woman who'd be his wife, but with Brandy. The woman always wearing flour in her black hair, fluffy socks in bed and holding his heart in her hand.

"Why this, then? More pomp?"

"I asked her on the water, surrounded by a million stars," Marty said, "But I wanted to hear the answer by the light of day. A life of both romance and...all that other boring stuff Eldon can't stop going on about." His brother groaned, but Marty didn't care as he spoke to Brandy. "I want you to want both."

She brushed her nose against the side of his, her lips parting to whisper, "It's always been yes."

"I love you," he answered back, the two of them entwining in a kiss to start a new journey between them.

And so, the princess of sugary dough and the dashing Latino librarian lived happily ever after.

Want to see more from this author?
Here's a taster for you to enjoy!

Some Like it Haunted: Ink
Ellen Mint

Excerpt

Ten minutes to midnight.
Ten minutes to Halloween.
Ten minutes to my birthday.

"Ah, shit!" I fumbled, my phone slipping to the unfinished staircase. Luckily it bounced, and the three zombie sours sloshing through my system didn't stop me from catching it.

"Careful, Layla!" my fellow nursing student Fariah called.

Dana stuck her head out of the back window and shouted for the entire block to hear, "Sorry your gift's late. But I swear, you'll *love it* when it arrives. Ten or twelve times a day until the batteries run dry."

I waved a hand at the girls, which was supposed to insist I didn't mind the lack of a gift, but that shot of whiskey rebounded and I slapped the mailboxes instead. "Sonnofa…!" The second curse of the night snapped to growling as I inspected the rising red welt thanks to my drunken buffoonery. Luckily, Fariah — our eternal DD — was already slipping off to shuttle the rest of the group home.

If they'd seen me, they'd have pulled out our anatomy books and come up with a dozen different treatments for 'drunk girl punches a wall'. Not that I was any better, my soggy brain wondering if I had a wrap back in the apartment while I stumbled up the stairs.

Slapping a wall, nearly breaking a phone and making a colossal fool of myself in front of the hot bartender would probably dim most people's birthdays. But honestly, compared to past ones, this year's was almost palatable. It helped that I'd stopped celebrating on the thirty-first when I was six. Last thing anyone wanted was to go to a kid's birthday party when they could be trick-or-treating.

As I rounded the stairs, checking twice that it was the right floor, I thought back to the bartender I hadn't been able to stop staring at. He'd had that whole 'I could model for a surf club' esthetic going on, complete with thick, medium-length dark hair and olive skin. But what'd had me drooling into my vampire bite were the tats. He'd known how to stylize his body, relying on black ink and the right amount of whorls and lines to draw the eye to all his best spots.

Shame that the rest had been covered by his shirt and the chance of me getting a peek had been negative billion. *Don't try to flirt when there's a pile of latex gloves in your pocket, is all I'm saying.* I can't even imagine the freaky shit he'd thought I was into.

"Seriously?"

Sitting before my door was a brown package, which was always supposed to be dropped off with the manager to cut down on theft. Not that it stopped him from refusing to keep said packages and just dump them off if we didn't collect within an hour. I checked the apartment number, thirteen, then the name on the box.

Layla Leeland. That was mine even if it was written in a super curly script my drunk ass had to turn around a few times to read. I'd bitch out the manager tomorrow... *No, that's Halloween. I'll bitch him out on November first.*

With that decided, I fumbled into my apartment. The door rattled open and smacked straight into the pile of laundry baskets I foraged from. Nursing school really took a bite out of everything in my life. Time, energy, the ability to connect with another human being.

I didn't even have a cake for my birthday. Most years I'd at least pick up a chocolate cupcake with orange frosting and cram a candle in it. But I couldn't bother this go around. Eh, what was twenty-five anyway but a reminder that a quarter of my life was over?

Dropping the box on my counter caused a trash bag to splatter to the floor. *I should really clean this place up. Put away my scrubs and dismantle bra hill. See if my vacuum even works anymore or if the spiders own it now.*

A yawn ripped from my throat, shattering any illusions I'd get my life in order. "I'll deal with it tomorrow," I declared to my apartment and the mystery box. It was probably more textbooks that cost the same as a new phone.

Shambling like a zombie on its last leg, I stumbled to my bedroom. Without bothering to shed my scrubs, or even wipe the makeup off, I fell face first onto my bed and embraced the ambivalence of sleep.

* * * *

What was that?

The sound of Jell-O shot out of a slingshot at speakers rocketed through my apartment. My heart jumped into my throat and my body tried to leap up. But I was still buzzing and had minimal control of my limbs. It was more of a graceful ooze to the floor.

In the process of righting my eyes, I caught a flash of light breaking from the living room. It kept strobing as if a lightning storm had crashed on my futon. If I wasn't partially hungover and drunk at the same time, I'd like to think I'd have done the smart thing. Called the cops, called the building manager, grabbed a weapon. Not walked out into the weird lights and sounds armed only with my exhausted hand on my hip.

As I stepped into the hallway, noting that my front door was still closed, a shadow crawled across the wall. It looked like a man rising to his feet when a pair of giant bird wings erupted from behind his back. They stretched wide, every shadowy feather straining as if this intruder were about to fly.

Did I turn around, grab my phone and wait for the police to sort this out?

Of course not. I ran straight into my living room and my jaw hit the floor.

It wasn't because a giant bird flew into my apartment and flapped about in pain. Or that one of my old angel costumes from a past Halloween had come to life and started dancing around. No, this was even weirder.

A gorgeous man with sun-kissed skin stood on my yoga mat. His hair was lush and reached his collarbones. His very exposed and cut collarbones. Which drew my eye lower down the rest of his body.

I could have offered to check him for moles for how naked he was. His chest glistened the only way hairless skin could, which he had puffed out to display his impressive pecs. A single line of dark hair revived itself under his labyrinth of abs. I tried to count them but lost track as I followed the treasure trail down to a pair of red satin briefs that barely covered his shame.

And it wasn't just because the fabric was tiny enough it revealed nearly his full bush to the world. No, whatever pipe he was swinging bulged so tight below his underwear it looked like it was vacuum packed for easy transport.

What if that wasn't the full show he had?

What the hell is wrong with me?

I lashed out with my hand and snatched up the first thing I could…which happened to be a pillar candle. Waving it about as if it were a club, I shouted, "Who the fuck are you?!"

The man laughed, his voice that deep 'roll through every nerve in my body' baritone. "Highly accurate," he said, raising and lowering his sharp eyebrows while a smile perched on his lips.

I shook the candle around, prepared to attack him if he didn't give me an answer. The stranger eyed it up, then said, "I am your incubus."

"What?"

"And I must say…" He placed a hand to his ab-alicious stomach and peered down. "I quite like your preferences. Ooh." His hand slipped under his red briefs and he started to jerk his hand along his full cock. Those dark eyes rolled back into his head and he shook his black hair while moaning.

I could nearly see the tip peeking above his underwear, his large hand yanking the waistband lower and lower. My toes raised my body up, trying to get me a better view, when I scowled. "Stop that!" I shouted as much at him as my own train-wreck libido.

The man pulled his hand away instantly then extended both out as if I had him at my mercy. *Ha. Sure.*

"Let's start again. Who are you?"

His infectious smile wavered, drawing my attention to how hawk-like his features were without the raised cheeks of a grin. I clenched my toes, afraid of what his anger would bring, but any ire snapped away in an instant. "I am yours, Layla. What more need be said?"

"Mine? How the shit are you mine? I've never seen you before in my life!" I shouted again, still brandishing the candle. To my surprise, he kept acting like it was a real threat to him.

His eyes stayed steady on the sweet pea pillar while he spoke. "I am here to answer your every desire."

My desire? Who the shit breaks in and... *No.*

Ah fuck, no. Dana and the rest did not chip in to get me a...an incubus, as he called himself. Did that mean a male prostitute?

She said my gift would arrive later, and I did give her a key to my apartment in case of emergencies. Did sneaking a male whore inside count as an emergency? I whipped back to my front door, noting the locks in place.

"Look, this is all very..." *Humiliating that my friends know I can't get a date to save my life.* "Flattering, but I don't—"

The stranger stepped closer, and my senses flooded with him. His heat burst across my skin like a warm bath. His scent, rugged as an alpine mountain, tingled down my spine and lit a fire inside me. And his look...*fuck me,* but he was even hotter out of the shadows.

Those eyes that'd been dark as night were in actuality an otherworldly amber. His sharp nose and harsh cheekbones combined with the full bottom lip made the word *pretty* almost perch on my tongue. But then I glanced down his body, the muscles taut and proud, his gait strident, those full-to-bursting briefs, and he was nothing but fire.

"I am yours to command, to will, to dance to your every desire, my lady," he announced, his head bowing low. My fingers ached to rummage through the thick hair before me, to tug on the roots and crush him to my lips.

His head popped up and a smirk greeted me. Shit, did he read the stupid horny thought on my face?

I stared at the candle. He didn't seem to be a threat, and if Dana booked him…?

I mean, it's never nice to return a gift unused, right? It seemed very impolite.

He rolled his hand around the candle, plucking it from me before I could even put it down. "I don't believe this is necessary, unless you were hoping to set the mood?" After placing the pillar on the coffee table, he turned and smiled. "Or intended to pour hot wax on my body."

"What…?" Fucking hell, what did she get me? Okay, the hottest incubus at the dude ranch. But, still —

"You seem…" he whispered while rolling his hands through my hair. It'd been a matted mess from a long day of school and drinking, but under his fingers the curls felt smoother and sleeker. Hot breath curled against my neck, causing me to shiver down to my toes. "…as if you require some relaxation."

Strong fingers dug into my shoulders, kneading away the stress. A moan slipped from my lips, this stranger making fast work of unraveling the tension I'd carried since I was nine.

"Now that is music for the ages," he said behind me. His hands released from my shoulders and flat palms caressed my weary ribcage before rounding right at the side of my breasts. Dressed in little more than an old bra and scrubs, I could nearly feel his skin on mine. It sent my heart racing.

"What's your name?" I spat out, clinging to the idea that if I knew who he was, then it couldn't be so pathetic. All the while, my body begged for him to touch more of me.

"Do we need names?" he asked and that pouty bottom lip caressed the shell of my ear. He didn't bite down, didn't lick, just placed it there telling me he could do anything at a moment's notice.

I spun in his hands, which settled right on my hips. The fingers kept tugging on the waistband of my scrubs, this incubus slapping the elastic back and forth. "What if I need to call you? Give you directions?"

His eyes blazed as the amber shifted to fire. "That should not be a concern. But if you are wondering what to shout to the rooftops while I devour you...?"

Fuck, how did he know that?

"I believe Ink will suffice."

"Ink?" I repeated, while staring the man up and down. "And...what are you going to do to me?"

Swooping his fingers under my shirt, he dug into the small of my back. I flew forward, his lips a breath from mine as he said, "Whatever you desire."

Home of Erotic Romance

Sign up for our newsletter and find out about all our romance book releases, eBook sales and promotions, sneak peeks and FREE romance books!

About the Author

Ellen Mint adores the adorkable heroes who charm with their shy smiles and heroines that pack a punch. She recently won the Top Ten Handmaid's Challenge on Wattpad where hers was chosen by Margaret Atwood. Her books, Undercover Siren and Fever are available at Amazon as well as a short story in the Lucky Between The Sheets anthology. Married, she lives in Nebraska with her dog named after Granny Weatherwax. Her hobbies include gaming, painting, and halloween prop making. The basement is full of skeletons because they ran out of room in the closets.

Ellen loves to hear from readers. You can find her contact information, website details and author profile page at https://www.totallybound.com

www.ingramcontent.com/pod-product-compliance
Lightning Source LLC
Chambersburg PA
CBHW021519240626
47154CB00002B/701